K E OSBORN
USA Today Bestselling Author

CAPTIVATE
The NOLA Defiance MC Series Book 5

K E OSBORN
USA Today Bestselling Authors

This book is a work of fiction. Any references to real events, real people, and real places are used fictitiously. Other names, characters, places and incidents are products of the Author's imagination and any resemblance to persons, living or dead, actual events, organizations or places is entirely coincidental.

All rights are reserved. This book is intended for the purchaser of this book ONLY. No part of this book may be reproduced or transmitted in any form or by any means, graphic, electronic, or mechanical, including photocopying, recording, taping, or by any information storage retrieval system, without the express written permission of the Author. All songs, song titles and lyrics contained in this book are the property of the respective songwriters and copyright holders.

Disclaimer: The material in this book contains graphic language and sexual content and is intended for mature audiences, ages 18 and older.
There is content within this book that may set off triggers, please see more information at the back of the book.

ISBN: 979-8387919671

Editing by Swish Design & Editing
Formatting by Swish Design & Editing
Proofreading by Swish Design & Editing
Cover model by Ryan Harmon
Photography by Reggie Deanching at RplusMphoto
Cover design by Designs by Dana
Cover Image Copyright 2023

First Edition
Copyright © 2023 K E OSBORN
All Rights Reserved

DEDICATION

To Nanna.
I may not have written about fictional historical romance heroine, *Lorna Doone* in this book for you, but I wrote about my female lead character becoming a writer.
I'd like to think that maybe she could write about
Lorna Doone for you...
And hopefully that will count and make you proud.
Also, I am smiling as I write this.
Love you, Nan. xoxo

NOTE FOR THE READER

For your convenience, below is a list of terms used in this book. Any questions, please do not hesitate to contact the author.

1% — When a 1% patch is worn, it represents the one percent of bikers who are outlaw clubs.

Cut — A vest with club colors.

Chapel – The room where the Defiance club members congregate to have their 'church' meetings.

Church – The name of important club business meetings where only patched members can attend.

Hammer Down — Accelerate quickly.

La Fin — Means The End. Also the Club's pet alligator.

Road Name — A road name is earned, given, and bestowed upon a biker. They usually have a story behind them.

The Heat — Police.

CHAPTER 1

RAID

It's hard when you're young.

But I'm working my ass off trying to make a life for Sophie and me. A good life—no, a *great* fucking life. She is the endgame for me. I may only be twenty years old, but when you know, you know.

As another morning breaks, and I make the mad dash to get ready for work—in my tech position for the government as an 'ethical hacker,'—I glance over my bank statements doing the sums in my head.

I'm getting close.

I've been saving for a down payment so Soph and I can finally move in together. But I don't want just any house. I only want the absolute *best* for my woman because she's worth it.

For now, I'm renting, and she stays over most of the time like last night.

Soph walks out of the bathroom, a towel wrapped around her naked body, her skin glistening with droplets of water, and my cock instantly reacts in approval. Taking a sip of my coffee, I shake my head, letting out a deep growl, trying to control myself.

I have to leave in five, and she knows it.

Damn temptress.

Strands of her long blonde hair stick to her face—the rest of it up in a towel curled atop her head—as she strolls into the kitchen, grabbing a piece of my toast and taking a bite. "Morning."

"You trying to make me late for work?"

With a wiggle of her brows, she slides her arms around my neck. "I mean... I wouldn't be against the idea..." She giggles. "Though I am still sore from last night."

My cock strains against my slacks, and I lean my forehead against hers. "You're killing me. You know that?"

Her beautiful crystal blue eyes stare into mine. "That such a bad thing?"

Groaning, I slide my lips against her neck, kissing her damp skin. She lets out a soft whimper as my fingers begin pulling at the edges of her towel.

Soph giggles again and swats my hands away. "Okay, stop. You need to go to work."

Exhaling, I take a step back and glance at my bank statements once more. "Yeah... by the end of the month, I should have saved enough to consider laying down that payment on a nice house for us to be doing this dance every morning. You can have your toothbrush permanently in place and shower whenever you want. No more going back and forth."

She smiles wide, leans in, and kisses me. My lips tingle as I kiss her back, my tongue gliding against hers with delight, but then she moans and pulls back. "Okay, we need to stop. I've got to get dressed for work. You have to leave. We will talk about this more tonight, okay?"

Smiling, I press my lips to hers yet again, take one last bite of my toast, and head for the door. "Love you."

She smirks at me. "Love you too. Now go before your boss fires you, and we can't get that final part of the money we need for the down payment."

Chuckling, I open the door and head out, making my way to work with a pep in my step.

The entire morning, I am buzzing, on a high, knowing that I'm so close to making my life with Sophie that much better. She is everything I could ever want. Everything I could ever need.

And at lunch, I send her my customary text to see how her day is going.

I wait for the reply, but I get nothing in return.

Eating my sandwich, I shrug it off.

She must be busy.

I'm not worried. It's not unusual for Soph not to text back. Her job is as busy as mine. So I text another message.

> **Me:** *I will meet at your place tonight after work. We can go over more of the décor for our new house. I was looking at furniture for the home office this morning, and I know we're going to disagree.*

I chuckle, sending the text that ends with a big grinning emoji because I know I am right.

But still, there's no response.

Furrowing my brows, I become a little concerned but continue with the day as I need to finalize some important work.

After waiting the entire afternoon to hear back from Soph, I make my way to her apartment and let myself in with my key.

As I open the door, my eyes wander around the mess, trying to figure out what it is I am seeing. There are boxes strewn all over the place and shit everywhere. It looks like there's been a mad dash of panic-related packing.

So I walk inside, my heart racing and a lump forming in my throat. Unease washes over my entire body. "Jesus, Sophie, what have you done?" I murmur to myself as I move to the coffee table where there's a note waiting with my name scribbled on top.

Inhaling deeply through my nose while closing and opening my eyes, I build up the courage to pick it up.

> *Jay,*
>
> *You've been so supportive of me, and I can't thank you enough. Our time together has been magical, but our relationship is moving WAY too fast. I don't want to move in with you. In fact, I had a job offer at work today to take a position at a gallery in Houston.*
>
> *I took it, and I had to leave immediately.*
>
> *I'm sorry I didn't call to tell you.*
>
> *I love you, but it's all too much, too soon. We're over.*
>
> *Don't try to track me, and do your hacker thing. There's no point. I am fine.*
>
> *I just don't want this anymore.*
> *I don't want US anymore.*
>
> *I'm sorry...*
> *Soph*

Shaking my head slowly, my heart feels like it's been ripped out of my chest. My body flops onto the sofa. Then letting out a long huff, I reach into my slacks pocket and pull out the ring box, placing it on the coffee table.

I'm not entirely sure what to do.

Something doesn't feel right.

We were so good this morning. Surely I would've spotted some kind of sign?

Yanking out my cell, I dial her number, and surprisingly, she answers.

"Hi." Her voice is low, somber, dull sounding.

It breaks my heart.

Sitting taller, I run my hand through my hair. "Soph, I'm at your place. What's going on? Are you serious?"

She exhales down the line. "Jay, I'm already in Lafayette. I have another three or so hours to go before I reach Houston. I'm sorry, I just couldn't stay. It was too much."

"Why didn't you talk to me? I could have backed off. We could have slowed down. You don't need to drive four hundred fucking miles to get away from me."

She sighs. "It's not just you, Jay. It's the *reminder of you*. I love you. That hasn't changed—"

"Then turn around now, and let's talk this through. Let me fix this." I'm not above begging at this point.

"I already took the job, Jay. I can't back out no—"

"Then I will stay in Houston with you while we work this out. I don't want to lose you, Soph. You mean *everything* to me!"

She is quiet for a moment, and then she exhales. "It's too much, Jay. Too much too soon. Saving for a house, the ring I know you bought me… we're moving too fast, and it's making my head spin. I need to start fresh. Somewhere I can breathe."

My eyes glance at the ring box on the table.

How the hell did she know?

"Soph, I can take the ring back. We don't even have to talk about that until you're ready. I obviously thought we were at the same place, and I read us all wrong, but we can get through this. It's just a speed bump."

"This is *not* a speed bump, Jay. It's the fork in the road. A full fucking roadblock. The end of the line. Do you need any more analogies?"

My chest squeezes tight upon hearing her talk so definitively.

"Soph, why didn't you talk to me? I thought we had good communication. I thought everything was fucking great between us. How long have you been feeling trapped?"

"I don't know, Jay." She sniffles. "When I found the receipt for the ring at your house, I guess? Look, you're going places in your career. You're amazing at what you do. I don't want to be holding you back. You need to be able to travel the world and go where the job takes you. I don't want to be a chain holding you down."

"You're not a fucking chain, Soph. You're my damn world—"

"Exactly! You'd drop everything for me, and I love you for that, but I don't want you ruining your life for mine."

"You're not making any sense."

"Jay… you can do amazing things with tech. You could work for the government… NASA… *fuck!* I don't know… you're brilliant. I don't want you to be held back. I need you to go out into the world and make something of yourself. Promise me."

"What's it worth if I'm not working toward a life with you?"

She's clearly crying on the other end of the phone line.

"Make a life for yourself, Jay. Don't do it for me. I'm not the girl for you. Not anymore."

"Sophie!"

"Don't come looking for me, Jay. You won't change my mind."

"C'mon, Soph."

"We're done! Goodbye, Jay."

"*Sophie*," I demand, but it's too late.

She ends the call, driving the hell out of New Orleans and right out of my life, shattering my world beyond repair.

Just. Like. That.

CHAPTER 2

RAID
Fifteen Years Later

It's been so long, and still, Sophie plays on my mind.

Since that goodbye phone call, I haven't had any contact from her. I tried to stay connected with her, but she cut me off.

Walking out of my den, I stretch my fingers and crack my knuckles.

They tend to cramp when I've been in there for hours on end working on shit for Hurricane, my club president. I've been at Defiance MC for years. I never thought I would be the type of guy to join a motorcycle club, being polar opposite from the guy I was in my early years.

But I guess trauma response changes people.

Most of my brothers have had harder lives than me, so I really have nothing to complain about.

I had a good childhood. A great education. An amazing job. I found the love I thought I would have forever, and all before I hit twenty-one.

I had a good fucking run.

But when Sophie left me, I lost all sense of self. That's

when I spiraled.

I didn't give a shit about anything and especially not caring about what happened to me, so I quit my high-paying job, almost straight away. Pissing away all the money I had saved for Sophie and me. I didn't need it anymore, so what was the point of hanging on to it. But I did need money to live, so I used my resources and the special techniques I had learned in my career with the government to hack into the dark web and found easier ways to make a lucrative living. Laundering for shoddy businessmen, moving assets and funds for less than virtuous people, I went from ethical hacking to straight-out dark web illegal shit in two point five seconds.

I didn't care if I got caught.

I had no one to fight for.

The money was good.

So why did it matter?

My name was getting thrown around the underworld of New Orleans.

Working for the criminals.

Getting the shit done that no one would do for them.

I was making waves.

No, more like tsunamis.

Which is how I fell into the MC.

Hurricane sought me out.

Maybe things ending between Soph and me was a good thing?

Defiance needed a tech guy, and it just so happened I knew how to ride a bike.

My care factor about being a model citizen was long gone. So breaking laws, kill or be killed situations, and that one percent badge didn't bother me in the slightest.

As a matter of fact, I couldn't have cared less.

It excited me.

Sophie turned me into a criminal.

She left me so I could better myself.

Well, what was the fucking point without her?
I failed her.
Or maybe she failed me...
...failed us.
I couldn't find it in me to care even one. Little. Bit.
Do I regret joining the club? Hell no.

By losing Soph, I found a brotherhood, a family that wrapped their arms around me and supported me like I never thought possible.

Sophie broke a part of me that will never be repaired, but maybe that's what love does to you when you lose it.

It seems my chest always squeezes tight when I think of Sophie. But lately, the tension relaxes and calms when I look at Frankie.

A woman with a gorgeous, enamoring smile that lights up the room.

While flexing my sore fingers a little more, my eyes flick to Frankie sitting with Kaia and Lani.

It's an odd sensation for me.

I have never let myself get close to another woman since Soph.

Not emotionally, anyway.

Physically, of course—I've fucked my way across New Orleans.

Emotionally—I can't connect, refusing to allow myself to open up.

Maybe it's fear.

Maybe I just can't be bothered with the bullshit?

I don't know.

The one thing I do know is that Soph was never far from my mind until Frankie and I started hanging out. Frankie is a club girl here at Defiance. The *head* club girl and this woman runs a tight ship.

When the guys at the club have an itch that needs scratching, Frankie is there for that, along with Storm and, previously, Davina, who is now dead because of her betrayal of the club.

I am a self-confessed manwhore, but Frankie and I have never gone there. I've always sought pleasure from Storm or Davina to get my fill when needed. Not because I'm unattracted to Frankie. *Just the opposite.* I think Frankie is the single most gorgeous woman in this place. But I respect her as a person and as a friend. So I haven't used her services as a club girl—as a club whore—because she means more to me than that *title* gives her credit for. Actually, I hate that fucking title—she is not that type of woman—but the MC gives these girls that title for a reason, and I can't argue with tradition.

The thing is, Frankie and I get along so fucking well. And yeah, we flirt, but friendship has always been our priority. She's a person I turn to, to talk with, and rely on. But she doesn't know about Sophie and how committed to her I was. How my world changed when Soph left for Houston.

But while I stare at Frankie, her nose buried in her English books as she studies her adult admission classes, I can't help but smile. She's finally taking some time to do things for herself. This woman, this strong independent woman, looks after us at the club so damn well that it's about time she did something for herself. To put her needs and wants first.

Kaia sits with her one-month-old, Imogen, cradled in her arms. Lani talks to her and Frankie as I walk over to the ladies. I step in beside Frankie and glance down at her textbook, folding the pages back to look at the cover of the book to check exactly what she's working on—'*Student's Book of College English.*' Frankie smiles up at me, and I smirk, loving that she's working on her passion.

"Still working hard on your studies, I see?"

"I never stop," she states with a large cheesy grin.

"Energy of a rabbit," I tease flirtatiously.

A flush of red crosses her cheeks. "Well, you know what they say about rabbits?"

My cock jerks a little in my jeans as I raise my brow while staring at her. The corner of my lips turns up. "What *do* they say about rabbits, Frankie?"

She leans closer. "They get the job done... again, and again, and again. They just keep pounding it out."

Smirking, I nod my head. "I bet they do."

If I said I hadn't thought about fucking Frankie, I would be lying through my ass.

I've thought about it—*a lot.*

But she is a friend.

A good friend, I remind myself.

And although we flirt insatiably, and the attraction is most definitely there between us, I feel like Frankie is the kind of woman I could surrender myself to.

And I'm not doing that again.

Our eyes lock, her intense hazel orbs holding my gaze. The way the light sparkles and reflects makes it look like gold glimmers, like she is literally glowing like a freaking angel. She's so fucking beautiful that it takes my breath away as I gaze at her. With my skin tingling and my chest tightening with anxiety, I continue to stare at this beauty in front of me.

I don't do emotions.

Goddammit! When I look at Frankie, I feel things.

Things I shouldn't.

She licks her kissable lips, the ones I so desperately want to taste, just as my cell pings, distracting me. Regrettably, I pull my eyes from Frankie, the moment between us now lost, when I glance down at my cell. Furrowing my brows, there's a proximity alert for the gate, so I swipe the screen to activate the camera. Clearly, there is a car with what appears to be a woman, and I can just make out a teenage child in the car next to her.

Because I can't determine who the people are, I turn to Hurricane. "Pres, we got a visitor at the gates. Looks like a woman with a kid."

Hurricane chuckles. "Anyone expecting someone?" he calls out, and no one replies. "Fine, Jesse, go see what she wants. Take the radio."

Jesse nods, running outside for the gate as I turn back to Frankie, winking at her. "Keep up the good work."

Frankie giggles—obviously flirtatious. "I will."

The radio crackles, then Jesse's voice comes through, and I bring it up to listen. "Raid, you there?"

I nod my head, even though Jesse can't see me. "Yeah, brother, I'm here."

"This woman at the gate... says she's here to see you. That you knew her from high school."

I scrunch my face. "Name?"

"Sophie Tait."

Well, fuck me!

My blood runs cold.

Tightness grips my entire body.

My throat is closing over as I crane my neck to the side—a tsunami of emotions rolls over me.

I haven't heard from her in fifteen years.

She wanted me to become something more.

She left so I could do amazing shit with my life.

Instead, I turned to crime and hacking for a biker club.

She is going to be so disappointed.

But why should I care what she thinks? She's the one who left me.

Who am I kidding? Fuck, my head is all over the place right no—

"Raid?"

My head snaps up, and I clear my clogged throat. "Yeah, let her in."

I start pacing, the eyes of the club firmly on me.

Frankie stands, placing her hand on my back to calm me. Her features turn to concern. "Hey, are you okay?"

"I haven't seen her in fifteen years. Why the fuck is she coming to see me. And how the hell did she find me?"

"Who is she?" Frankie asks.

I look at her, clear sadness in my eyes as I sigh. "The woman who broke me."

Frankie swallows hard as Sophie walks into the clubhouse, escorted by a teenage girl.

But the sight shocks me to the core.

Sophie is wearing one of those beanies you don when you're sick.

The terminal kind of sick.

She's still beautiful as all hell, but I can tell she has lost her lustrous flowing blonde hair, and the beanie is hiding a bald scalp.

I take off, rushing for her. "Sophie, is it really you?"

She weakly smiles as my eyes shift to the young girl who's holding Sophie up and is wearing a somber expression on her beautiful young face. "Yes, Jay, it's me. It's so good to see you again."

"Someone, grab her a chair," I call out, and Frankie rushes a chair over for Sophie.

She exhales while taking a seat, but I can't take my eyes off the young teenager beside Sophie. The scowl she has directed toward me isn't going unnoticed. She clearly has a problem with me, but I have no clue who she is, though a sense of familiarity looms over me.

I just can't place it.

"Sophie, don't get me wrong, I'm so glad you're here, but…" I scratch my head. "Why *are* you here?"

She glances up at who I assume is her daughter, then back to me. "If you haven't guessed, I am dying… breast cancer. The doctors don't think I have long."

The words are like a bullet straight to the chest. The oxygen leaves my lungs as I stumble a little on the spot, my chest squeezing so damn tight I might be having either a panic attack or a heart attack. I can't be sure which one.

"Jesus, Soph, I'm so sorry."

She reaches out, grabbing my hand. Her fingers are frail. Cold. Nothing like the Sophie I knew, and it breaks my damn heart. "Jay.

When I took off all those years ago, when I left without telling you why… there was a reason."

I shake my head because right now, I don't even give a shit.

Sophie is dying, and I want to spend whatever time we have left together.

"It's okay, water under the bridge. It's been fifteen years, Soph. We don't have to worry about—"

"Jay… I was pregnant."

CHAPTER 3

RAID

A damn fucking nuke goes off.

My chest explodes with grief.

I turn to the girl standing beside Sophie. The girl with long blonde hair...

...just... like... me.

The girl with green eyes...

...just... like... me.

The girl with a freckle on her right collarbone...

...just... like... me.

And I stop dead still.

"Surprise, *Dad!*" The young teenager mocks.

I let out a long exhale, tilting my head, wanting to ensure I am getting this correct. "You're saying... *you're* my kid?"

"I'm as surprised as you are. Mom told me you were dead. I only found out last week. So if you think *you're* angry, imagine thinking your dad was dead your entire life only to find out he's a fucking criminal!"

"Addilyn Quinn!" Sophie chides.

A wave of resentment and anger curdles inside me as I breathe harshly in and out of my nose and turn back. "Sophie, you raised my daughter for *fifteen years* without telling me?"

"I'm fourteen. Mom was pregnant with me for nine months. Can you *not* do basic math, dumbass?"

I jerk my head back, raising my brow at my daughter, who seems to have a severe attitude problem.

Especially with me.

Sophie scowls, rubbing the tension from her forehead. "I'm not proud of what I did, Jay. But what's done is done. I'm trying to rectify it now before I'm gone."

My nostrils flare. "So what? You want me to be a part of her life? She *clearly* doesn't want to be a part of mine."

"I have no choice. I have no family to look after her when I go. Legally… you're her next of kin."

My eyes widen, and I shake my head. "You want her to come live *here?*"

"If you have *any* love for me at all and for the love we once shared… you'll learn to love Addi too. She is a part of us both, Jay. Believe it or not, she's *so* much like you."

"Pfft!" Addilyn groans, folding her arms over her chest.

I already noted the physical similarities. There's no doubt she is mine.

I just can't believe I let Sophie go.

I can't believe I didn't fight harder.

I can't believe I didn't drive down to Houston and demand to know why she didn't fight for us.

And now I know…

… because Sophie was pregnant.

It still doesn't make sense.

She ran because she was pregnant?

I need more answers.

And the only way I am going to get them is if they are here—both of them.

I have to figure out what Sophie's motives are, and I need to connect with Addilyn. I never saw myself as the father type, but it's been thrust upon me now.

There's no choice.

No option to say no.

I have got to step up.

As I glance over my shoulder, my eyes meet Frankie's.

Shit.

Frankie.

With Sophie here, any thoughts of being with Frankie will have to stop.

Surely she will understand.

We are only friends. That's all. But even as the words filter through my head, I know it's a lie.

Frankie weakly smiles as if she can read my rambling mind.

I turn to Hurricane. "Pres?"

Hurricane shrugs. "This is your family, Raid, *your* family is *our* family, you know that. You do what you gotta do. We'll always make room."

I spin back to Sophie. "If Addilyn is staying here, then you are too. You need people to take care of you."

Frankie's eyes widen as Addilyn's eyes begin to glisten, then she leans down, embracing her mom. "Thank you."

Nodding, I run my fingers through my long hair and turn back to face Frankie. My eyes meet hers for a brief moment. "Can you make their room ready for them?"

She nods, something unspoken being said between us.

We all know we've been dancing around our connection for a while, but I've just been hit with an insta-family. *This takes precedence over everything in my life.*

Frankie gently grips my arm in a show of support, then turns, walking off for the hall.

I let out a breath I didn't know I was holding and spin back to Sophie. "We have a lot to discuss."

Sophie dips her head, but I can tell it's a strain. "Is there somewhere we can go to talk?"

"You can use the Chapel," Hurricane offers.

"Thanks, Pres..." I turn back to Sophie. "Can you walk? Do you need me to carry you?"

Sophie smirks incredulously. "Jay, really? C'mon, have I ever needed anyone to help me?"

I shake my head. "You've always been extremely stubborn. It's why we got along so well."

"Because you were a pushover and did whatever I said?" She smirks.

"Pretty much... c'mon. Let's go talk this through." I point. "Just in that room over there."

"Hold onto my arm as you walk, Mom. You might not accept help from him, but I won't take no for an answer," Addilyn demands.

"Stubborn like your mom... got it," I murmur, and Addilyn scowls at me. *Again.*

Note to self—*don't take it personally.*

This kid doesn't know me.

I don't know her either.

So I can't judge on our two-minute interaction.

What I can tell is that she adores her mother. Would do anything for her. And the fact that she is dying right before our eyes is slowly killing Addilyn too.

I'd say that's why she is so defensive with me—she's hurting.

And her mother is forcing me into her life right now when she thought I was dead, which is a whole other conversation in itself.

This is going to take time.

Problem is, I don't know how much time Sophie has left.

By the look of it—*not long.*

Addilyn slowly helps her mother up from the chair, and we all carefully walk toward the Chapel. The eyes of the entire clubhouse are on our backs when I open the door and walk through. I let Addilyn take Sophie inside then I close the door

Captivate

behind us, locking us out from the prying ears of the rest of my family.

Here, in this very Chapel, is a family I didn't even know existed.

And I need a second to process that fact.

I close my eyes, taking a deep breath, my hand resting on the closed door while trying to keep myself in check.

"Jay?" Sophie whispers.

Opening my eyes, I clear my throat and turn to see Addilyn's eyes assessing me like she has no clue what she expects me to say or do next.

Honestly, I don't even know what I will say or do next.

There is no handbook for this kind of situation.

The woman I wanted to spend the rest of my life with is sitting right in front of me, visibly dying before my eyes, and as if that isn't enough to deal with, she's thrown a kid into the mix that I knew nothing about.

What the fuck am I going to do?

Walking to the opposite side of the Chapel, I slide into the seat and rest my hands on the table. My eyes meet Sophie's. "How long have you known you were sick?"

"I was diagnosed six months ago, but it went metastatic quicker than the doctors thought it would. It took us all by surprise. If that's the word you want to use for it."

"So it's spread?" I ask.

Addilyn's eyes begin to water as she clings to Sophie's hand.

Sophie nods. "They found the first lesions in my lymph nodes, then they did a full body scan, and that's when they saw lesions in my liver, lungs, scattered through my bones, and there's one in my brain."

A tear slides down Addilyn's face as the sheer torment of the situation shows in her tight posture and full body tremors.

My stomach recoils, wanting more than anything to empty all over the table. My body wants to run. Wants to hide from the world and the unjust fucking bullshit it's serving me on a nice silver platter.

I've spent the last fifteen years wondering how Sophie was doing.

Wondering if I would ever see her again.

Wondering if we would ever be reunited.

But never... *never* in my wildest dreams did I ever... *ever* picture this.

"Okay... so what are your treatment options?"

Addilyn sniffles, letting her mom's hand go and drift to her lap. The silent tears are tearing up my insides, watching this kid lose all sense of herself.

I see it clearly—all hope is gone.

Sophie exhales, and when she does, the stuttering breath tells me she's weak. Exhausted from the simple act of talking. "There are no treatment options, Jay. I need to be kept comfortable until—"

Addilyn begins to sob, which cuts Sophie off. She turns to Addilyn and picks up her hand, giving it a tight squeeze before looking back at me.

Watching my child—a kid I never knew I had—in this much pain is tearing at my heart.

I want to protect her.

From a pain we both now share.

I want to bond with my daughter, but *not* over something like this.

"Do we need to think about hospice?" I ask, and Sophie smiles.

"Maybe... as a last resort. I want to spend as much time with Addi as I can. Make as many memories as possible. She starts as a freshman at the high school tomorrow, and I want to try and make these last few weeks as easy as they can be for her. There's been a lot of upheavals. Moving cities. Moving schools. Meeting you. Moving in here... it's a lot for her. I need to make sure..." she takes a deep centering breath, "... to know that you and Addi will be okay once I am gone."

My eyes shift to Addilyn, and if her eyes are any indication, she isn't convinced.

I'm not so sure I am, either.

Is a biker club the right place to bring up a teenage girl?

Am I even equipped to take this on?

"Maybe this isn't the right time, but I need to know... *why*, Soph? *Why* did you leave and not tell me you were pregnant? Help me understand because you *know* I would have been *all in*. You *know* I would have been over the damn moon."

Addilyn widens her eyes like she wasn't expecting me to say that, and Sophie exhales slowly. "I do know that, and it's *exactly* why I left. Jay... you were going places. Your career was skyrocketing. You were so good at what you did. I didn't want to hold you back. You were supposed to forget about me and make a go of it. That's *why* I left. Because I didn't want to tie you down and ruin your chances at the man you were going to become... a gifted specialist in your field."

I snort out a grunt. "Sophie, you left. I fell apart. You were *every-fucking-thing* to me. There was no reason for me to keep going. I couldn't have cared less about my career. You were the reason I was succeeding. You gave me a reason to succeed. Without you... I gave up. I didn't want anything but you."

Her eyes begin to sparkle, and she wipes away a stray tear. Her eyes shift around the Chapel, looking to the ceiling lined with neon lights that shine down over the walls which are littered with club memorabilia, bike merchandise, and New Orleans hometown homages. Then, she glances to the table Hurricane had made specifically for the club. The plexiglass top sits above a piece of a petrified tree log that branches out underneath, giving it an otherworldly feel—perfectly New Orleans. The fleur-de-lis is etched into the middle of the plexiglass, representing our home.

Sophie's hand gently glides over the top of the clear plexiglass. "So... you became a biker? I mean, I always knew you loved your motorcycle, but this? I never pictured *this* for you."

My chest tightens because we both know it's true, and I take a moment before I answer, "Hurricane, my president, sought me out when I started going off the rails. He brought me in and put my talents to good use."

"So you hack for the club?" she asks.

"I'm the tech guy here. Make sure security is in check, run the numbers, and yeah, hack if need be."

Sophie sighs. "Is any of it legal?"

I tilt my head. "Soph... we're one-percenters. We don't live under the constraints of the law. We find ways around it, but only when necessary. We don't hurt good people. And we don't do bad shit just for fun. The guys here are a good bunch. They're my brothers. My family. They're respectful. *Especially* toward family and women."

Sophie's shoulders relax. "That makes me feel better."

"How did you find me, Soph? How did you know to come to the club?"

She swallows hard. "I went to your old house. Of course, you weren't there, but the man who lived there said he thought the guy that lived there before he moved in fifteen years ago joined the local biker club. So I did some digging. We went to a bar for lunch... Revel Rose, I think its name was. Turns out..." she smiles, "... the owner knew you guys well."

I let out a laugh. "Marcel?"

"Yeah, great guy. Not extremely chatty, but once I told him who we were and how we knew you, he told me where the club was located. Said he was going to call ahead, but I asked if he could let us tell you about Addi in person. He wasn't so excited by the idea of holding back, but I think he understood that you needed to hear about *all* this directly from us."

"Mmm... I'm glad I heard about it from you. Don't get me wrong. I like the guy. But you're family. And honestly, I'm glad you're both here."

"That makes one of us," Addi snaps, folding her arms over her chest—her defiant attitude a direct reflection of mine.

I shift my eyes to my daughter. *Holy hell! I have a daughter.* "Do you prefer for me to call you Addilyn or Addi?"

She shrugs, and the annoyance in her eyes shines bright. "Everyone calls me Addi."

"Okay, Addi. Everyone calls me Raid."

Addi turns up her nose. "As in the bug spray?"

I can't help but smirk. The kid's funny.

"No, as in a RAID system. It stands for Redundant Array of Independent Disks. Basically, they work together to have speed and reliability. And they protect data in case of drive failure…" I trail off because I know I have lost them with the technical jargon. "That's kinda like my job here at the club. Speed, reliability, and to protect data which in turn protects our club like a RAID system. Hence why they called me Raid. Plus, when the cops raid the clubhouse, I am in charge of locking down our systems and making sure the heat can't gain access to anything." Sophie smiles at me, understanding perfectly that this is a job I was made for, but Addi simply rolls her eyes.

"Lame. You sound like a nerd."

"Technically, I am… and although I know you meant that derogatory, I actually love the term, kid."

Not only does she roll her eyes, but an audible huff goes along with it.

"Addi, I know you're hurting, but please try to remember that Jay… sorry, Raid… isn't the bad guy in all this. He had no clue you even existed until fifteen minutes ago. You've got to cut him some slack."

Addi stands abruptly, and with so much force, her chair falls over. Tears well in her eyes. "You think this is easy for me, *Mom?* To come here and see you with this guy that I have zero connection with and watch him fawning all over you like a damn puppy? He obviously loved you, but *you* left *him!* You deprived *me* of having a father my *entire life* because *you* wanted *him* to do better, and now he's a *fucking* nerd *fucking* criminal!"

"Addilyn, language!"

"No, Mom. You're gonna die! You've made this huge mess, and you're leaving me here to pick up the pieces *you* made. And now, in your last few weeks on this Earth, you've gone and made me angry with you when all I want to do is to *spend time with you!*" Sophie sinks into her chair, closes her eyes, and breathes out heavily. "How *could you, Mom?* How could you just leave him like that? Leave *me* without *my father!*" Addi bursts into tears and runs for the door, making Sophie and me stand.

"Addi!" Sophie calls out, but Addilyn is out the door before we have a second to say anything else.

Sophie has to lean on the table for support.

I race around to grab hold of her. "Whoa, now... I got you." As a tear slides down her face, I help her back into the chair.

"I never meant to hurt the both of you. I thought I was doing right by you, Jay. I *honestly* thought I was..." She sobs, her whole body wracked with grief.

I pull out the chair in front of her and sit, grabbing her hands. "Okay, it's been a really long time for us. We have a lot of catching up to do. Don't worry about Addi. Everyone out there will look after her. I need you to tell me *everything* about my daughter. Every milestone I missed. Every single thing Addilyn has done to this moment in time. I want to know it all."

Sophie smiles hesitantly and nods. "Okay... I'll start from the beginning."

CHAPTER 4

FRANKIE

Raid's ex turning up with his daughter on our doorstep like that has my stomach swirling.

My heart hurts for him and what he must be feeling right now. Not only has he learned that he is a father and has missed out on fourteen years of his daughter's life, but his ex is clearly incredibly ill, and even though they're not together, that has got to be the worst kind of pain.

I don't know much about Sophie. In fact, I'm not sure I've even heard her name mentioned. But I do know that Raid had one woman who broke him in the past, and I'm willing to bet Sophie *is* that woman. The way he was looking at her, the way his face contorted when he saw her walk in, yeah, those feelings don't just disappear.

And by the look of things, the way his eyes met mine, I can tell things between us—whatever this fun flirtation was—are over, at least while Sophie is here.

It makes sense.

And I totally get it.

We were never a couple, so his loyalty must lie with the family he never knew he had.

Sophie does not need to witness him flirting with another woman, especially considering she is virtually on her deathbed. That simply would not be fair to her. And it wouldn't be fair of me to expect anything from him right now.

It is what it is. We've been dancing around our feelings for years and never acting on anything.

Raid's the one brother besides Jesse who has never made a move on me. I mean, it's what I'm here for. Though I must admit, over the last few months, those services have dried up, with more club brothers finding women of their own to scratch that itch. Not all of them have old ladies, but it seems the brothers go elsewhere since they have been watching our banter.

As I finish making the bed, I stand back, hoping the room is okay. It's the single twin room. I thought it would be best for them. I don't know if Addilyn wants to share a room with her mom, but I figure she'll want to spend as much time as possible with her. I am hoping a single bed is going to be okay for them. Otherwise, I will have to rethink the bedroom situation.

Letting out a heavy exhale, I walk over to the desk and make sure there is plenty of supplies for Addilyn. She's going to be doing her homework in here, I assume. So she is going to need notebooks, pens and all things school. Once I've grabbed a few supplies, I pull a laptop from the storage room and take it down to charge. She probably already has one, but I will provide one just in case.

I want them to feel as welcome and accommodated as they can.

Because that's *my job.*

Also I want Raid to know that I am on his side.

And that he has my full support—whatever he needs.

Because I care about him.

Probably more than I should.

The whole thing with our 'relationship' is that there is more than friendship feelings involved—at least, there is for me. But I think there is for him too, which is why Raid never knocked on my door. Because if we took it there, it might mean something.

My title as club whore means I don't get the luxury of falling for a brother.

It's just not how it works at an MC.

And now he has far more important things to worry about than me. So I will give him his space and let him deal with what is happening, but I will still be here if he needs me.

Even though it's hard.

Even if it kills me to step aside.

I sniffle, knowing I have lost something.

A friendship that was solid.

A relationship that was building slowly.

I have lost more than I care to admit.

I clear my throat and straighten my shoulders. "You got this, Frankie. You're the toughest bitch you know." I give myself a little pep talk, nod my head, then turn and walk out of Sophie and Addi's bedroom into the hall.

As I walk the long corridor, the Chapel door bursts open, and just as I am about to walk past, Addi rushes out, slamming the door behind her. She turns straight into me with a thump, and I let out a gasp when she hits me with a jolt. Her feet slip out from under her, and she falls flat on her ass with a thud.

"Shit!" I call out, but she doesn't make any attempt to get up, simply wraps her arms around her legs and flops her head to her knees. The sound of sobbing is evident when she begins to rock back and forth.

I widen my eyes as I check the Chapel door waiting for Raid or Sophie to exit, but they stay inside, obviously giving Addi the space they think she needs.

What *I* think Addi needs right now is someone to give her some attention.

I let out a long exhale and slide down onto the carpet next to her, crossing my legs. "You don't have to say anything if you don't want to. Just know that I will sit with you until you're ready to talk."

Addi's head slowly rises, her eyes blotchy and swollen. I reach inside my tank top, to my bra, and pull out a Kleenex, handing it to her.

Finally, she manages a smirk. "You carry random tissues in your titties?"

"First of all, I'm not sure if you're allowed to talk like that..." I chuckle. "But yes, that's one thing you need to learn as a growing woman..." I pause for dramatic effect. "Your titties are your best friend when it comes to storage."

Addi lets out a small giggle. "I wish I had boobs like yours."

I shrug. "I paid for mine, and trust me... I do *not* recommend doing that. Stay natural, honey. While big boobs might look aesthetically pleasing, the dramas that come with implants are no fun at all."

Addi's smile falls. "But then again, boobs are bad. Look at what's happening to my mom all because of her boobs."

I nod and wrap my arm around Addi, pulling her closer. "I know. It fucking sucks. And I am sorry this is happening to you, Addilyn. It must be a lot to take in."

Addi cuddles into my side, obviously needing the comfort. "I love my mom... *so much.* She's all I've ever known. It's been us against the world. She's never lied to me, *ever.*"

"It must be nice to have such a tight relationship—"

"That's the thing... now I'm questioning our entire relationship. Because if she can lie to me about something as huge as my father being dead, what else is she capable of lying to me about?"

My shoulders slump because I don't know the answer to that unenviable question. "I don't know your mom's reasons, but she must have thought it was the right thing to do at the time. For you, for Raid—"

"How can keeping me from my father be the right call? I mean, he's a nerd which is weird. I never thought my mom would go for someone from *The Big Bang Theory*, but he also has long hair, and well... he's just *not* what I pictured my mom would go for... *at all*."

I smirk at her quick assessment of Raid. "I get that you think Raid is a geek, but I think you're confusing smart with dorky. Raid is highly intelligent. But he doesn't go around on weekends wearing a Spock costume if that's where your mind is going. He loves art. He loves riding his bike. He is loyal to a fault. He is fiercely protective of those he cares about. He can be funny. He can also be very serious when he needs to be. Raid is an amazing man, and I think if you gave him a chance, you might get to know him like we all do."

"He's my dad..." Addi's eyes glisten, a single tear rolling down her cheek. "I have a *d-dad*." Her voice cracks on the last word.

I weakly smile. "Yeah, honey... you do."

She wipes her nose with the tissue, then lets out a long exhale. "Are the kids at school going to tease me about Raid being a biker?"

I pull her closer. "If they do, you have an entire club ready to teach those kids a lesson."

The corner of her lips turns up. "The whole club will look out for me?"

I turn and look her straight in the eyes. The eyes that are the spitting image of her father's. "You listen to me, Addi... you're part of this club now. That means you're family. *No. Matter. What.* We look after our own through thick and thin. We got your back. Anyone hassles you... they answer to us."

She tries to hide her smile. "That's kinda cool."

"You know, Addi, if I know Raid like I think I do, then he will do everything in his power to be the kind of father you deserve. He missed out on fourteen years with you already. He's going to be feeling this pain as much as you are. But, don't forget, he didn't know about you either."

"I just keep thinking... if Mom didn't get sick, would she have even told me about him?"

"I can't answer that for you. That's a subject you need to talk to your mom about. But just know that she loves you. She adores you. You are her world. And for her to bring you here, knowing how this would affect you and Raid, that's brave. She could have let the secret end with her. But she put her dignity on the line, so she knew you would be taken care of. Because in her heart, she knows Raid is a decent guy. And he is going to move Heaven and Earth for you."

"You really think he is going to accept me into his life? He doesn't know anything about me. I was dumped on his doorstep, and Mom just expects him to take care of me."

"He won't accept you into his life, Addi," I tell her, and her eyes widen in fear, so I quickly continue, "You will *become* his life. Like I said, I know him. You're a piece of him, and he's going to take care of you even if he has to give up *everything* he loves to make sure you're happy... you have *nothing* to worry about. You will want for nothing. And though he *will* be strict with you, I think you'll be able to walk all over him because he will forever be trying to make up for lost time with you. So you see, you have the upper hand. But if you want this relationship with him to work, I wouldn't take advantage of that if I were you. Work *with* him, not *against* him. Everything will be an adjustment. You're a smart girl, and we *know* he's a smart guy. Together you could be unstoppable... you just *have* to work at it together."

Addi's eyes narrow on me like she is assessing me. "Is he your boyfriend?"

I weakly smile. "No. But he is a good friend."

"Then, are you a motivational speaker or something?"

I let out a small laugh. "Or something. Part of my job at the club is to be an ear for everyone. To talk to people when they want advice. Maybe I've just gotten good at dishing out the motivational quotes?"

Addi sighs. "You're really nice, you know that?"

I rest my head against hers. "Thanks. But it's not hard to be nice when you're so easy to get along with."

She turns to look at me. "I just unloaded all of that on you, and I don't even know your name?"

I smile, placing my hand out for her to shake. "Hey, Addi, I'm Frankie. Nice to officially meet you."

She takes my hand and shakes it once. "Hey, Frankie, sorry about all the blubbering."

"No sweat. Us girls gotta stick together, right?"

Addi swipes under her eyes again and nods. "Right."

I move to stand and place my hand out for Addi to help her up. "C'mon, let me show you your room."

She rolls out her shoulders and lets out a long, exaggerated huff. "Okay, that would be nice."

We start to walk off when the Chapel door opens to Raid holding onto Sophie as they move to exit the room.

Addi darts past me toward her mother and props her up on the other side. Raid spots me, his eyes darting from Addi and then back to me. He smiles, nodding his head in thanks.

Addi talks softly to her mother, something I can't hear, then she says, "C'mon, Mom, let me show you to our room." Addi takes Sophie, and Raid lets her go, stepping back to me as we fall a couple of steps behind them.

I reach out for his arm and ask, "You okay?"

"I don't even know how to answer that question." He lets out a soft mocking laugh. "But thank you for taking care of Addi while I talked with Soph. She gave me a baby picture of Addi." He pulls it out of his pocket and shows me.

Addilyn is in a crib, and he simply stares at it.

And while he is doing that, my heart breaks.

That he's missed all these precious moments with her.

That he's now faced with raising a child he has no idea about.

It especially breaks for the lost look on his face right now.

I gently caress his back while he exhales.

"I've missed so much, Frankie."

Nodding, I pull him close. "I know. But she's here now. And you have a lifetime to get to know her."

He nods, placing the picture back in his pocket, and we walk up the hall. "It's this one here on the right," I call out to Addi, and she escorts her mom into their new bedroom. Addi edges Sophie to the nearest bed, and we stand back while Sophie sits on the side, completely out of breath.

"You need to rest, Mom. It's been a huge day," Addi suggests.

Sophie waves her hand through the air haphazardly. "We just got here. I need to be social."

Raid scoffs, shaking his head. "Addi's right. You rest up. Take all the time you need. We're not going anywhere. We'll all be here when you wake. You are a part of this family now, Soph, whether you want to be or not, and we're *all* going to take care of you. So please, take the time to rest while you're here. Spend time with Addi, and let us pamper you both."

She sighs. "That's not why we came here, Jay."

"But it's what you're going to get."

Sophie weakly smiles and nods. "Thank you." She takes Addi's hand in hers. "You have no idea what it means to me to have you and Addi here together."

Raid glances at Addi. "I'm just glad you finally brought her here. Everything else doesn't matter. You're here, and we take each day as it comes."

"You were always so good to me, Jay."

Raid dips his chin. "We'll get you guys something to eat while you settle in. We will be back in a little bit. You take some time to get used to your new room. You can set it up however you like."

"Thanks, Jay."

He reaches for my arm, and we walk out of their room, closing the door behind us. As I go to walk off, he grabs me, spinning me back to him. One arm slides around me, pulling me tight to him, his fingers on his other hand digging into my hair while he holds me, just taking in a couple of deep breaths.

My heart aches for him.

He obviously needs the comfort.

"It's gonna be okay, Raid," I tell him. "We'll get through this."

He exhales with a low grumble as he slowly pulls back from me, his eyes meeting mine. He's looking at me like he's desperate to kiss me.

I'd love nothing more.

The energy around us explodes as we stare at each other. Goose bumps tingle all the way up and down my body while butterflies flutter in my stomach.

Closing his eyes, he leans in, resting his forehead on mine. My heart rate increases, and I take a stuttering breath.

But then he pulls back, lowering his eyes, the chemistry instantly fizzling out when he takes a step back, putting some space between us. "I know this probably isn't what you want to hear, but I need to concentrate on Addi right now."

I smile, but my chest squeezes so hard I can't breathe. Not because I'm upset but because I am proud of him for proving to me that he is the man I *knew* he was. "That's what I told her... that you'd be all in."

He sighs. "Thanks for being there for her. I really appreciate it."

"I am here for you too... if you need me. That doesn't change. That will *never* change. I'm still here however you need me. In whatever capacity you need me. I'm here."

"Well, I don't know anything about fourteen-year-old girls, so I have a feeling I am going to need *all* the help I can get."

I chuckle, nudging his shoulder. "I got your back. Now though? What can I do for you right now?"

He glances from their bedroom door to the end of the hall and back. "Maybe grab them something to eat?"

Nodding, I smile. "That I can do."

His hand comes up, gently caressing the side of my cheek. "I'm sorry... for what it's worth."

My hand touches the side of his face. "Family comes first...

always. I understand that. We were just flirting, Raid. If we were going to take this further then maybe this is a sign that we're supposed to wait?"

"Yeah... maybe. We have no choice now either way..." He swallows hard, his hand dropping. "I better get back to them."

I inhale sharply, nod, and begin to back away. "Yeah, of course. I'll prep some food for y'all and bring it on in." I turn to walk off, feeling a heavy weight on my chest, but he reaches out, grabbing my wrist.

"Frankie?"

I turn back, my eyes blinking to keep any tears at bay. "Mmm..."

His bright green orbs, heavy with the burden he now carries, stare into mine. "Thank you... for everything."

I lean in, planting a tender kiss on his bearded cheek. And I can't help but linger for a few seconds longer than I should. Then I inhale and turn to walk toward the kitchen, leaving him with his new family. My eyes instantly flood with tears at losing what could have been.

If only we had acted on our feelings sooner.

But there were already obstacles in our way and issues with us being together...

... including his hang-up on Sophie.

And the fact I'm a club girl.

So maybe this was the sign we needed to point us in the *right* direction.

The direction of where we are is just *not* meant to be together.

Let's face it club girls don't get to ride off into the sunset with their biker prince. Brothers rarely consider the idea of being with a club girl, so happy ever-afters are not something I can entertain.

Raid will need to concentrate solely on Addilyn and Sophie, and I must take a step back emotionally from him. I'll be here, of course, for whatever he needs, but I have to detach my feelings because the only person who will get hurt is *me*.

Raid will have Addi to distract him, and I'll be left to pick up the pieces of my own heart when this all goes to hell with Sophie.

So I need to safeguard myself for now.

Before the devastation of all this is too much to bear.

CHAPTER 5

RAID
The Next Day

While lying in bed, I stare at the picture of Addi when she was a baby, feeling like I have so much to catch up on. She is a stranger to me, and I have no idea how to broach anything with her.

Do I try to act like a friend?

Do I try to be a father?

The problem is I have no idea how to even be one.

Never mind the fact Sophie is here at the clubhouse, and I have to process that I am finally seeing her again after all this time, only for her to be at death's door.

Where's the fairness in that?

Do I still love her? A part of me will always love her, but the way she left killed our relationship.

It destroyed a part of me.

So do I still love her? Yes, but not like I did all those years ago when she was my everything.

But Addi? That's a different story. The second I knew she was mine, I felt this unbreakable bond. This unwavering protective instinct kicked in, and it was mighty powerful. She may not be receptive toward me, but I know I will always be there for her no matter what.

Because that is what fathers do.

No matter how hard she tries to push me away.

Normally, I'm eager to rise and get ready for the day, but today I'm hesitating. I am lingering in bed because I just don't know how to start the day. Let alone what do I do with Frankie? I feel like I have waited for so long to make a move with her due to my commitment issues because of Sophie, and now it appears we have missed our shot.

I'm fucking gutted because I like her, but I know I was probably only going to hurt Frankie in the long run.

It's better this way.

A gentle knock on my door pulls me from my thoughts. I hop out of bed, wearing just my briefs. "Yeah?" I call out, expecting it to be Hurricane needing me for something.

The door opens, and Sophie walks inside while I look for my jeans.

My eyes widen when she takes in my practically naked form. "Shit, let me put some clothes on."

She chuckles, rolling her eyes. "Jay, we have a kid together. You don't have to be embarrassed around me. Though, you *have* filled out a lot since we were twenty."

My lips turn into a grin, but I continue getting dressed as she sits on my desk chair. "You should be resting," I tell her.

"Just because I'm here doesn't mean life stops. I have to take Addi to her first day of school. That's why I'm here..." She's hesitant. I can read it in her eyes. "I wanted to see if you would like to come. Meet Principal Schneider?"

I stop and turn to face her. "Seriously?"

She nods. "When I'm gone, you will need to do all the school stuff. So it's best you're involved right from the start."

Nodding my head—that makes sense. "Right... yeah. Let me get my shit, and we can head out." While internally panicking because

I don't know how to do any of this shit, I start gathering my things.

Sophie stands and walks over, grabs my arm, making me turn to look at her. "Hey, you're going to do fine. Just... be yourself. Addi is currently contending with the upheaval of her life, so she might be hard on you, but give her time. She'll warm up. She's a great kid but is going through a lot."

I nod once and let out a stuttered breath. "Okay." I reach for my cell, shoving it in my jeans pocket, then smile at Sophie. "Let's go to school."

We walk out to the main clubroom, where Addi is dressed in a private school uniform. *I should've guessed.* But honestly, as long as Addi is getting the best, that is all I care about.

We walk up to her while she chats with Frankie.

"Ready for school?" I ask Addi.

"What? You're coming with me?" Addi asks.

"I've missed taking you to school for years, Addi. So yeah... I'm taking you to damn school."

She folds her arms over her chest. "You don't have to step up now just because Mom roped you into this, you know? I can look after myself."

Sophie sighs.

"You're a minor, Addi, and that's not even the issue here. You're my daughter, and if I had been in the picture from the start, I would have stepped up. I have a lot of making up to do. So get used to the fact that I am going to be in your life from here on out. I'm here, Addi, and I'm not going anywhere."

She groans. "Fine! Enough with the sentimental drama. Just take me to school."

My eyes shift to Frankie. She winks at me, and I move my hand to Addi's back and usher her to the club pickup truck. I help Sophie into the front passenger side as she's clearly weak, but she manages, then we're on our way.

The journey to the school isn't far, but the tension in the truck is thick as I try to make conversation with Addi, though she shuts me down at every turn.

"So, what's your favorite subject at school?" I ask.

She huffs. "Do we really need to do this? I'm trying to text my friends back in Houston about how stupid this all is."

"Addilyn, c'mon... we're all trying here," Sophie berates.

"Maybe you should have tried harder when you found out you were pregnant, Mom? Like telling Raid I existed, for starters."

Silence falls over the truck because no one can argue with that statement.

I glance into the rearview to see Addi scowling at her cell, and I exhale. "Addi, we can't change what happened. But we're together now, and the only way this will work is if we all make an effort."

Addi's eyes meet mine in the rearview. "I'm sorry if having to go to a new school in a new city today is kind of playing on my mind right now. You don't know what it's like starting over, being the new kid with family drama. Everyone is going to be talking about me, and *I'll* have to deal with that. *Not* you. So forgive me if I'm a little... *preoccupied.*"

My shoulders tense, and I glance at Sophie. High school was easy for us. We had each other to lean on. Unfortunately, Addi is starting over and hasn't got anyone she can turn to for support right now. "I understand high school can be shit but know that if anyone starts anything with you, they'll have me to deal with."

"Right! Like I'm going to send my *absent father* in for me. Thanks, Raid, but no thanks."

I have to admit that stings.

Sophie spins back, facing Addi. "Young lady, that's not fair. Raid didn't have a choice in this. Remember that!"

Addi snorts out her disgust. "Oh... I do."

We pull into the school's parking lot and file out in silence, with me helping Sophie. I can't help but notice some of the kids staring at Addi, talking in their groups in hushed whispers as we walk toward the entrance.

Addi groans out a huff. "Great! Could you have *not* worn your damn leather coat thing? For my first day, at least? Now they're all going to think I'm a biker brat."

Grimacing, I feel like shit for giving these asshole kids any kind of ammunition against Addi. My cut is something I automatically slip on in the morning. I don't even think about it because it's like another layer of skin.

Dad Lesson Number One...Don't wear my cut to school.

The thing is that it's not such a big deal—it could be helpful. So I say, "It will only show those fuckers who *not* to mess with. You'll see."

Sophie is quiet as I help her walk inside the building and straight to the office for our meeting.

Addi is silent while we wait for Principal Schneider, but as she opens the door and spots me, there's a clear hesitation in her eyes. "Addilyn, I am ready to see you and your parents now," Schneider says, her eyes still focused on me.

Damn! I really should have taken off my cut.

We stand and make our way inside her office. I hold out the chair for Sophie and help her to sit. Addi stands, pacing around the back of the office while I take the spare seat next to Sophie. Schneider places her hands on the desk. "Mr. and Mrs. Tait, I would like to officially welcome you and Addilyn to Prescott Hills High."

Widening my eyes, I glance at Sophie, and she back at me. I figure we don't want to start school on the wrong foot, so I correct her. "Sorry, it's just Sophie and Addi with the surname Tait. My name is Jay Goodwin."

Schneider widens her eyes, looking through the files. "Oh heavens, I do apologize. Actually, now that I look over the files, it seems we don't have records for you on Addilyn's admissions, Mr. Goodwin. We may need to adjust her forms while you're here if Ms. Tait would like you to be added as a guardian?"

Sophie sits forward. "Jay is Addi's father, and as you can see, he will need to be a point of contact as well as myself. I am currently suffering from a stage four cancer diagnosis, so I need Jay to be on the contact list."

Addi scoffs, folding her arms over her chest.

Schneider dips her chin. "I am sorry to hear that, Ms. Tait. And Addilyn..." she looks up, "... the school is here to help you with anything you need. School wise, and also emotionally through this transition period."

Addi curls up her lip. "Whatever! I just want to get to class. Can I get out of here?"

Schneider picks up a folder. "Sure, Addilyn. Here is your schedule. If you need anyone to help you, you can ask any of the teachers, or—" Addi yanks the folder from Schneider's grip and races for the door, totally ignoring her.

"*Addi*," Sophie calls out, but she slams the door so hard behind her a book falls from the bookshelf.

We are left alone with the principal, and I exhale heavily at my daughter's anti-social behavior.

Sophie turns back to Schneider. "I am so sorry," She sighs. "Our daughter is having such a tough time adjusting to all this. I swear she's a good kid—"

"Don't worry, it's fine, Ms. Tait. Addilyn is going through a lot."

Sophie's eyes glisten, and she nods. "Yeah. She's not coping with all..." Sophie points to herself, "... this."

"How are your treatments coming along?"

Sophie shakes her head. "We've stopped all treatment. They only make me worse, and for the last few weeks or months, or however long I have, I don't want to be hunched over a toilet and incoherent."

Schneider's eyes show clear sadness as she turns to me. "It's a good thing that Addilyn has a strong father figure to look out for her."

I roll my shoulders. "She's known me twenty-four hours. I don't know how much of a father figure I am to her right now, but I intend to be the best father I can be."

Schneider widens her eyes, and Sophie sighs. "Jay and I were together young. I found out I was pregnant, and I left without telling him. He never knew about Addi until I showed up yesterday and told him. Equally, I told Addi her father was dead because I didn't want an unplanned pregnancy to stop Jay from making a career for himself. Apparently, all I did was screw everyone up by walking away that day."

Schneider cranes her head to the side. "So you're telling me Addi has only just found out she has a father…. yesterday?" We both nod. "Okay, that explains why she is resisting everything right now. This does make her case a little more delicate. She has a lot going on, so we will keep a close eye on her. If there is any trouble, who should I call?"

I turn to Sophie, and she weakly smiles. "They should call you, Jay. I'm in no fit state to be taking charge anymore. Plus, when I'm gone…" she trails off.

An intense sense of fear rolls over me.

My palms sweat.

My stomach rolls with nausea.

But I know I have to do this.

For Addilyn.

"Okay, yeah, call me."

Schneider pulls out a form and slides it over. "Mr. Goodwin, please fill out this form so we can add you to Addilyn's file, and then we can make you her first point of contact."

Taking a deep breath, I pull out a pen and start writing everything down, feeling a huge weight pressing on my shoulders.

I have a whole person I have to take care of now.

It's such a massive responsibility.

My entire world has changed in the blink of an eye, and I have no idea how to handle it.

All I know is that I want to provide for Addi the best way I can. I just don't know how to do that.

After filling out the forms and creating an action plan for Addi with Schneider, Sophie and I leave her office and walk past Addilyn's classroom. I pop my head over the door to see Addi sitting at a desk, with her head in a book. A slow smile crosses my face.

Sophie wraps her arm in mine. "Don't worry. She'll be fine. She's a tough kid."

I glance at Sophie. "She takes after her mother."

"No, I think she takes after her father in the tough department."

We walk back to the truck quite slowly. This outing seems to have knocked the wind out of Sophie.

It has been a whirlwind since she arrived, and we haven't had any time together to just talk shit out, so as I hop in the driver's side, I turn to Sophie. "I want to take you somewhere."

She smiles. "Okay, where?"

"Just somewhere we can talk for a bit. Is that okay?"

She nods with a warmth about her I fondly remember. "Yeah... I'd like that."

I start the truck and drive a short distance to the nearest park. When I pull up, I hop out and walk around to help Sophie out. Then I lead her to the bench beside a manmade pond. The sun shines down over the glistening water, and I glance out at the ducks swimming on the pond without a care in the world, unlike the monumental changes that have happened for me in the last twenty-four hours.

I reach out and hold Sophie's hand, and she tightens her grip on mine.

"I'm so sorry, Jay," she almost whispers, a tear sliding down her cheek.

My stomach churns as I stare out at the sparkling water.

I want to yell at her...

... then hug her.

I want to scream at her for taking something so precious from me...

... then hold her.

To tell her...

... I missed her.

I am so fucking angry.

I'm so fucking sad.

So undeniably... lost.

All these mixed emotions cause havoc in my body, making me feel fucking sick.

"How could you *ever* think taking my child away from me was the right call, Soph?"

She shakes her head slowly. "I know it wasn't. I thought I was being unselfish. I thought I was doing the right thing by you. But all it did was ruin us all. I'm sure the guilt and stress of it has played a hand in making me sick."

I wrap my arm around her shoulders and pull her closer. "You can't think like that. While I don't understand what you did, and I can't justify your reasonings... what's done is done. We don't have time to point fingers and place blame. We've got to enjoy what time we have left and be a united front for Addi."

"You were always *far* too good for me..." She takes a deep breath. "You had a ring."

My stomach knots as I look at her, her face pale, her head covered by that damn beanie. She looks like a shell of the Sophie I once knew, but I smile down at her. "Yeah... I had a ring."

She shakes her head. "That day at lunch, I took the pregnancy test and freaked out. Then, the job offer came in, and everything happened so fast. Before I knew what was happening, I was packing and on the road. But I want you to know if things were different, if the test was negative, I would've turned down the job in Houston and said yes to the ring."

I don't know if that makes me feel better or ten times fucking worse.

Sighing, I hold her tighter. "But instead, we have Addi, and you've had fourteen good years with her."

"Fourteen amazing years. She really is a great girl, Jay. She's just a little broken and lost right now."

Nodding, I sigh. "She's hurting, lashing out because that's all she can do."

"I need to know you'll be there for her when I die."

My entire body tightens upon hearing Sophie use *those words*, and bile rises in my throat. "Soph—"

"No, Jay, we need to talk about this stuff. When I go, and I know it's not going to be that far away, Addi needs to be kept to her routine. She can have a day or two off school, but then she needs to go back because if she is left to wallow, it will eat her alive. She will fight you on it. She may even try to run away. But I need you to promise me that you'll take good care of her."

"I don't know her, Soph. You've landed our daughter on my doorstep, and you expect that she is going to accept me into her life. I'm not going anywhere, but it might not be as seamless as you expect."

Sophie nods. "I know. That's on me. I left it too long. And this is *all* my fault. You have no idea how often I wanted to call and tell you what she'd done during the day. When she took her first steps, I was so excited I actually called your cell, but your number had changed, then I took that as a sign that you weren't supposed to know. I am *so* fucking sorry, Jay. I honestly thought I was doing the right thing. I was so young, so stupid, and so damn naive. I wanted you to do something with your life... I had no idea me leaving would stop that path anyway. I never even considered the damage my leaving would cause you. *Young and stupid*... they don't say those words for no reason, right?"

"No one can predict the future. You had no idea what I was going to do when you left. Should you have told me about Addi? Absolutely. But what's done is done. We've both lived our lives and have gone down roads we can't change. We just have to play the hand that's been dealt as we have it now."

Sophie nods. "So... Frankie seems nice."

Subject change!

"Don't even start with me, Soph."

"What? She's gorgeous. You think I didn't pick up the chemistry between the two of you?"

"It's complicated."

"Because of me? *Please* don't let it be because of me."

"It's more than just you, Soph. I have to put all my attention on Addilyn right now—"

"Okay, I get that. But for you to be good for Addi, you have to be happy with yourself. If Frankie makes you happy, then you need to lean into that, Jay. From what I have seen, she would move mountains for you."

"It's not that simple... she's a club girl, and I'm a high-ranking brother. It's just not something that normally happens."

Sophie snorts. "Pfft, since when did you ever follow the damn rules?"

"We're not here to talk about me, Soph. We're here to talk about you and Addi."

"On the contrary. I need to know that my... sorry, *our* daughter is going to be taken care of. Is going to have a loving home to support her when I'm gone. Frankie has already shown a supportive arm around Addi's shoulders. I like her, Jay. She's a good fit for you."

"This conversation is starting to feel fucking weird."

Sophie chuckles. "Like you're getting my blessing?"

"Something like that."

"Maybe that's what I am doing, letting you know that I realize I fucked you around. I recognize I hurt you. I know I have already said this, but... I'm *so, so sorry* I left you the way I did. Just know I never stopped loving you. Watching Addi grow and seeing how much of you is in her reminded me of you every damn day. It broke me too. It's just... the longer I left it, the harder it became to tell you and Addi the truth."

"Until it was too late."

"Until it was too late, and I had no choice."

"If I said I wasn't angry that you took off and kept her from me, I'd be lying. You deprived me of my daughter. Of the first fourteen years of her life. I'm a stranger to her because of you, Sophie. I'm fucking angry as hell…" A single tear slides down her cheek as I glance back to the pond and take a centering breath. "But the fact you found some inner courage to come and find me, knowing the hurt you would cause both Addi and me in the short term for the long-term gain, makes it all worthwhile. If Addi accepts me into her life, it will *all* be worth it." I take a steadying breath, not wanting to let my emotions get the best of me.

Instead of telling her, I feel fucking cheated.

That *she* stole fourteen fucking years of my life.

And how dare she come to me in *her* time of need.

But fuck if seeing her wilting in front of my very eyes doesn't do my head in.

I have a daughter.

She's here now.

That's what matters.

Sophie smiles. "She will… she's so affectionate when she opens up. She has a heart full of love, and she will need someone to pour that into when I am gone."

"Don't worry. Me and the club are gonna take good care of her. In the meantime, let's get you back to the clubhouse, and I'm gonna get Hoodoo to check you over because you're looking a little pale."

"I'm fine. It's just been a big morning. What with taking Addi to school, and now we're here talking about painful memories. I just need to rest."

"Then let's get you back home."

We walk to the truck, with me almost carrying her, then drive to the clubhouse. With all the excitement this morning, she is deteriorating quickly. So when we arrive, I know she can't walk. I pick her up and carry her toward the entrance. With my adrenalin pumping at how fast she is fading, I race through the doors while everyone looks at me, but there is only one person I want right now. "Hoodoo!" I call out as I run through the clubhouse straight for Sophie's room, placing her on her bed.

Hoodoo is behind me in a flash. "What happened?"

"We were out all morning dealing with Addi's school and talking, and on the way back, she started zoning in and out. She's so fucking pale, Hoodoo. What's wrong with her?"

He leans in and checks her vitals as I stand back, pacing the bedroom floor, hoping I haven't made this all go faster than expected by me needing to talk about our past. My heart races so damn fast I feel like I'm hyperventilating as I stare at Sophie, her breaths short and shallow.

Hoodoo stands and looks at me with a somber face. "It's okay. She's exhausted. She is going to get like this Raid. She can't do too much at one time… she's at the end of life, and she should be in a hospice right now. All we can do is make her as comfortable as we can. But it's only going to get worse from here on out. I'll get her some HydraLyte to make sure she is well-hydrated. But she needs to rest and take her pain meds."

Letting out a heavy sigh, I grip his shoulder. "Thanks, brother, appreciate it."

"Best thing you can do now is to let her sleep, and you go back to work."

I gently caress Sophie's face, pulling her beanie down over her ears and tucking her in further, ensuring she is kept warm. Seeing her so frail like this is heartbreaking. But I step back and walk out of the room to let her recover, feeling like shit for wearing her out.

The last thing I want to do is send her to the grave earlier because I had to clear the damn air. What's done is fucking done. I want her to be around for as long as possible for Addi because I don't want to see Addi hurting. I want to protect her from that inevitable pain because I know she is going to experience it because I'm going to feel it too. And if I can protect Addi from that pain for as long as I can, you can bet I am going to do everything in my power to achieve that end.

Because she is blood.

And I protect what's mine.

CHAPTER 6

RAID

Hurricane glances over me as I approach but waits for me to talk first.

I need to focus my attention on something else. Something other than the clusterfuck that my life has turned into right now.

"What's on the plan for today?" I ask.

Hurricane simply nods, like he understands I need to get on with work and club business. I don't want to talk about Sophie and Addi, I need to get lost in the club.

"There's been an incident with the Iron Chains MC. They've been linked to the traffickin' of women and launderin' money 'round the casinos, startin' race turf wars and all kinda shit we don't want in our city. So we need to call a meetin' and inform 'em while we share our streets out of courtesy that they gotta toe the line or get the fuck out of New Awlins."

Nodding my head, I smirk. "You want me to send Frost a message?"

Hurricane grunts. "Na, we better pay Frost a little visit. Let's gather the guys and mount up."

Hurricane sends a whistle through the clubhouse, and

everyone turns. "Brothers, we're riding out to the Iron Chains MC. Gotta straighten 'em out a little."

Everyone dips their chins and heads for the exit as my eyes shift to Frankie. She weakly smiles at me. *Goddammit!* I want to tell her everything about my morning, but it will have to wait. So I simply grin, then turn and walk out for my ride.

My muscles are tense as shit. It's no wonder, given everything going on right now. Hopefully, this ride will ease the strain. Riding always soothes my nerves.

Throwing my leg over my bike, I start the engine, revving a few times to warm her up. The deep drawl of the motor makes me feel a little more human while the rest of my brothers bring their Harleys to life beside me.

We take off, out of the yard, toward our destination.

To an allied biker clubhouse, the only other one in New Orleans allowed on our turf.

The sole reason? Because the founding president was one of us.

Frost came from Houston Defiance.

He went out on his own once the brothers started getting old ladies and having kids. That life wasn't for him. Frost didn't like the family atmosphere the club was diving into, so he defected and created his own club. He couldn't create another chapter of Defiance because we already existed in New Orleans, so he formed the Iron Chains MC.

Defiance has a code of conduct that Frost didn't want to adhere to. The Iron Chains are breaking boundaries, and so that's why we're paying them a visit. To stop them from turning New Orleans into a fucking shit show where bikers are concerned. We need to strike while the iron is hot and shut this shit down.

Riding up to the old, converted church they use for their clubhouse, where the gates are high and ethereal, it's the opposite of what you would expect from bikers, but that's the point. They want to give off the impression that they're not as bad as they are to the community around them.

As Hurricane pulls up to the gates, a prospect aims his weapon until he realizes who we are, then he lowers it again. "Fuck, guys, maybe announce you're coming next time, so I don't freak the fuck out when a bunch of bikers ride up unannounced?"

Hurricane chuckles. "But where would the fun be in that?"

The prospect smirks. "I swear my asshole is still puckering. I had no idea how I was gonna take on all y'all."

We chuckle, and Hurricane says, "First thing you shoulda done was radio through for backup if you weren't sure, Prospect."

The gates begin to open, and Frost and his VP, Dirty, step through. "He *did* call for backup," Frost replies with a big smile as Dirty sprays some hand sanitizer on his hands. The guy's a walking contradiction. They call him Dirty because he's such a fucking clean freak.

"Glad you're teachin' your prospects somethin' right then. Apologize for the unannounced visit. We need to run a few things by you. Can we come in?" Hurricane asks, and Frost waves his hand.

"My clubhouse is your clubhouse. You're welcome here anytime. Park your rides. Come on in for a beer... on me."

Frost and Dirty step to the side to let us ride in, and we enter their clubhouse lot and park our rides behind theirs. Jumping off my bike, I don't feel as relaxed as I was hoping from my ride.

Maybe I'm just wound too damn tight.

Hopefully, a drink with the guys will help.

We all walk to the main door and follow Frost and Dirty inside.

This place never ceases to amaze me. The interior is painted gray and white. The stained-glass windows are still intact and sit tall just below the high ceilings.

The guys have their pool table, dart board, and pinball machines at the mezzanine level. It's like a bachelor pad up there. Underneath the mezzanine is the living area with sofas and coffee tables, not to mention a projector television screen against a white wall.

To the left are the stairs leading up to the mezzanine. Then to the back of the living area, which leads to the housing quarters, where I assume the chancel was located in the original church. The club has built onto the church from behind, where their sleeping quarters are situated, and the stained-glass doors leading from the main club rooms to the sleeping quarters give it that extra churchy vibe. It's a contradicting look that somehow works.

The bar sits almost at the front of the space where an aisle would have been to the left. I know there must be other rooms that run off this main one, but I haven't been here enough to know where they are. All I know is that this clubhouse is unique as hell, or is it heaven in this case?

Club members greet us along the way, welcoming us with a mix of confusion and hesitation. "Hey, fuckers, what the hell are all y'all doing here?" Salt asks, slapping me on the back.

"Here to talk business, asshole." I smirk.

Frost glances at Hurricane. "Well then, let's not waste any time. Chapel?" he asks, and we nod as he leads us through to what was previously the priest's chambers.

We take a seat at the long oval table, and Frost sits back, hands behind his head and his eyes focusing straight on Hurricane. "So… what brings you to this side of town?"

"Frost, I've known you since you were a member of Houston Defiance. You went out on your own, and because of your affiliations with Defiance, we let you have your club on our territory. But you're startin' to do shit we don't approve of, and word is gettin' back to us that you're causin' chaos in the streets of NOLA." Hurricane is straight to the point.

Frost chuckles while shaking his head. "Why would I do something like that? I know New Orleans is your property. We pay the tax to ride here. I wouldn't *dream* of stepping on your toes, Hurricane," he states too easily.

Apparent tension floods the air as Hurricane huffs. "Good. See that you don't! Or we're gonna have a *very* big fuckin' problem, you and me."

"Won't be an issue, Pres. You have my word. Now if you don't mind, we were about to head out for a ride." Frost shakes Hurricane's hand and gestures for us to stand.

Hurricane hesitates but stands, signaling for the rest of us to move. We head for the exit, seeing as we're more or less being ushered the fuck out. But considering how I thought this would go, it was pretty damn smooth.

Maybe a little *too smooth.*

"While I understand your reasoning for dropping in like this, Hurricane, a little warning next time, yeah?" Frost states, and Hurricane chuckles.

"Yeah, brother. I'll call next time. Catchya 'round."

We walk out to our rides, Frost and Dirty hanging back inside their clubhouse, all talk of a beer on Frost now gone.

City, Bayou, Hurricane, and I gather around in a circle.

I raise my brow. "That felt *way* too easy?"

Hurricane clears his throat, keeping his voice low. "Raid, I need you to monitor them. I know you have a lot going on right now, but you think you can handle this as well?"

"Yeah, Pres. I got this."

"Okay, let's get the fuck outta here."

We all jump on our bikes, revving them a few times for good measure, then take off to ride back to our clubhouse by the bayou. The vibration of the engine sends a shot of adrenaline through me. Today has been a crazy fucking day, and feeling the hum of my beast beneath me is cathartic.

I need this.

To feel the wind flowing through my long hair as it whips at my face.

Being free, at one with the highway, feeling completely open to the elements—yeah, it's totally intoxicating. There's nothing like it on this earth.

After a problem-free ride, we pull into the clubhouse gates. I spot Frankie standing outside waiting for us, and I can't help but smile. Seeing her makes everything a little fucking brighter.

Hopping off my ride, the early fall sun smacks my skin, causing a bead of sweat to drip down my temple. Swiping it away with the back of my arm, I walk over to Frankie, and she hands me a drink.

"Am I getting special treatment?" I take the cool glass of beer from her delicate hand.

She chuckles. "Maybe just a little, but I want to talk to you about something."

I take a generous sip of the nectar of the gods and nod. "Butter me up with beer first, huh?"

"Something like that. I was thinking..." she pauses while assessing me, "... what do you think about me spending some time with Addi? I felt a connection with her yesterday, and I want her to know she has someone she can confide in who isn't related if shit gets too intense for her here. I won't be in her face all the time. I only want her to know I'll be here for whatever she needs."

I smile and my heart squeezes in the way it does when I'm around this woman. "Appreciate that. It'll be a big help. If there's anyone I want to help guide Addi through all this, it's you."

Frankie smiles. "Really?"

"Yeah, Franks, you mean a lot to me. I want Addi to feel safe and cared for, and I know you can do that for her."

"I sure as heck want to try my hardest."

"Addi seems to have an attitude toward me, but if she can connect and trust you, then at least when Sophie goes, she will have someone she can talk to about how she's feeling until I can break through that barrier with her."

Frankie gently caresses my arm. "She'll come 'round. She'll have to love you. I mean... how can she not?"

My eyes meet hers, a moment shared between us. "Thanks, Franks." Letting out a long exhale, I glance down at my watch and grimace. "Shit! I have to go pick up Addi from school."

Frankie shrugs. "Let me come seeing as Sophie is still resting."

Rolling my shoulders, I could do with the backup. "Great! You're really helping me out here. Honestly, I have no fucking clue what I am doing."

She squeezes my shoulder. "You're doing just fine. I don't think there's a handbook on how to play this kind of situation, Raid, but the way you're stepping up for Addi and Sophie, well... most men wouldn't be as proactive as you are being."

"They're family," I simply say with a shrug of my shoulders, and Frankie smiles.

"So then, let's go get your daughter."

I glance at my beer, thinking better of drinking the rest before driving, then place the glass on a keg, and turn for the pickup.

We jump into the truck, and I take off feeling like this day is just one damn thing after the other.

Frankie places her calming hand on my bobbing knee, which is exactly what I need right now. She's managed to calm my rampaging thoughts without even trying.

I glance over at her and smile. "Glad you're here."

"Wouldn't be anywhere else." She squeezes my thigh.

Pulling out of the clubhouse, I start the short drive to the high school, and Frankie fills me in on what she's been up to today with her studies. I have to admit it's awesome distracting myself from my life, even if only for a moment. But as we pull up at the school's curb, I glance across the yard to witness a kid pushing Addi over. Her books scatter across the lawn when she falls to her knees. My hands clench around the steering wheel when I turn the truck off and race to Addi faster than I thought possible, with my fists balled at my sides.

"Raid! *Raid*... remember he's just a kid," Frankie calls out behind me.

I don't fucking care about that fact, as a bunch of fucking asshole cunts circle around Addi, laughing at her.

My feet pound the ground so damn hard I feel like the earth is quaking beneath me.

No one picks on my daughter.

No. One!

Upon reaching the kids, I hear them laughing and joking at Addi's expense, and I shove my way through the fuckers, not caring who I hurt in the process. A kid goes flying to the ground as I shove him out of the way to reach Addi. Leaning down, I pick her up out of the dirt. "You okay?"

She glances up at me, tears streaming down her face, but a look of complete shock adorns her eyes when she realizes it's me. "Y-yes."

My pulse races so fucking fast as the little brats stare at me, clearly scared shitless, as I hand Addi over to Frankie, then turn back to the assholes who were hurting Addi, pointing at them with intent. They all flinch, jerking back like they think I'm going to smash their heads together.

I *really* fucking want to.

"You pick up Addi's stuff, *right... fucking... now*, and do it nicely."

The little shits rush around, picking up her books and her bag, and sheepishly hand them back to Addi. She takes them, swinging her bag over her shoulder as I step forward, staring the assholes down.

"You start shit with my kid, and it won't just be me who comes to protect her next time. My whole club will. And trust me... they're not going to be as lenient as I am *right now*. You hurt her again, she gets even *one... single... scratch* on her, I will find where you live and make your parents suffer so painfully that you'll hear their screams for the rest of your *miserable... damn... existence*. You understand me, *you little pricks?*"

They all nod their heads backing away slowly, then one turns, scurrying away like a scared little rat, and then like a flock of sheep, they all take off, scampering away like the little chicken-fucking-shits they are.

My blood boils as I turn back to Addi.

Oh shit!

Her face is contorted, her eyes wide, and her face red.

Is she angry? At me?

She crosses her arms over her chest. "Did you seriously just threaten bodily harm to their parents? They're going to tell Principal Schneider, and I will probably be suspended or expelled. Great first day. Thanks a lot, *Raid!*" She storms off to the truck, slamming herself inside.

My shoulders slump as I let out a long, drawn-out exhale. "Fuck."

Frankie pats me on the shoulder. "For what it's worth, I think you showed those little assholes who *not* to mess with."

So why do I have a sinking feeling that I may have just made shit so much worse?

"Let's get her home."

CHAPTER 7

FRANKIE

The tension in the air is thick, and as I look in the rearview, Addi is still crying softly, so I know I need to try and fix this somehow. Turning in my seat, I face her and reach out, placing my hand on her leg. "Hey honey, you know Raid was only trying to help the situation?"

She snaps her head up at me. "If Mom was here, she would *never* have threatened those guys. She would have gone to the teachers, but she would *not* have done *that*. I'm going to be in so much trouble."

Raid shifts uncomfortably in his seat while he continues to drive.

I sigh. "It will sort itself ou—"

"I want to go home. Back to Houston. Where I had friends and everything was normal. Where Mom wasn't sick, and everything was fine."

"Hey, you listen and listen good... you have family here. A big family now, and we will do *everything* we can to support and care for you. I know it may not feel like home, but it is, and everyone is *so* happy to have you here, Addi. This club will support you no matter what. We may do things a little differently, but it's always with the best intentions. No one will take care of you and support and guide you like your father is going to, young lady. You need to open your eyes and see it," I tell her.

Addi sniffles, her eyes falling to her lap as she remains quiet.

So I spin back around, facing the front.

Raid glances across at me and dips his chin in thanks. "How about we get something to eat on the way home? Beignets?"

"I've never had them before," Addi replies, and Raid smiles.

"Beignets it is. We'll get enough to share with your mom too."

We make our way to Café du Monde, buy far too many beignets, and then head back to the clubhouse.

Addi's spirits are lifting as we all walk toward their bedroom to take the sugary treats to Sophie. When we enter the room, Hoodoo is standing over Sophie's bed, taking her vitals, and Addi stops in shock.

I hold onto Addi with one arm wrapped around her body to steady her.

"M-Mom, are you o-okay?"

Sophie lifts her head from the pillow, and it's easy to see that the strain of doing that is taxing her. Her pale, hollow face reminds me of how sick she really is, and for some reason, it shocks me. I mean, I know she's terminally ill, but today has brought home just how long she might have left.

Sophie smiles, and although she tries to put on a brave front, it's more than obvious she is weak and incredibly unwell. "I'm fine, sweetheart. It's merely a down day."

I let go of Addi, and she rushes over to her mom, sitting on the edge of the bed.

Hoodoo steps up to Raid and me. "Her blood pressure is low, so don't let her get out of bed, okay?"

I nod. "Is it okay for her to have some beignets?"

Hoodoo smiles. "The sugar will do her good, actually. But if she needs to get out of bed, she must have help. She's too weak at the moment. Tomorrow she may be okay again, but right now, she needs rest… lots of it."

"You got it," I reply.

Hoodoo walks out.

After I watch him leave, I walk the beignets over to Sophie and Addi.

Addi smirks. "Raid came to the school and decided to Hulk Smash one of the kids who was picking on me. Said he was going to their parents and shit."

Sophie laughs while Addi scowls. "It's not funny, Mom. They're gonna expel me."

"Then we'll enroll you in another school, Addi. It's no big deal. At least he was protecting you from those little assholes."

"You're on *his* side?"

"There are no sides, sweetheart. I think you're overly emotional and not seeing the bigger picture."

"Which is?"

"Those kids will be terrified of you now. They won't come after you again."

"Bullshit! They'll come after me worse. I'll probably have my head flushed tomorrow."

Sophie slides some hair behind Addi's ear. "So young, still so much to learn. He threatened their parents. If the bullies think their parents are going to find out they've been intimidating kids at school, they will be terrified of getting shit at home. Bullies are often the victims of bullies, sweetheart. They're copping it at home… I'd be willing to put money on it. They bully you to make themselves feel better about feeling like shit when they're at home. You threaten to tell their parents, it's a whole world of hurt they don't want raining down on them. You watch… Raid did you a favor."

"Maybe…" Addi deflects with, "Anyway, we stopped off at Café du Monde and got you some beignets."

Sophie smiles. "Maybe I'll just have one bite to see what all the hype is about."

She pulls out a beignet and looks it over, waggling her brow at Addi. "Have you tried one yet?"

Addi shakes her head. "No, I was waiting to have one with you."

"Well then, kiddo, let's do this."

Addi pulls one out of the bag, and Sophie and Addi both take a bite. Their faces light up, and I chance a glimpse at Raid, seeing him smile for the first time in hours.

"These are *good*! Thank you for getting them, Frankie, and for being here to help with Addi," Sophie says.

"It's my pleasure. I want Addi to know I am here whenever either of you needs me."

Addi stands, leans across, and wraps her arms around me in a tight embrace. My eyes widen as I look across at Raid, and a wave of what can only be described as relief crosses his face. I cuddle her, letting her know I genuinely care. Addi slowly pulls back, her eyes meeting mine. "I feel like you're the only one here who understands me, Frankie."

Sophie exhales. "That's just not true, Addi."

Addi glances at her mother. "I didn't mean you, Mom. You go without saying."

Sophie frowns. "Do you really hate it here *that* much?"

Sophie's eyes widen like she's terrified, and Addi sinks back into herself, finally realizing that she is hurting her mother by being a damn brat.

"No, I don't hate it here. I just miss home. I miss my friends."

An idea pops into my mind, so I say, "Well, I think I might have a fix for that. We have another girl living here. She is a couple of years older than you. Her name is Clover, and she is new here too. Maybe you two might find some common ground?" I tell her.

Sophie smiles. "I think you should meet her, Addi. Try and make a friend."

"I should stay here with *you*, keep *you* company."

"Sweetheart, I'm going back to sleep in about two point five minutes. I'm going to be no fun. You go... investigate the clubhouse and have some fun with Clover. And... *do your homework*!"

Addi groans. "Yes, Mom."

I wrap my arm around Addi and lead her out of the room, leaning my head against hers and smile. "You're going to be just fine. C'mon, let's go meet Clover."

"You think she's going to wanna talk to me?"

I guide Addi to Clover's room, offering some reassurance. "I think she'll be happy to have another teenager in the clubhouse with her, for sure."

We stop at Clover's door, and Addi turns me to face her. "What if she hates me like the other kids at school?"

I grab her shoulders and look into her eyes. "Impossible! And the kids at school don't hate you. They were simply hazing the new girl."

"You really think so?"

"I know so." Placing my fist out, I knock twice on Clover's door, and Addi tenses all her muscles. She puts on this tough girl act in front of Raid, but actually, she is an insecure young girl who just wants approval.

Clover opens the door seconds later. "Oh, hey... I heard there was a new girl at the club." She smiles wide. "You must be Addilyn?" Clover places her hand out for Addi to shake, and she widens her eyes like she wasn't expecting Clover to be so welcoming.

"Oh... hey, yeah, it's just Addi. And you're Clover, right?"

"Yeah, my brother calls me Clo. You know... I think I saw you at school today. You go to Prescott Hills?"

Addi smiles wide. "Yeah, started there today."

"Great! I mean, I'm a couple of years above you, but I'd be happy to sit with you and show you around at lunch and stuff."

I smile, loving how Clover is taking on the 'big sister' role. Just like I knew she would.

"Really? That would be amazing. I was picked on today, so it'll be nice to have a friendly face around campus."

"Of course. You're a freshman, yeah? I bet it was Trey Miller and those dicks who were picking on you, right?"

Addi nods, and Clover snorts. "Figures. Guy thinks he owns the school. God help us all when he is a senior."

"So, how do you fit into all of this, if you don't mind me asking?" Addi queries.

"My brother Jesse is a prospect."

Addi stares blankly at Clover. "I don't know what that means."

Clover looks at me for clarification.

"Basically, he's a biker in training, like a probationary biker. He's the lowest rank in the club and has to do all the grunt work until he can prove himself and gain his patches. Then, once Hurricane and City think he's done his time, he will make rank and be a full member. They will give him a road name as well."

Addi shakes her head. "I have so much to learn."

Clover giggles. "Tell me about it. I'm still learning it all. We can study together if you like."

"Deal!"

My chest warms at seeing Addi finally smiling. It's good to watch her getting along so great with Clover, and I know I need to let this friendship blossom on its own. "Okay, girls, I'm going to go and do some club girl stuff. You two going to be okay in here? Not going to cause too much mischief?"

Clover and Addi giggle. "We'll be good."

I wink at Addi before Clover leads her into her room.

"Thank you," Addi mouths to me, and I dip my head at her before turning to leave.

Yeah, Addi is going to be just fine.

CHAPTER 8

Frankie
The Next Day

As I pack a light bag, I'm being torn in two.

Part of me—a major part—is telling me to stop everything and stay here at the club. To put my life on hold and ensure I am here for Raid and Addi. But as I place my *Student's Book of College English* textbook in my bag, a sense of accomplishment rolls through me.

I've been a club girl for so damn long.

I've worked so freaking hard to get this placement.

I can't throw it all away now.

This could be my only shot at getting something better for my life.

Don't get me wrong. I adore this club and everyone in it. Helping run this place has been a lifesaver, but I need *more*.

I want *more*.

I deserve *more*.

That's why I took this English course. Hell, it may not lead to anything, but I won't know if I don't try, and throwing in the towel now because life is getting hectic will only hurt me in the long run.

So I straighten my shoulders, shove the textbook in my bag, zip it up, and throw it over my shoulder. I smile at Storm, who's watching me.

"You were just having a complete conversation with yourself in your head then, weren't you?" Storm grins.

"Am I that obvious?"

She wipes down the bar with a chuckle. "For what it's worth, I think you need to do what's best for you, Frankie. This club can function for a few hours without you. I'll hold down the fort. And if anyone in particular…" she glances past me to where Raid is chatting with Hurricane, "… needs you, I'm sure they'll call."

Letting out a heavy exhale, I nod. "You're right. Of course, you're right. I'm gonna go. I'll see you when I get back."

"Make me proud, learn all the things," she calls as I take off heading for the club parking lot.

My stomach twists because I feel like I'm letting Raid down. I should be here for him. But I have to admit it's hard having him be so close and yet so untouchable. I know we've never taken that step over the friend's barrier, but it felt like it was just within reach.

Now my heart hurts knowing we probably missed our shot.

Because he has far more important people in his life to be concerned about.

I don't begrudge him that at all, but I can't deny that it really freaking hurts.

Shaking my head from the thoughts that seem to be inundating my mind lately, I let out a deep breath as I reach for my car door handle. Thunderous footsteps pound up behind me, making me turn to Raid. My heart flutters a beat or two at the sight of him. His long dusty blond hair is pulled back half up, half down. His chiseled jawline is so strong and covered in a slight beard. His muscles ripple, wrapped in so much ink I could get lost in the designs for days. This man is spectacular to look at, and I instinctively clench my thighs together to dull the ache forming there as he steps up to me.

"Hey, where you off to?" he asks with a smile that could make any girl's panties fall to the floor.

"I have classes today, but if you need me to stay—"

"I don't want you to stop your life for what's happening in mine, Frankie. I appreciate you helping me with Addi, and I will always accept that help where she's concerned. Because fuck knows, I have *no* clue what I am doing. But please... don't stop what you need to do because of me. You have to go to class, don't ask for my permission."

I weakly smile and nod. "Okay. I'm going to class then."

Raid smiles. "Good... I'm taking you."

My eyes widen as he grabs my hand and drags me toward his bike. I dig my heels in and stop him in his tracks. "Raid, no. You need to stay here for Sophie. What if Addi needs yo—"

"Addi is at school, and Sophie is sleeping. Probably will be all day. I know I can't give you much right now, but what I can give you is protection to and from class. With all this upheaval, I need to know you're safe, Frankie. So please, with my mind in constant chaos, let this not be another thing I need to worry about."

My shoulders slump, and I know he was trying to make that sound like it was about him, but I read between the lines. He wants to make sure I am safe. He wants to spend time with me to make sure I'm okay.

And I am good with that.

Plus, I'll take any alone time with Raid that I can get.

"Can you go really fast, though? 'Cause I'm running late," I tease.

He grins and we start walking toward his bike. "I can run all the reds if you'd like?"

"Hey now, let's not get too carried away." I chuckle. "I'd like all my limbs intact."

He reaches over, handing me a helmet, and I gaze at him with a raised brow. "Really?"

"Especially if I am going to be riding fast. Safety first."

"Fine!" I plop it over my red hair. He leans in, doing up the strap for me. Our eyes lock, the air around us sizzling with intense energy. My breathing quickens as I lick my bottom lip. I want him to kiss me so damn bad.

With my helmet secured, he rests his forehead on mine, and my breathing picks up, our breaths mixing. Even though I know we're not in the right place, my heart says otherwise, beating erratically at his nearness.

He slowly pulls back, clearing his throat. "You ready for the ride of your life?"

I snort. "I dunno, Raid. I'm a club girl. I've done a lot of riding in my time."

He turns to me, scowling. "Yeah, but you've never ridden me or with me."

I smirk. "Touché. Then you better throw your leg over and show me what ya got."

He grins, mounting his hog.

Fuck! That move was sexy as sin.

I move in behind him, my arms sliding around his waist, holding on tight. I inhale—his scent of leather and sandalwood surrounds me. He smells so damn good my clit instantly begins to tingle. He starts his bike, and as it roars to life, the vibration makes me slide closer to his ass.

He duckwalks the bike back, reversing it out of the parking lot, then takes off. The gate opens, and we dart out onto the street so fast I don't have time to think. I let out a surprised squeal, feeling his torso shaking with laughter as he goes.

Fucking bastard.

But you can't wipe the smile from my face.

This is precisely what we both need—to let loose and unwind from the stress that landed on our doorstep four days ago.

Raid pushes the bike to its limits as he accelerates down the street. The wind whips my hair, flowing behind me, while his tickles my face as it jostles in the breeze. I don't mind, though. I adore his gorgeous hair.

I wish I could run my fingers through it.

Hold onto the strands while he fucks me relentlessly hard.

There are so many things I'm not sure we will ever get to do.

But I won't let the 'what-ifs' ruin this ride for me because I am enjoying it far too much. I hold onto him tighter, resting my cheek against his back and cuddling into him. His hand slides back to rest on my thigh, letting me know he's in this moment too. Right now, it's just us, the wind, the open road, and not a damn care in the world.

It's so fucking nice.

Eventually, he pulls into the campus parking lot, and my energy and excitement begin to dwindle as he slows the bike and comes to a stop. His hand leaves my leg when he cuts the engine and leans the bike to kick out the stand.

Reality sinks back in, and regretfully, I let him go and slide off the back. Then, swallowing hard, I turn and start unbuckling the helmet.

"Here, let me help," he states. So I move closer, and Raid helps, his fingers sliding under my chin to ease out the tight straps. He gently pulls the helmet off my head, and I flick my long hair from side to side, running my fingers through to help with the wild knots that have occurred on the ride over.

Raid shakes his head.

"What?" I ask.

"Nah, nothing."

I shove his shoulder playfully. "What?"

He sighs. "You really are fucking beautiful."

A lump gets caught in my throat, and I bite my bottom lip. "I better get to class," I murmur because, quite simply, I don't know what else to say.

We know we can't act on this attraction.

The whole no-yes, yes-no is giving me whiplash.

And this isn't helping.

"What time do you get out?" Raid asks.

"About one. Why?"

He looks directly into my eyes. "I'll be here—"

"Raid, no. You don't have to do that. I'll catch an Uber or some—"

"Frankie... I'll be here!" His tone is more forceful, lower, and demanding, like he's not giving me a choice.

I have to say it's kind of sexy.

I like this alpha side of him.

"Okay... I'll see you after class." I turn to leave, but he reaches out, grabbing my wrist to stop me.

He grins. "Wait! Before you go... I need to know one thing."

My heart begins to race, and my breath catches when he looks into my eyes longingly. "Yes?" I whisper.

"Was I the best ride of your life?" He smirks.

I roll my eyes, shove him, and turn to walk off. "See you at one."

His low chesty laughter fades as I walk toward the campus building with a pep in my step. Sure, there's a huge dark cloud hanging over the clubhouse, but a tiny glimmer of light was shining on us just now. I don't know what's in the cards for Raid and me—*probably nothing*—but these little moments with him mean the world to me.

Walking up the stairs to the building, I watch all the younger kids moving about campus. I can't help but wonder what they think about someone like me, a thirty-year-old, coming in and taking adult classes. Sure, they have the special class set aside for us 'older' folk, but I'm sure these college-age kids hate the fact that adults come in every few days.

I'm sure they think we cramp their college style.

This course is new. The college is trial running an adult course at the same time as the general courses during the daytime, so I'm the one who lucked out getting to attend.

Walking inside the building, I hoist my backpack higher and make my way to the classroom, the other college kids moving about the halls like they own the place.

I guess they do.

It makes me wonder how different my life would have been if I actually went to college straight out of school. *What if I didn't join the club and tried to make something of myself.* No, I need to stop those thoughts. I must remember that all good things take time, and I am trying to improve my life. It might have taken me a few extra years, but I am doing my best right now.

And that's all that matters.

A fellow adult student, Jasmine, spots me as I enter the classroom. Her eyes light up, she waves me over, and I immediately make my way to her to take a seat.

"Hey! You look nice today. I love that color on you," she says.

I smirk, looking down at my casual clothes, and shrug. "This old thing? I've had this forever, but thank you. Do you think Erin is going to drone on about the importance of Shakespeare again today?"

Jasmine groans. "I assume so. Professor Prim and Proper seems to be obsessed. I'd rather learn more about how Stephen King got so dark and twisted."

Snorting out a laugh, I sink further into my seat. "I think that title suits Erin perfectly. But you have to hand it to her, she is a great teacher."

Jasmine nods. "Yeah, she is. But seriously, fuck Romeo, gimmie Jack Torrance any day."

I raise my brow. "The dude from *The Shining*? Trust you to pick a psychotic writer. That's so you, Jaz."

She smiles wide and nods her head. "I know." She flicks her blonde hair over her shoulder happily like she gives zero fucks that she might be slightly unhinged. But I think that is what draws me to her, the fact she's not afraid to be so unapologetically her.

Movement to my side has me glancing up at Daniel, who is standing above me. His dark hair flopping over in a coif, dangling a little on his pale face. His iridescent blue eyes linger on me like they always do, and his bright smile lights up the room. The guy is gorgeous and has an old-worldly feel about him. He could be a dead ringer for James Dean in an old '50s movie with his tight white tee, chain around his neck, and black jacket—though I'm not sure it's genuine leather. I like to think with all the time at the club that I'm a bit of a pro at spotting *real* leather.

It doesn't matter, though. He wears it well.

"Hey, Frankie, it's always nice seeing you here," Daniel states, his eyes lingering on mine.

I smirk. "Hey, Dan... you get your homework assignment done?" I ask, striking up a conversation.

He tilts his head. "I would have gotten it done quicker if I had some people over for a study group. The offer is still open if you guys wanna come join me after class one time. We could grab some snacks, maybe some drinks, and work on the assignments together?"

I turn to Jaz, and she grins. "Don't you think that's something they do in *real* college? Aren't we all a little too old for study buddies?" Jaz chuckles.

I tend to agree, plus I don't have much spare time. With the club and my duties there, and wanting to help out with Raid, Addi, and Sophie as much as I can, I know I can't spare the time to hang out with my new friends to study. As it is, I have to make time at the club to do my assignments when I can. "Sorry, Dan, I have so little spare time. So I have to study when I find the small spaces in my schedule to fit it in. It sounds nice, though. Maybe one day."

He dips his head. "I'll take that, and hey, if not for studying, then maybe I can take you out for a drink, Frankie?"

I squish my eyebrows as Jasmine giggles beside me—the traitor. My stomach clenches, immediately thinking of Raid. Every inch of me wants to be with him. But honestly, with Sophie and her condition, and now Addi in the picture, I don't see us ever being able to make it work.

Maybe I should cut and run.

Take another opportunity when it's being presented.

Dan is hot. He's always super friendly, and we have a lot in common.

Would it be so bad to leave my options open?

"I have to get back to the club today after class, but maybe next week. We can play it by ear."

Dan grins so wide that the dimples in his cheeks pop in, making him appear even more gorgeous. "I'll take it. And, Jaz, the offer is open for you too."

She smirks. "I think I'll sit this one out. Let you two enjoy some time together."

I widen my eyes, and she winks.

"Catch ya after class," Dan says, patting my desk twice, then walks off to his seat.

Jasmine chuckles, rolling her shoulders. "Oh, man, that was so much fun to watch."

I let out a long groan.

Jasmine narrows her eyes on me. "Now, that's not the sound of a woman who just got hit on and is happy about it. So what's going on in that beautiful flaming red head of yours?"

I rest my chin on my hand as I lean my elbow on the table. "There's a guy at the club... Raid. We're close, but there's been this whole thing..." I trail off but then start again. "A woman showed up with his long-lost daughter, and it's kind of put any flirtation we may have had on hold."

Jasmine purses her lips. "Oh... yeah, that old chestnut. So he had no idea he had a kid?"

"None, the kicker is, the mother is sick, real fucking sick. The kind of sick you don't come back from. So Raid has found out he has this kid and that the mother doesn't have long, so he has to prepare for the fact he is not only a father but going to be a single dad sooner rather than later."

Jasmine grimaces. "Jesus, that's a heavy burden. No wonder your relationship was put on the back burner. Bad for you, though.

You really liked him?"

Nodding, I let out a long exhale. "So much. But Raid has his hands full. I can't expect him to factor me into his life when he has to think about his daughter. I'm there to help, but that's all I can be at this point..." I sigh heavily. "I know I have to let him go, even though there are moments, glimmers of hope, but I know there isn't any."

Jaz places her hand on mine, her eyes flicking behind me to Dan. "Then, in that case, you need a distraction. And while Dan isn't a badass biker, he does have that bad-boy vibe down pat. And he might just be a moody, broody writer, and surely that's just as good, right?"

I scrunch up my face in reaction. "Is it?"

Jasmine laughs. "No... a biker is way more badass. But seriously, you don't need to marry Dan. But he could be just what you need for now to help ease the pain."

I glance at Dan—his head is buried in a textbook—and sigh.

Maybe Jaz is right.

Maybe I do need a distraction.

If only there was a sign that Raid and I could make this work.

A sign that I shouldn't start looking at other people for a distraction.

People like Dan.

Please, Raid—give me a sign.

CHAPTER 9

RAID
Two Days Later

Holed up in my den, I've been monitoring the Iron Chains MC, checking out their business dealings.

Hacking into their servers was easy, so now I'm searching through their history. They need a better tech guy. I laugh at the amount of porn in their systems and shake my head. I'm sifting through the bullshit when there's a ping at my door.

I check the security camera—Hurricane—so I slide my chair over to the door and open it for him. He walks in, cradling Imogen. His one-month-old daughter is sleeping soundly in his arms.

Fatherhood looks good on him, I think.

"Hey, makin' any progress with this?" he asks.

I smirk as I click on a link and show Hurricane the porn folders on Frost's personal computer. "The guy's a total sex addict, but I am finding a whole bunch of shit."

"Good… good. On another note, how are ya copin' with Sophie and Addi bein' here?"

Running my hand through my hair, I let out a long exhale, sinking back into my chair. "It's an adjustment, but I think we're doing okay so far. Goddammit! I don't think Soph has long." I exhale again, long and hard this time. "I'm *real* fucking sorry for bringing this into the club, Pres. I had no clue it was coming."

"Not on you, brother. I'd rather have her here than fendin' for herself in Houston and havin' no one out there to take care of Addi. We're gettin' used to havin' Clover around, so what's another teen girl running 'round here anyway? Gotta get used to it with this little one growin' up here." He chuckles, holding onto his tiny daughter and cradling her.

I snort. "We need some more testosterone around here, pronto."

Hurricane chuckles. "You're tellin' me! This place is gonna be overrun by ovaries before we know it."

I smirk, then spin to my desk to show him what I've found on the Iron Chains MC. They're running guns, lots of them, trafficking girls... their latest shipment was last night. Even after our little chat with them, they didn't stop.

Hurricane growls. "Frost is jerkin' our chain. He's bein' an arrogant ass and thinkin' he can get away with it under our damn noses."

"So where to from here? Do we pay them another visit?"

"Yeah... we do. Let's mount up."

I log out of their systems and stand, walking with Hurricane into the main clubroom.

He sends a loud whistle through the large space. "All right, we need to head out and visit our good ol' friend, Frost, and his band of merry fuckwits. Even though we told 'em to lay low, they're still doin' shady shit. Time to get serious, brothers."

City and Bayou step up to us.

"What's going down?" City asks.

I pull out my tablet showing him Frost's shipment details from last night. "The Iron Chains had a shipment go out last night of women, even though we told them to stop."

City groans. "Fucking dickheads."

Bayou glances over at his Old Lady, Novah, then back to us. "You think they're gonna cause a problem, Pres? Do we need to prepare for a fight here?"

Kaia steps up and takes baby Immy from Hurricane, her eyes focusing on her fiancé. "I don't want you heading over there looking for trouble. I need you to go there peacefully and tell them to pull their heads in. You have people who need you here."

My eyes shift to Frankie as she sits on the bar stool doing some homework. My chest squeezes, thinking about if shit did hit the fan, I could be leaving Addi behind. "Kaia's right. We don't need to go in all guns-a-blazing. We can do this amicably."

Hurricane nods. "Yeah, we do this right. But we gotta let Frost know we mean fuckin' business this time." He leans in, planting a tender kiss on Immy's head, then one on Kaia's cheek. "We'll be back soon."

"Okay, be safe." Kaia smiles.

"Always, Sha. Always."

We turn and walk out of the clubroom and hop on our rides, making the half-hour journey to the converted church. Again, we haven't announced ourselves, so we're not expecting a warm reception from Frost when we arrive.

The same prospect is at the gate as we pull up, but he lets us through without question this time. We pull up in the parking area to hear what sounds like a party going on inside.

Maybe I was wrong?

Maybe the party's still raging from last night, and they haven't even gone to bed yet?

Jumping off my ride, my eyes flash to Bayou, and he groans. "Great, this should be fun."

Grit chuckles. "C'mon, it will be fun. It's like they've thrown a welcome party for our arrival."

City smirks. "I don't think they're going to be in any kind of position to talk to us by the sound of what's going on in there, Pres."

Hurricane groans. "Let's head inside and see what state they're in. We can assess once we know how coherent Frost is."

We make our way inside the clubhouse, and as we enter, the music blares, the bass vibrating through my body. Scantily clad women are chained by their necks to poles like they're fucking slaves as they dance for the guys, and the sight makes me curl up my lip in disgust. The guys are visibly drunk.

Salt, their SAA, rubs up against one of the girls. Tears stream down her face—all these fuckers taking advantage of these clearly underage girls.

This is *not* how we do things.

This is *not* okay.

Frost spots us, his eyes widening as a young girl sits on his lap. He shoves her to the side, and she doesn't have time to catch herself before she tumbles to her knees on the floor.

I grimace as the asshole saunters over to us. His eyes are bloodshot, he's noticeably high, and a fog of dope haze lingers in the air, the pungent odor assaulting my nostrils as he steps up to us. "You're late to the party, Hurricane."

"Clearly. Seems you've been havin' a *real good time*." Hurricane grunts the words out, aggravation in his tone.

Frost rolls his eyes. "Relax, man, you're so uptig—"

Hurricane lunges forward, grabs Frost by his cut, and shoves him against the nearest wall.

We all tense, but his guys are too busy partying to even care what is happening to their president.

Frost tries to struggle against Hurricane, but Hurricane is so much bigger than him. "We fuckin' told you to stop doin' this shady shit in our city. Last night you trafficked women. Some of them are obviously still here. The girls you got chained up barely even look fuckin' legal, and they certainly don't look like they'd have immigration fuckin' papers."

Frost chuckles, even though he's still being held by Hurricane. "You'd be correct on both assumptions."

"That's *not* how we do business in New Awlins!" Hurricane shoves him harder into the wall.

Frost grins like he doesn't give a shit. "And you call yourselves one-percenters?"

Hurricane doesn't even blanch at the words. Instead, he pulls his fist back and slams it into Frost's jaw. Frost slips down the wall a little, his hands gripping his knees as he spits a line of blood.

Hurricane turns, running his fingers through his hair to walk off his anger. "We *are* one-percenters, asshole. You can respect women and be outlaws. There's no need for degradation and abuse. We're *not* about that life."

"That's a *you* problem. And anyhow, how do you know we did a deal last night?"

I step forward. "I was monitoring you. To make sure you kept to your word."

Frost scowls. "You're tracking us. I thought we were allies?"

"We are, so long as you keep to the rules. *Which. You're. Not. Doin'*. Turn the women you bought over to us, and we'll forget you made a damn deal last night. Cease any further traffickin', and we won't take any disciplinary action," Hurricane states.

Frost chuckles. "I paid for them, to sell them off. You think I'm gonna just hand them over and lose out on a payday? They're worth a fortune. They are Cuban virgins, Hurricane."

"I don't care if they've got fuckin' gold-plated pussies. They're comin' with us. You're gonna deal with the loss because you shouldn't be sellin' 'em in the first place, dickhead. Rules are there for a reason, asshole."

He growls, his brows furrowed and his teeth clenched. "Fine... but only because I want to keep the peace with Defiance. I owe you that much."

"Good. Get the girls out of those damn chains, and fuckin' get them some clothes. They're comin' back to our clubhouse. *Now!*" Hurricane's voice is so intimidating even I feel a shudder go down my spine.

Frost hesitates for a split second but then turns and walks over to Dirty, who is motorboating one of the poor girls. Frost talks to his VP—once his head is removed from the girl's cleavage—and they discuss shit amongst themselves.

Dirty walks over to the sound system and turns the fucking incessant sit music off, and all their guys groan, finally turning to notice us.

"We're takin' the girls."

Salt raises his brow. "You're the buyers? I didn't think you were the type. Hurricane, you old dog."

Frost waves his hand through the air. "Salt, grab the keys. Defiance is taking the cargo. We told them yesterday we would stop transporting women. We already had this shipment en route. I couldn't stop it from arriving, so they're taking the girls."

Salt's eyes widen. "Are they fucking paying for them?"

I let out a mocking chuckle. "You wanna keep your club in New Awlins, or... you want us to run you out? Think about that before you ask any more dumbass questions, Salt," I snap back at him.

He glares but says nothing.

The rest of the club falls to silence, clear tension rising in the air.

Yeah, the Iron Chains MC are losing money on these women, but they stole them.

These poor women have no clue what they were in for. Every one of them appears terrified and are being forced to do shit against their will.

They deserve better.

Dirty unlocks them all while another club member hands them some clothing. They slowly get dressed like they're unsure of what's happening. I walk over to them, along with Bayou, and usher them toward the exit. They're hesitant, but I weakly smile to let them know we're not going to hurt them like these fuckers have.

"We won't hurt you," I tell one of them, but it's clear she doesn't speak much English.

We walk outside toward my bike. I don't know what Hurricane is saying to Frost, but I know it's going to be an earful about respect and not doing anything else to damage what little trust our clubs have left between us.

There are four girls and five of us, so City, Bayou, Grit, and I each have a girl on the back of our bikes. Hurricane gets a free ride, but he is also on the lookout to ensure nothing comes our way as we ride.

My girl clings tight to my stomach like she has never ridden on a bike before, so I glance over my shoulder and smile. "I got you. You're safe now."

She trembles, and I can't help but feel so utterly gutted for her. A red ring around her neck from where they had the collar locked around her makes me want to run back in there and punch Frost myself. But the best thing I can do right now is to get her the hell away from this place.

So we start our rides and take off to head back home.

Once we get these girls back to the clubhouse, we can figure out how to help them. Then what we're going to do with the Iron Chains MC, they have become a burden to Defiance and to everyone around them.

As we pull into the clubhouse lot, I park my ride. The girl slowly steps off the ride, her eyes falling immediately to the ground. I bring my finger up under her chin, making her look up. "You're safe, you understand?"

She shakes her head, dropping her eyes back to the ground. I have no fucking idea how to make her feel comfortable. So I gently wrap my arm around her shoulders and walk with her and the other guys inside.

Frankie's eyes meet me instantly, along with Kaia and Lani. The three girls rush over.

"What have we here?" Kaia asks.

Hurricane leans in, placing a tender kiss on Kaia's lips. "Hey,

"Sha, I need a favor. These girls were at the Iron Chains compound, taken by them to be sold. They had 'em chained up and were partyin' with them. They're underage and undocumented. We don't know if any of them speak English, so you might have your work cut out. Can you and the girls take care of 'em for a while? Feed 'em, get them some decent clothin'?"

Frankie grins, dipping her head, and Kaia smiles wide, linking her arm with Lani. "We got this. Don't we, ladies?" Kaia chimes.

"Yeah, we can help them for sure," Lani states.

"We can get Izzy to look at any physical injuries they might have and grab Novah to handle any immigration stuff we need through her social work connections," Frankie suggests.

"Great idea, Frankie," I reply, and she smiles at me. That damn amazing smile always makes my cock ache for her.

"Okay, well, you ladies take care of all that while we go discuss the Iron Chains issue," Hurricane states.

We go to walk off, but Frankie gains my attention. "Raid..." she calls. I turn back and raise my brow. "Look at the time."

I glance down at my watch and exhale. "Fuck! Pres, I gotta get Addi from school."

Hurricane nods. "Go. We can deal with this until you get back."

Frankie smiles. "You want company?"

"Always."

We walk out to the pickup truck, and I open the passenger side door for Frankie. After she climbs inside, I close the door, then walk around. When I hop in, she's buckling up and I shake my head. "I can't believe Frost had this kind of shit in him. He always seemed so decent when we saw him in Houston. It's funny how people change."

Frankie reaches out, placing her hand on mine, and I turn to face her. "People are who they are. Frost is lost. He wants his club to outrank you guys. It's not up to this club to make him better. All you can do is tell him how New Awlins is gonna be run, and if he doesn't get it, then..."

"You couldn't be more right. I just hope he comes to the party."

I take off toward Addi's school, and Frankie slides her hand down to rest on my thigh. I love the feeling of her touching me, even if it's just in some small way.

Frankie keeps her eyes forward, looking at the road ahead as I drive.

"This may not be the right time... but we don't seem to get a lot of alone time, not anymore, so I just wanted to take this opportunity to tell you that I am so proud of the way you have stepped up for Addi... and Sophie. They rocked up on our doorstep, and you didn't have to take them in, but you did without a second's hesitation. They have completely uprooted your entire life..." She pauses, then continues, "You're an amazing man, Raid. I'm in awe of you."

I glance at her briefly, then back to the road, my hand moving from the gearstick to her hand on my thigh, and I give her a little squeeze. "Frankie... that means a lot. I know it's uprooted your life too, and you've taken this all in your stride. Honestly, I don't think I could be as tough navigating this without you."

She snorts out a laugh. "Raid, you can handle Addi. Yeah, she has an attitude, but what fourteen-year-old girl doesn't? You'll figure out how to work her. You'll find a rhythm. I know you will."

I turn to face her, her eyes so bright as she stares back at me.

Fuck she's beautiful.

My heart races, and my mouth goes dry. I wish I could tell her how I really feel, but the damn timing is all wrong.

Fuck! I want to kiss her.

Those plump, supple lips, her gorgeous—

"Eyes on the road, Raid." She giggles, gesturing with her head to the windshield.

Widening my eyes, I snap out of my Frankie trance and spin back to the road to see I am veering toward the curb. I jerk the steering wheel while my heart leaps into my throat. "Fuck, sorry."

She chuckles, squeezing my thigh. "Normally, I would love you staring at me, just not while driving a three-quarter-ton truck."

"Noted," I state.

Not long later, I pull into the pickup line at Prescott Hills High. I don't see Addi just yet, so I wait, turning to Frankie again and smile.

She rolls her eyes. "What, now?"

"Nothing. You look *real* good today."

Frankie slides her red hair behind her ear. "Are you flirting with me?" She waggles her brows.

I chuckle. "No, just telling how I see it."

"Raid," she whispers, glancing down and letting out a soft exhale.

I bring my hand up, caressing her shoulder. "I know."

Her breathing increases as she tries to avoid eye contact with me, the air around us filling with lustful tension. My hand on her shoulder slides up, caressing her neck. Then I move, cupping her cheek and letting my thumb whisper against her skin. She lets out a heavy breath, closing her eyes, while my fingers slide into her silky strands. My pulse skyrockets, my cock throbbing with the sexual tension, which is so heavy you could cut it with a knife. I begin to edge her face closer to mine. Our lips are only an inch apart.

We're breathing fast and heavy. I've never wanted to kiss someone more in my damn life. "Fuck, Frankie, I need to taste you."

She whimpers, her hand on my thigh moving higher while I grip her hair tight, pulling her closer. Our lips barely touch as the back door opens. Reluctantly, I pull back from Frankie before our lips make a significant impact. My chest is heaving, and my cock is rock hard.

Addi throws her backpack on the backseat and slams the door shut. "I had such a great day today! It was nothing like yesterday," she chimes like she has no idea what she's interrupted.

Swallowing, I quickly glance from a smiling Frankie to the

backseat at Addi—she's practically glowing. "That's good news." I turn the key in the ignition, put the truck in gear to keep the line moving and head off.

Frankie spins in her seat. "I think that was my sign," she whispers like she's saying it to herself and not to me.

Addi and I both stare at her in confusion.

"Huh?" Addi asks.

Frankie smiles and waves it off, facing Addi. "Never mind, just talking to myself. Now, let's get to you. Tell… me… *everything!*"

"Well, you know those bullies from Friday?" Addi chimes.

"Mm-hmm…" Frankie nods.

I tense, glancing in the rearview ready to go back and commando kick those kids in their cocks if they gave her any more shit today.

"They did a complete backflip and treated me like a queen today. I've never felt more welcomed in a school before. It was honestly like something from *The Twilight Zone*. And once I got past my anger at them being such assholes, and we all got to talking about our mutual childhood trauma, they're actually pretty normal kids. They apologized, and we're all good. I even told them about Clover, and we hung out with her for a bit too. They all said it was so cool that we're living together at the clubhouse. That it's unique and kinda badass."

Relief floods me that I *did* make the right choice, but I don't want to rub it in.

Frankie chuckles. "See! Raid was only looking out for you. He knew what he was doing with those little pricks."

I may not want to rub it in, but I'm totally okay with Frankie doing it for me, and I can't help but smirk.

Addi smiles. "The bit that really made me wanna puke, though… was that all the girls were totally drooling over you, Raid. I kept telling them you're my dad, and they were like, "He's totally like Jax Teller from *Sons of Anarchy*, just with longer hair." I told them you're *waaay* cooler than Jax Teller."

I look at her in the rearview, my chest filling with pride. "Cooler, huh?"

"Totally. I told them you could one hundred percent kick people's asses too."

Frankie turns to me and smiles while I grin from ear-to-ear hearing Addi finally talk me up. "So I'm not just a nerd now?"

Addi chuckles. "You're still a nerd, but you're a badass nerd."

"I'll take that." I nod.

She leans forward, her head popping through the two seats, and I glance at her. "Thanks for sticking up for me. I know I was a bitch about it then, but it actually helped. So… thank you."

I know that would have been hard for her to say, so I'm going to take the win and be grateful for it. "You're welcome, Addi. I'm always gonna do right by you. That's what a father does."

She sinks back into her seat, letting out a soft sigh. "I wouldn't know. Never had one."

For some reason, that really strikes my heart, so I dramatically pull the truck over to the curb and turn back to face her. Her eyes are wide as she stares at me like I have lost my damn mind.

"Well, you're never going to have to worry about what it's going to be like to live without one again. I'm here. I'm *not* going anywhere. And I want you to know, Addilyn, that if I knew about you, if I had *any* inkling whatsoever about you, I *would* have been in your life. I *would* have been there for every milestone, every celebration, every heartbreak along the way. I *want* to be here for it *all*, Addi, and I am *so* fucking sorry that I missed so damn much of your life up to now. But I am gonna make it up to you by *being* here. By being present for *everything* else for the rest of my life. For… *every… single… thing* you need me for. I won't let you down, Addi."

Her bottom lip trembles as she swipes a tear from her face, then she sniffles with a slow smile creasing the corner of her lips. "I still think you're a nerd."

I laugh loudly and spin back to face the road, putting the truck into gear. I head back out into the traffic with my heart full. "I can live with that."

Frankie glances over at me and I smile.

It's not often I let my emotions out for everyone to see, but Addi is my kid, and I need her to know that I will *not* abandon her. I need her to know that I am here, and whether she believes it or not, she is stuck with me.

Once we arrive, we make our way to Sophie's room, who's half awake when we all walk in. Addi's too excited and runs in, throwing her backpack on the desk with a thud, making sure Sophie is now fully awake. "Mom! I had such a great day at school today."

Sophie blinks a few times to gain her bearings as Addi slumps down on the bed next to her, and Addi adjusts Soph's beanie.

Sophie chuckles, making herself more comfortable in the bed. "Did you now? That *is* good news."

"I'm going to be a popular kid before we know it, and it's all because of Raid."

Sophie raises her brow. "Oh, is that so?"

"Just made my patch known at the school. You know, the usual overprotective father shit."

Sophie chuckles. "Well, I am glad that it's all working out. Wouldn't want to have the club going in and offing some students for being assholes now, would we?"

Addi laughs.

I shake my head. "I mean... I wouldn't want to, but if a kid treated Addi like shit enough, it might force my hand."

Addi snaps her head around to face me with her mouth agape. "What?"

I chuckle while shaking my head. "I'm kidding. I wouldn't hurt a kid. I'd certainly scare them if they fucked with you, but I would never hurt them. Unless they hurt you, then all bets are off. Anyone hurts you then I'm gunning for them."

She smiles. "Thanks for having my back."

"You got it."

"Hey, Mom?" Addi turns to look at Sophie to finish whatever she was going to say, but we all see Sophie has fallen back asleep.

Frankie walks over to Addi and wraps her arm around her as Addi's happiness seems to disappear from her face, and concern washes over her instead. "How about we let your mom rest, and you go find Clover to hang out with for a while?"

Addi weakly nods her head. "Yeah… Mom needs to rest," she says so softly it's hardly audible. It's like she's validating the fact in her mind but knows deep down that these are her mom's final days. No one knows how hard this must be for Addi, but all I can do is to make sure she's well taken care of and step up and be the father she deserves.

My heart hurts for Addi when she walks out of the room.

My eyes fall on Sophie.

She's so tired.

So weak.

It won't be long now.

My stomach somersaults in anxiousness as Frankie steps up to me, and we walk out of Sophie's room together, closing the door behind us with a soft click.

Frankie slides her arm around me, and I let out a heavy exhale. "It's just so fucking sad."

Frankie nods, holding me tighter. "I know. I'm sorry, Raid. I am here for you… you and Addi."

I hold her tighter as we walk out into the main club room.

Frankie takes my hand and starts leading me toward the kitchen. "C'mon, let's get you something to eat."

We walk in to the smells of something amazing cooking on the stoves and Lani, elbow deep in food. "Hey, guys, you wanna try my new recipe?"

Frankie picks up what I think is some kind of cookie and hands it to me. "You should eat something."

I take it and have a bite. It is, of course, delicious, as is everything Lani makes. "It's *real* damn good, Lani."

She beams from ear to ear. "Thank you. Just trying to keep myself occupied. I have an appointment with my doctor, and they'll tell me how everything is going healing-wise for my burns. I mean, it's been four months, so I am still healing, but some places are a little slow."

"You do whatever you need to recover, Lani. We got your back," Frankie states.

"Cooking helps. It's like therapy."

"And we reap the rewards of that therapy," I jest.

"I'm just glad y'all like what I cook."

"You've never failed us, Lani. But I gotta get back to working on this Iron Chains shit for Hurricane and getting Novah in here to get these girls situated, or Hurricane will have my ass."

Frankie exhales, her eyes focused on me. "You did good with Addi today."

"You think so? Because I'm trying to be in her life without stifling her."

"You're doing great." Her beautiful hazel eyes stare into mine intensely, something being said in that look that I can't quite comprehend. My mind shifts to the way our lips almost touched in the truck only a short time ago, and I'm pretty sure she's thinking about the exact same moment.

The air around us is sizzling with the same intensity that electrifies us constantly. My chest rising and falling with my faster breaths as my cock reacts to the way she is looking at me. Her lips part, her tongue gently licking her bottom lip in a way that is so fucking sexy, I almost fucking come in my jeans.

I inch forward.

Wanting to touch her.

Wanting to taste her.

She is the object of every single one of my desires.

I need he—

"Hey, Frankie, can you give me a hand with this for a second?"

Lani asks from the other side of the kitchen, breaking our moment.

Our eyes shift from each other's when Frankie snaps her head to look at Lani, who is trying to pop an electric mixer together unsuccessfully.

Frankie turns back to me. "I better..." Then she gestures to Lani.

I point to the door and rush for it—I have no fucking clue what I am doing.

I'm supposed to be staying clear of Frankie.

No romantic intentions.

Now is not the time.

I must focus solely on Addi.

And I cannot get swept up in Frankie and allow my attention to waver from Addi, not even for a second.

Not even if every part of me is screaming for Frankie.

She a drug I can't seem to do without.

But I must put myself last for the first time in my life.

No matter how much it fucking hurts.

CHAPTER 10

FRANKIE
The Next Day

Raid has been a little distant from me today.

I thought with our 'almost kiss' yesterday that it was a sign we were on the right track. I needed something, a hint that I should stick this out and wait for him.

I was positive, at that moment, that was it.

Now I'm not so sure.

I know he wants to keep things cool between us.

Maybe yesterday, he let things go too far.

He let the signals become tainted.

I know he likes me—that's never been the question. It's whether we're going to act on it. Whether I should hang around and wait.

The problem is, with Addi and Sophie in the picture, there's no way of telling how long I will be waiting. And this push and pull we have going will drive me insane. Hot one minute, icy cold the next! The whiplash is an injury my heart can't take.

So I am heading out for an hour or so. I need a break from constantly wondering where my life is heading. And as I drive, my fingers tap on the steering wheel to some latest hit I don't know well, but it talks about buying your own flowers—a full girl rock anthem that's empowering and just what I need right now.

After pulling into the parking lot, I take off for the French Quarter to Café Envie. Jasmine is sitting at a table waiting for me when I walk past the window. She waves cheerfully, and I can't help but smile.

Making my way inside the café, I head straight for her. "Morning!"

She glances at her watch. "Well, it's practically lunch. But sure... good morning."

"You ordered yet?" I sit and place my bag on the floor at our feet.

"Yes, and I got you an omelet. That okay?"

My stomach growls in appreciation. "Perfect, you're the best."

She places her hands on the table in a tight ball and furrows her brows. "Okay, so I *know* you didn't want to take time out of your busy schedule because everything is all sunshine and roses at the club. Is shit going down with Raid?"

Groaning, I slump back into my seat. "So much."

She chuckles. "Okay, if you want to talk to someone who doesn't have a vested interest in the club and its members, I am here. I won't pick sides. I'll just listen."

Rolling my shoulders, I sigh. "I shouldn't talk club business with outsiders, but I have no one to talk to about this stuff."

She gestures that her lips are sealed, then leans over, placing her hand on mine. "Look, Frankie, it's hard for me to make friends. People think I'm either too much or I'm a little too weird for them. But you... from the first moment you met me in class, we clicked. I'm glad to have a friend like you, and I cherish that fact. So please... if it will help you feel comfortable and safe like you make me feel, then please, let me help you."

My chest warms with the thought that I have made a real friend. I squeeze her hand back and nod, then start talking,

"Okay... so yesterday Raid and I went to pick up Addi from school, and we were in the truck waiting for her, and there was this... *moment*. A *definite moment* when we were about to kiss, but Addi jumped into the car before we touched lips."

Jaz chuckles. "Aww... she's cock blocking her own father... little shit."

I smirk but continue, "Thing is... I thought we were good after that. I thought it meant we were on the same page. That we had feelings, and we shared them, and maybe we could try."

Jaz grimaces. "He's not on that page with you, though, is he?"

Shaking my head, I exhale a long breath. "No, hardly spoke to me today, if at all. Complete cold shoulder. Like he regrets the entire thing."

Jaz slams her hands down on the table, making everyone look at us. "Fuck him!" she yells loudly with a great big smirk.

I burst out laughing, then turn to the people nearest us. "Sorry, she's invested—"

"This guy's being a total dick to her. So I'll say it again, *fuck... him,*" she says louder making the people beside us laugh.

"I agree, hon, if he's being a dick, then fuck him," the girl at the next table agrees, and the man with her chuckles.

"Hang on. Maybe he has a solid excuse?" The man tries to stick up for Raid even though he doesn't know him.

The woman with him slaps him on the arm. "Don't stick up for him just because he's a fellow man. If the guy is being a dick, then he should be treating her better."

I smile. "Thank you, but there *are* extenuating circumstance—"

"See! Guys aren't just dicks for the sake of being dicks. There's generally a reason, Cami."

Cami, who I assume is her name, smirks. "You're being a dick right now, *James.*"

He chuckles playfully. "Yeah... but you still love me."

Cami rolls her eyes. "I do, but anyway... sorry we *fully*

interrupted your conversation. Moral of the story... all guys are dicks, babe. Even the ones you've been with for years, like me and James. I think you need to really process whether this guy's dickiness is worth getting past or getting over."

Jaz nods her head. "I couldn't agree more. You need to figure out whether Raid is worth the head fuck and whether you want to stand around waiting for him or simply move on with your life. You know *his* situation isn't going to change, but *yours* can."

James shrugs. "I can't give you any solid advice. I don't know the ins and outs, but if he's treating you badly, it's for a reason. So I'd start with finding out what that reason is. If you already know, the answer to your question might lie there."

With a nod, I exhale as the waitress brings over our food. "Thanks, guys, you've actually been really helpful."

Cami smiles. "We'll let you enjoy your meal. Hope you figure it out with your dick guy. Because when you find the right one, even if he can be a shithead sometimes..." she reaches out, grabbing James' hand, and he smiles up at her lovingly, "... it can be the most rewarding thing ever."

My chest squeezes when I look at them.

They do look so utterly in love.

And I want that with Raid.

To have witty banter between us as a couple but still have him look at me like James is looking at Cami.

"Thanks again. Enjoy your day," I tell them.

They turn back to their table, and I focus on my omelet.

Jasmine lets out a small chuckle. "I swear you can make friends with anyone."

I snort out a laugh. "I think that comes with being a club girl. I have to be open and communicative with everyone. It's part of the job description."

Jaz takes a bite of her smoked salmon bagel, narrowing her eyes at me. "So, you've never told me what it is you do as a club girl."

I clear my throat. "It's complicated."

"Frankie, c'mon, I'm not stupid. I'm pretty sure that if you're living as a 'girl for the club,' I know what that entails. I'm no prude."

I've never been shy about what I do for the club. I have never been ashamed about being a club girl. I love sex, and I love everything about the Defiance MC. They look after me, and in return, I look after them. But I'm trying to make something of myself with this college course. Trying to be better. And I don't want the people there looking at me differently.

But there's something about Jaz that hits close to home. Something that makes me feel like a kindred spirit to her, so I bob my head. "Yeah, it's exactly what you think. I'm the head club girl. So I run everything, make sure to keep everyone in line. I maintain the cleanliness of the club. Stock all the groceries and keep the laundry done. Basically, like being the mother of the club, but at the same time, if any of the guys have an itch they need to scratch, they can come to my door at any time and ask me to scratch it, although not so much lately."

"And they pay you to do this?" she asks, not in a way that sounds like she is offended but more intrigued.

"They give me money toward things like school tuition, I have a roof over my head, food in my stomach, and a wage for working at the club. I don't look at it as "I'm getting paid for sex..." " I use air quotes, "... it's just a part of what I do. I've always enjoyed that, though. You have to love sex to be a club girl. You can't sign on and not have a basic need for it, even be a bit kinky in some ways."

"So how does that work with you and Raid? Doesn't he know you've slept with some of the guys he lives with?"

"Yeah, he knows. But we don't bring it up. And most of the guys go to Storm now. I'm not sure if that's because they know there's a connection between Raid and me, and it's a respect thing, but I haven't had a brother come to me in quite a while. Honestly, I'm in a dry spell."

"Maybe that's clouding your judgment too? The fact you haven't gotten any?" Jaz states.

I let out a snort. "Probably. I just wish I knew where his head is at."

"Maybe I should come to the club and meet him?" Jaz suggests.

I widen my eyes. "So you can yell at him and tell him how much of a dick he's being? No, thanks."

She giggles, bobbing her head. "Okay, so you got me there. But really, I'd love to come to the clubhouse and see it for real. This whole club girl thing has me intrigued. I'd love to see what you do if I can. I mean, not in detail. I'm not into voyeurism or anything, but seeing you interacting at the club and watching how it all works would be really interesting."

I snort. "Not into voyeurism? You don't want to watch me getting it on with a hot biker?" I tease.

She raises her brow like she is considering it. "I mean... when you put it like *that...*" She bursts into laughter as I smile at her.

"Okay, let me text the club president and see if you can follow me back to the club. You can meet everyone and get a feel for the place."

Jaz bobs in her seat excitedly. "Seriously?"

"Don't get too excited. Hurricane might deny the request, but if he says yes, then yeah, for sure, I'll take you, show you around, and introduce everyone," I reply as I send the text to Hurricane.

Jaz shovels more bagel into her mouth. "Thanks for this, Frankie. I've never felt so accepted by anyone before. I'm so glad we met."

"Me too." I feel warmth when I'm around her. There's nothing but a clear connection. I place my cell on the table and shovel in a mouthful of omelet when an alert comes back from Hurricane.

Pres: *As long as she isn't a psycho like Maddie, sure...*

I smirk at his response because no one could be as psychotic as

Grit's ex, Maddie. She tried to burn Lani alive. She *did* burn Grit's father and Davina alive, which was intense and heartbreaking. Maddie was a cult member and one hundred percent crazy town. Maddie left this world, and if I am honest, she deserved everything she got. She made Grit and Lani's life pure hell.

Yeah, Maddie was a real doozy.

Jasmine snickers. "Someone send you a dick pick?"

I curl up my lip while imagining Hurricane sending me a dick pick. "God, no, just a text back giving you the all-clear to come to the clubhouse as long as you're not a complete psychopath. Which from what I can tell, your psychopathic tendencies are marginal at best."

"Hey, they only come out on a full moon and in Mercury retrograde, so you should be safe... *for now.*" She waggles her brows, making me laugh.

"Okay, we'll finish our food, then you can follow me. I'll introduce you to everyone, and you can see what all the fuss is about."

She grins widely. "Can't wait!"

***

As I drive into my parking space, Jasmine pulls her car beside mine. I can't help the smile that forms because that used to be Davina's spot, and it's nice to see the space being filled again. As much as Davina hurt me by betraying us all, I still miss her.

She was a part of the club.

She was a team member working under my care.

And I let her down.

I should have taken better care of her.

I most definitely should have noticed the warning signs that she was unhappy.

And I carry that guilt every damn day.

We never truly know what a person is capable of until it's too late. And in Davina's case, she sided with and helped Maddie achieve her endgame—the destruction of Grit and Lani. Luckily she never accomplished the final phase of enlightenment for the cult, but it came close and at a massive cost to everyone in the club.

Shaking off the thoughts, I watch Jasmine step out of her car and plaster on a fake smile as I jump out to greet her. The look of awe and wonder crossing her face is clear as her eyes practically bug out of her head. I chuckle, sliding my arm into hers, gripping tight. "You ready to meet everyone?"

"I mean, yeah... this is so exciting." She giggles. "Why do I feel like I'm about to break a dozen laws, and that fact only is so incredibly fucking exciting?"

I snicker. "You're not breaking any laws by being here. Sorry to burst your bubble."

She shoves me playfully. "Shut up! Let me pretend I'm being bad for once."

"Okay, just by driving through the gates, you can be hauled in for consorting with known criminals and charged with propagating violence toward Defiance enemies."

Jasmine's entire body shudders, a big smile lighting her face. "I think you just made me wet."

I burst out laughing as I drag her toward the entrance. "C'mon, you freak."

"No, but really, keep talking like that. I need to hear more..."

I shake my head while dragging her through the front door and into the clubhouse. Her eyes widen as she takes in the main area and all the people inside. Her jaw drops, and she clings to me a little tighter.

Hurricane is the first to move, and he walks over, bobbing his head. "Frankie, this your friend you texted me about?"

"Yeah, Pres, this is Jaz. Jaz, this is Hurricane. He's the big boss man around here."

Jaz grins wide, looking him up and down, and lets out an

exaggerated exhale. "*Jeeesus*! Do they all look like you?"

I smirk while Hurricane scrunches his brow. "Look like me?"

"So damn fine. I would sell my soul just to lick your abs."

I burst out laughing at her lack of tact.

Hurricane tenses all over, looking increasingly more uncomfortable.

I tighten my grip on her. "Sorry, Pres, Jaz has no filter."

"Ah... I only let *one* woman lick my abs, my Old Lady. She's over there nursin' my daughter. So, thanks for the compliment, but... I'll pass."

Jaz shrugs. "No harm, no foul. You're committed to your woman. I like that..." she leans in closer to him, "... but it does make you sexier!"

The corner of his lips turn up. "Okay, well... I'm gonna go sit with my woman and kid. You two don't get up to too much trouble while you're here. And just holler if y'all need anythin'."

"Will do. Thanks, Pres," I tell him, and Jaz waves as Hurricane walks off, shaking his head.

"He's so fucking hot. No wonder you like it here with guys like that strutting around."

"They're nice as well as hot, you know?"

"Have you fucked him, though? With you being a club girl?"

I smirk. "That's confident—"

"Oh... my... God, you have! Is he *big*? I can imagine he would have a huge co—"

"Is who big?" Raid asks with a quizzical look crossing his face when he steps up to us, effectively cutting her off.

My palms become clammy while butterflies flutter in my stomach. Finally, I clear my throat after just staring at him for a moment before Jaz sticks her hand out toward him. "Hey, I'm Jaz... Frankie's friend from college."

Raid takes her hand, shakes it, and smiles. "Nice to finally meet someone from her class. I'm Raid."

Jaz nods her head. "Mm-hmm... so *you're the one*. It all makes sense now."

"*Jaz*," I scold as Raid furrows his brows.

"What? It does! He's like a Norse fucking god."

Raid smirks. "Thanks?" he replies, but it's more like a question.

"Oh, it was *definitely* a compliment. There must be something in the water here because, so far, the guys I've seen have made my pussy tingle in ways I can't even explain. Someone needs to call Mulder and Scully because it's like the damn *X-Files* in here. An unexplained phenomenon of god's gift to women everywhere I look. It's not *natural!*"

I chuckle, not knowing what else to do.

Raid raises his brow, trying to hide his smirk. "You have a very active imagination, Jaz."

"I guess that's why I'm studying English at college. To help me with my creative writing, just like Frankie."

"So, what brings you to the club?" Raid asks, trying to steer to conversation away from 'hot men.'

Jaz glances around, taking in the atmosphere. "Honestly? I wanted to see the club for myself. Frankie can't sing its praises highly enough, and I just want to see if it is as amazing as she's said."

Raid shrugs. "And?"

Jaz beams from ear to ear. "She didn't do it justice. It's *sooo* much better. The perks of this place sound amazing. I can't see a downside."

I raise my brows. "You sound like you want to be a part of it?"

Jaz looks at me with a more serious expression crossing her face this time. "I mean… I wouldn't be opposed to the idea. You said the club could help pay for things, and I'm struggling, Frankie. I can barely make the payments for my college class. I'm living in my car if you want me to be *real* honest because I can't afford my rent anymore…" She sighs. "The way you talk about being a club girl, the things the job entails, to me, it sounds fucking amazing."

Well damn! I had no idea. She always seemed so put together.

"Jaz, it's not for everyone. While this club looks glamorous and fun, there are times when it's dangerous and scary. I *don't* want that for you."

She reaches out, taking my hands in hers. "Frankie, I love sex. I love living dangerously. I love the thrill of new things. And more importantly, I need help. So, please, can you and the club *help me*? Take me on as a club girl?"

I turn to Raid, and he shrugs. "It's your call, Frankie. She's your friend, so you'll need to vouch for her. If needed, I can take this to Hurricane and do the introductory searches."

My stomach twists. Having Jaz here would be *so* good. We get along like a house on fire.

But... can I give her this life?

I guess it's not up to me to decide whether this is worthy enough for her.

If she wants a helping hand, I should be able to give it to her and let Jaz decide for herself.

"Take the offer to Hurricane and see what he says," I tell Raid.

He dips his chin, his eyes narrowing on Jaz. "I'll have to do a thorough background check. Anything I should know?"

"Nope, clean as a whistle. I can tell you anything you need, and I will help with what you want. I *need* this, so whatever I have to do, I will do."

Raid dips his chin. "Okay, I'll talk to the pres, see what he says. I need your full name."

"Sure, Jasmine Wilde."

He dips his chin. "I'll go talk to Hurricane now."

I reach out, grabbing Raid's hand. "Thanks."

He smiles. "Anything for you, Frankie." Then he takes off for Hurricane.

I turn back to Jasmine and widen my eyes. "Is this really what you want?"

She relaxes her shoulders. "After seeing this place and the people here, yeah. I need the help."

"Why didn't you tell me about your situation?"

She slumps her shoulders. "I didn't want you to think less of me. So I try to put out this persona that I have my shit together when I'm barely holding on in reality."

My stomach falls through the floor, and I rush forward, pulling her into a tight embrace, not having any idea she was in this much trouble. "We're gonna help you, Jaz. Even if it's not as a club girl, I'm gonna find some way to be there for you."

I mean it.

If Jaz comes in as Davina's replacement, I will teach her everything I know so she can be the best damn club girl she can be.

Even if I have to teach her every single thing myself.

Because she deserves a good life.

And I want to help her have exactly that.

CHAPTER 11

RAID

While making my way over to Hurricane, I can't help but feel a little surprised that Frankie has brought in someone to take on a club girl role. I mean, she did lose Davina, so she does need someone to pick up that slack, but I sometimes forget Frankie is still into the club girl life.

I don't see her with my brothers any more, and I know that's on me. I had a quiet word about leaving her alone while I made up my mind about what I wanted. I know it wasn't fair of me to do that, but I don't fucking care. She means a lot to me, and I don't want her with my brothers.

She's more about doing the day-to-day chores around the club.

Which I have to admit I am grateful about—it would do my head to watch her leave with one of my brothers. I know I couldn't fucking cope knowing what was going on behind closed doors. It would fucking kill me.

That's just not happening.

The guys know *not* to go there.

But, at the same time, if one wanted Frankie, there's little I could do to stop it. She is club property.

She's not mine.

Maybe Frankie feels the same as me, and that's why she wants her friend to come into the club. So the guys can go to Jaz instead of Frankie.

Or maybe I'm just reading too much into all this shit.

Maybe I'm just being hopeful.

Because I clearly have no right to want no one to touch her.

She's not mine.

I haven't claimed her.

Hell, I haven't even fucking kissed her.

So I can't say shit.

All I can do is my best to minimize the problems in my mind, and the way to do that is to make sure Jaz comes on board to take my single brothers' attention. So I approach Hurricane as he cradles Immy in his arms. Kaia sits next to him, and they look up at me.

"Pres?"

He raises his brow. "Yeah?"

"Frankie's new friend, Jaz... she's asking about becoming a club girl."

Hurricane squishes his eyebrows which causes wrinkles to form in the corners of his eyes. "Seriously? Do we need another one? The last one kinda put a dampener on the whole damn thing."

I shrug. "Yeah... I get it. Davina was a wild card. Not one of us here saw her turning on the club like that. But Jaz needs our help, and I think with Frankie going to class, she could probably do with an extra set of hands around the club to help her and Storm out."

Hurricane smirks. The bastard sees right through my plan. It's why he's the president—he's always one step ahead of us all. He knows that if Jaz is here, there's more chance the guys will use her instead of Frankie.

I'm being obvious.

But I don't fucking care.

Hurricane dips his chin and stands. "You do a thorough background check. I want every single inch of her life scrutinized. I don't want any damn surprises. Any inklin' of a red flag, you fuckin' tell me."

"You got it, and don't worry... I'm gonna be looking into her hard. If there's anything there, I'm gonna find it."

Hurricane grips my shoulder. "She's part of Frankie's life, so I know you're gonna do everything to protect her and the club. I know I've been hard on ya and the work you do here in the past, but I want you to know I appreciate you, brother. You got this."

I have to admit, that's fucking good to hear.

"Thanks, Pres. All right, I'm gonna go run some checks. I'll let you know what I find?"

He nods. "If she is squeaky, then she can come on board. If she is dirty, then she can get the fuck outta our clubhouse, and we'll warn Frankie to steer clear."

"Shouldn't take me long... hour tops."

"See ya in an hour," Hurricane states, and I turn, walking for my den.

Glancing over my shoulder, I give a subtle head bob to Frankie, letting her know I'm off to run the checks. She smiles, wrapping her arm around Jasmine, and they walk off toward the kitchen.

While letting out a long breath, I open my door to get ready to do some digging. I don't know what, or if I am going to find anything, but it's going to be fucking good to have something to occupy my mind with something other than the fact my ex is here dying, my daughter is constantly testing my patience, and Frankie? Well, I have no idea what I am fucking doing there.

Sitting at my desk, I run the search on Frankie's college class, checking for Jasmine. Her surname pops up straight away.

Jasmine Wilde.

So I run an initial search, and nothing pops up, which is always a good sign.

Then it hits.

Twenty-nine years old.
Born in New Orleans.
Lived here her entire life.
Engaged briefly to a Jarrod Simms, but they broke it off when he cheated and left her with nothing. Even took the damn dog.
She has a rental on the outskirts of the city.
Her bank account statements show she is barely making the payments on the rental and is on the verge of being kicked to the curb.
She got a payout from a car accident when she was a teen. Her parents were killed as a result of the same accident.
The payout was not significant, and she is using those funds to pay for college, but there's not much left, and it will dry up within a few months.
All her money is going on college tuition fees, which means she can barely afford ramen, let alone anything else.
She has been applying for jobs but is denied because she can't work the hours needed due to college commitments.

"She must really want to do this college course if she would rather go there than spend the money on rent and food," I mumble to myself.

Jasmine has been scarred emotionally by her parents' deaths and her ex-fiancé. It seems that she has a lot to prove by doing this college course, and she wants to find a way to get through the shit she's buried knee-deep in. She wants us to help pay for her tuition and give her a roof over her head.

If she has to be a club girl to do it, then she's okay with that.
She wants to feel like she belongs.
Like she has people who truly care about her.

I don't find any red flags.

Jasmine is a broken woman looking for redemption.

She's passed all the tests so far.

But I will keep digging because Lord knows we've had our fair share of crazies walk through our doors, and I don't want to be the one responsible for missing a warning sign, especially when it involves Frankie. I also need to bear in mind Sophie and Addi. I've got to safeguard them all, and I am the first line of defense regarding checking Jasmine's credentials.

So I run a more in-depth search that checks not only the legitimate World Wide Web but also the dark web, deep web, and other more seedy sides of the internet.

I'm damn well going to do my due diligence and make sure I get this right.

***

With a folder in my hand, I make my way to Hurricane.

His eyes shift to look at me as I approach. "She pass?"

I pop the folder on the table and slide it in front of him. "With glittery, neon colors. Girl's clean as a damn whistle. Yeah, there are skeletons in her past, and I expected that. Hell, if there weren't, I'd know her file was doctored. She's broken, but what potential club girl isn't? Her parents died in a car accident when she was a teen… she was in the car and survived. She received a payout and uses the money to fund her college, but it is quickly drying up. She can't afford her tuition and rent, so her rent is slipping. I'm pretty sure they're gonna toss her ass. She's definitely on struggle street, Pres. She needs our help. I have checked, double-checked, and then gone into every fucking sinister corner of the web I can think of and then triple-checked, but again, she's clean. Jasmine's looking for a handout we can easily give her."

Hurricane rolls his shoulders, glancing from me over to where Frankie and Jaz are sitting at the bar. "Well, if you trust her, then I trust you."

"I trust what I saw in my research and Frankie's intuition. If Frankie thinks Jaz is the right fit for the club, I see no reason not to offer her a spot."

"Then we should tell our newest member the good news."

Smirking, I turn, and Hurricane stands. We walk together to the bar, where Frankie's eyes widen in curiosity as we approach. I subtly nod, giving her the answer to her unasked question, and her lips turn up into a bright smile.

Jasmine sits taller upon noticing Hurricane and me approaching. "Hey! If it isn't the two sexiest men in the club," Jasmine chimes.

I laugh.

"Jaz, I had Raid run your history to ensure you're on the up and up. We know about your parents, the fact you're payin' for everythin' from your payout money, and that it's almost gone."

Her eyes widen, and Frankie weakly smiles, reaching out and taking Jasmine's hand. "It's okay, Jaz. This is all part of the process."

Jaz nods, but her eyes give away her surprise. "My education means so much to me. I don't know what I am going to do when that money dries up. I can't even afford my rent right now. They've already started talking to me about eviction."

I knew it was close but didn't realize the process had started. "That's why we're coming to you now, Jaz. I thoroughly searched your history, including every social media account and every infringement you've ever made. Every mark against your name. Anything I could find, and there's nothing that constitutes a red flag for me."

Jaz inhales sharply through her nose, her eyes shooting to Frankie, then back to me. "So what does that mean?"

"Welcome to the club, Jasmine." Hurricane smiles. "On one condition..."

She lets out a small squeal and jumps off the bar stool in

excitement. "Oh my God, really?"

Frankie giggles.

Hurricane tilts his head. "On one condition... focus, Jasmine."

"Shit, sorry. Yes, of course. What is it?" she asks, calming herself down.

"Hittin' on me has to stop. Save that shit for the single brothers."

Jasmine giggles, dipping her head. "Right, sorry. I understand completely. Thank you so much, Hurricane. I won't let you down. I will be the best club girl... *besides Frankie*... there is. I promise you."

"Take your cues from Frankie. You have the best mentor in her. We don't tolerate cattiness or in fightin', so you gotta get along with Storm too."

"Got it. That's not me. I'm all about lifting each other up and straightening my friends' crowns."

"Great! Frankie, I'll let you get her settled in Davina's old room."

"Thanks, Pres. I really appreciate this," Frankie says.

Hurricane dips his head and turns, walking off.

I make a move to walk off too, but Frankie reaches out, grabbing my arm. "Thank you. This couldn't have happened without your help."

My eyes meet hers.

Fuck she's beautiful.

What I wouldn't give to have one moment alone with her.

Goddammit! I know it's not plausible right now. Still, it doesn't make me not want it any less.

I've got to think of Addi.

I must focus on Addi.

My relationship with my daughter is super important, so unfortunately, I can't get lost in Frankie even though *every single inch* of me is screaming for her.

Gently I pull my arm free. "It was my pleasure. I'll always help you whenever I can, Frankie."

Her eyes fall, like me pulling away from her physically caused her pain, but she nods and wraps her arms around herself. "Appreciate that."

The air around us is electric, but I can't tell whether it's in a good or bad way. So I need to leave before we fall victim to the storm surrounding us. "Welcome to the club, Jaz. I'll catch ya 'round, Franks."

"Yeah, see ya," Frankie offers.

Jasmine gives me a small wave and a wink.

Spinning on my heel, I let out a long exhale, heading for my den.

Jesus Christ.

Frankie and I need to find a way to deal with the sexual tension brewing between us because there is no way we can keep going like this.

I've got to find a way to cool my shit when I am around her.

The problem is, she's so fucking gorgeous I don't know how I'm going to be able to stop.

CHAPTER 12

RAID

My mind is beyond exhausted as I crawl into bed—with thoughts of a particular redhead, which never seem to lessen—when a knock on the door grabs my attention.

"What?" I holler, not wanting to get up, knowing my semi-hard cock will tell whoever is on the other side just what is about to go down with me and my hand.

The door swings open, and *she* pops her head in, waves of red flowing over her shoulder. "Raid, got a minute?"

Internally I groan, my cock rigid at the sight of her. She's not wearing a bra, her perfect, fake tits stretching her black tank top to the tearing point. Not daring to sit up, I prop myself on an elbow while lying on my side, ensuring my rock-hard cock stays hidden. "Of course, Frankie. What's up?" I ask, patting the space next to me on the bed.

"You sure? We can chat tomorrow."

I wave my hand for her to come on over, and as soon as she takes a seat, I know I've fucked up. Her glorious tits are at eye level, and I want to fucking bury my face in them. Get lost in the abyss. Drown in her perfectness. With each breath she takes, the movement has her chest rising and falling, hypnotizing me.

Is it possible to be jealous of a piece of clothing? Hell, yes, it is!

When I don't respond, she gives me a playful shove. "Hey, eyes up here," she teases.

"Sorry, Franks, I know what I like," I say with a wink, shrugging my shoulders. "What can I do for you?"

I know what you can do for me.

Somehow, I behave and keep that thought to myself, but the thing with Frankie is we have an easy connection. Flirting has become second nature between us.

"I wanted to thank you for helping me with Jasmine and getting her involved in the club. I couldn't have done it without you."

"I'd do anything to help you. You know that," I tell her honestly, sitting up and leaning against the headboard.

In my new position, the sheet falls away, baring my shirtless chest, and I don't miss the hitch in her breath as she stares. I clear my throat. Now it's my turn to tease her, "Eyes up here." My voice is gruff, and when her eyes meet mine, heat burns intensely between us.

"Uh... yeah. I... I just hate the timing of everything. I'm not saying I wish Addi and Sophie didn't show up because I would *never* wish that. I'm just saying, I wish we acted sooner," Frankie admits, and sadness has now replaced the heat we shared a second ago.

"Yeah," is all I can reply because I feel it too.

So damn much.

I caress her cheek, offering support, but the ache in my cock is unbearable. "I hate that it's like this. I hate that I haven't had a chance to taste you," I confess, brushing my thumb closer to her sexy full lips she has painted glossy pink.

She leans into my touch, closing her eyes. Then, when she opens them, meeting my gaze, she lets out a small sigh. "I wouldn't stop you if you wanted to taste me. I want you. I want this."

My cock fucking jerks, the traitor. The air around us sparks with insatiable, lust-fueled desire. "Fuck, Frankie. I'm not strong enough to say no," I confess, sliding my hand to the back of her neck and pulling her to me. I slam my lips to hers in a bruising kiss.

All the build-up leading to this moment is bound to be explosive. Our tongues collide—she tastes so fucking sweet—and I can't get enough. I devour her, a soft whimper escaping her mouth while we kiss frantically. This is no lovey-dovey first kiss. It's hard, strong, and full of fucking passion, just how I like it.

My cock's so hard when I run my hand into her hair and grip it tight, then pull her back and watch as she catches her breath. "I'd like to see this shade smeared around my cock when you're done taking me down your throat," I tell her, using my other hand to smear her pink lipstick with my thumb.

At my words, Frankie crawls onto the bed, straddling me, then presses her lips to mine. I groan, grabbing her hips and grinding her pussy against my already throbbing hard-as-stone cock. I growl against her mouth and pull back slightly to bite her bottom lip until she whimpers. "I don't think so, Franks. I need to taste your sweet pussy."

Gripping her hips, I toss her back, and she lands on the bed with an audible "oomph." Her body bounces on the mattress a couple of times from the force. Her amazing tits bounce so perfectly I can't wait to see them in the flesh.

Immediately, she props herself up on her elbows, watching me and panting for breath. "Don't make me wait, Raid. I wouldn't want to have to make myself come," she threatens, a new, mischievous sparkle in her eyes I haven't seen before.

In an instant, I'm on my knees. "Now is *not* the time to taunt me." I growl the words, stripping Frankie of her tank top and freeing the most exquisite breasts. I quickly make work of her jeans, yanking them down her legs with probably more force than necessary, but I *need* to be inside her.

A groan echoes through the room at the sight of her shaved

pussy, already glistening with need. "No panties?" I ask, sliding my fingers through her folds. "Fuck, this better be for me," I warn, moving between her legs.

Before I know it, she has a hand wrapped tightly in my hair, shoving my face to her pussy. "Raid, stop fucking talking and eat me like you mean it."

Lapping my tongue through her folds, I settle on her clit and nip, causing her hips to buck right into my face.

Fuck she tastes so damn sweet.

I can't help the smile that spreads as I push two fingers into her soaked pussy. Frankie gasps when I slide them against her G-spot, then I focus my tongue on her clit, working my fingers in and out of her until she's writhing. Her walls clench around my fingers, telling me she's close. As much as I'm dying to taste her release, I want to be buried deep inside her when she comes, so she will have to wait.

Plus, delayed gratification is so much better.

In her bliss, I free myself from her hold and move over her. "Not yet, sweetheart. I need to be inside you when you come. Then I want your sassy mouth around my cock, taking everything I fucking give you." I don't wait for a response, sinking myself until my hips are grinding into hers. A shudder wracks my body from how wet and tight she is. "Fuck, Frankie."

She feels so damn good.

Frankie moans out her pleasure, wrapping her legs around my waist and pulling me deeper. I groan, pulling back, then slam inside her.

"Yes! Harder," she cries.

Leaning down, I nip my way along her neck to her breast and bite her nipple. Instead of letting go, I keep my teeth firmly in place. Then every time I thrust into her, the motion causes me to tug. A whimper catches in her throat, her legs locking me against her and her pussy squeezing my dick. "Frankie, Jesus... you're so tight. It's too much," I say, releasing her nipple.

Captivate

She scratches her nails down my back, and I know it's going to bleed from the sting it leaves behind. I rock my hips forward, needing her to get there. Frankie's back arches, thrusting her gorgeous tits right into my face. I can't resist biting them, marking her.

This woman is mine!

"Raid…" she trails off, my name on her lips as she lets go.

Knock. Knock. Knock.

"Fuck, I'm coming…" While releasing inside her, my body seizes, and I'm left panting.

"Well, hurry the hell up," a voice calls in the distance, and my head begins to feel light. I can't breathe as everything turns black, and the constant knocking becomes louder.

I gasp for air, but my mouth is muffled.

What the fuck!

I pull back, realizing my head is buried in my pillow, and I am biting down on it.

What in the fuck!

I move my hips feeling the complete mess I have made of the bed beneath me.

"We're gonna be late!" Addi calls out through the door, waking me completely.

What the actual fuck!

I jerk awake.

Well damn! I just fucking imagined my first kiss, my first fuck, my first everything with Frankie.

I groan, running my fingers through my hair.

I'm lying in my own fucking cum.

Jesus Christ, Frankie, you know how to work a guy up, even in his sleep.

"Raid, I need to go to school," Addi calls out again.

"Okay, fuck! Gimmie ten to get dressed, kid. I'll be out soon," I yell back at her.

"Urgh, fine! Mom would *never* be this late." She groans for good measure just to make sure I know how frustrated she is, and then I hear her storming off down the hall.

"Fuck!" I mumble to myself while hoisting myself up out of bed. With the mess, I've got to have a quick shower and wash the memory of Frankie off me so I can do what I need to do—*concentrate on Addi.*

But damn, does it make me want to question things.

Because if being with Frankie in a dream could be that good, imagine what it would be like in real life.

But is that all I can do—*imagine.*

I have a daughter out there.

Waiting on me.

Relying on me.

And as much as I'd like to put myself first, I *must* put Addi first.

Right now, I have to put one foot in front of the other and get myself moving.

First things first—shower.

Then focus on getting Addi to school.

Then somehow—and I have no idea how I am going to manage this part—I have to find a way to look Frankie in the eyes without remembering how it felt to be inside her.

Fuck. My. Life.

CHAPTER 13

FRANKIE
Two Days Later

"How are you feeling?" I ask when I sit on the edge of Sophie's bed.

She lets out a long exhale, looking pale as I hand her her breakfast. "I think I'll go bungee jumping today and maybe go take a walk around the French Market, eat some gator bites. Do a swamp tour. Oh, and go to a Voodoo shop, buy a voodoo doll, and think about all the people I *don't* like."

I can't help but weakly smile, knowing she can't do any of those things. She's simply trying to make light of a bad situation. "I can't imagine you not liking anybody. You're too sweet for that."

Sophie chuckles. "Don't let me fool you. I'm a real badass underneath all this." She waves at the beanie covering her bald scalp, and I grin.

"Oh yeah, you give me *real* serial killer vibes."

Sophie exhales, picks up her coffee, brings it to her nose, smells it, then curls up her lip, pushing the mug away. "I'm so sorry, Frankie. Thank you for making breakfast for me. I just don't think my stomach can handle anything right now."

Nodding, I stand, take the tray away and place it on the desk.

"That's totally fine, honey. I'll leave it here in case you change your mind?"

She nods, a somber look crossing her face. "Thank you... for taking care of me. For looking after Addi and for being there for Raid. I truly appreciate you. I want you to know that."

I walk back over and sit next to her, taking Sophie's hand in mine. "It's easy to take care of the three of you. It's an honor."

"Raid is lucky to have you in his life."

The way he's been avoiding me the last couple of days? Pretty sure he doesn't feel the same.

"He's a great guy, but his focus is on you and Addi. That is as it should be, and I am here to ensure that Addi is taken care of. She's the main priority."

Sophie dips her head. "I agree. Addi must be taken care of. But you and Raid need to be happy too."

I inhale sharply, standing to move for the door. "I have to get to class, but Storm will be here all day if you need anything, okay?"

Sophie smirks. "I'll be fine. You go have fun."

I reach the door but turn back and smile at her. "Thanks, Soph, for your support. It means a lot."

She smiles, sinking back down into her bed. "It's easy to give when I know you're such a wonderful person, Frankie."

My chest squeezes, and I have to blink my eyes to stop the tears from falling. I despise the fact that Sophie is so damn sick. In another life, I think we could have been great friends.

Why is the world so cruel?

"Rest up. Eat if you can."

She smiles, saying nothing because we both know she isn't going to eat anything, and she curls up under the blankets as I walk out of her room. I close the door with a small click, lean with my back against the door and take a second just to breathe.

Sophie's so fucking beautiful.

Such a kind soul.

Life's not fucking fair.

I wipe a stray tear from my face, shake my head, and straighten my shoulders.

Pull yourself together, Frankie!

Taking off, I grab my bag and walk to where Jasmine is waiting. "You ready to go?" I ask.

She nods her head as Raid steps up to my side. It's the first attempt he's made to talk to me in two days. Honestly, I thought he was avoiding me.

"You headed to class?"

I nod. "Yeah, we're both going in now."

He rolls his shoulders. "You can ride with me. I'll take you."

I shake my head. "That's not necessary. Jaz and I will carpool together."

He takes a step forward, reaching out for my hand. "Franks, I always take you to class and pick you up. This isn't a negotiation. It's for your safety."

"And so Jasmine's safety doesn't come into it then?" My hand goes to my hip in some sort of defiant stance.

Jaz widens her eyes, trying to look anywhere but at the two of us like she is avoiding this confrontation.

Raid looks at Jaz and exhales. "I'm sorry, Jaz. Of course, I am concerned for your safety, but Frankie is my main priority here."

Jasmine places her hands in a reassuring gesture. "No, I understand perfectly."

I fold my arms over my chest and decide to have this out with him. "So why are you *now* deciding to take care of me when you've been ghosting me for two days?"

Jaz purses her lips together, trying to fight her smile.

Raid groans under his breath. "Why are you being so damn stubborn, woman? Just let me take to you to your cla—"

"*Me*... stubborn? Just answer the question, *Raid*."

A low rumble growls deep within his chest, and he runs his fingers through his long dusty blond hair. "You know what? Go with Jaz. Safety in numbers, right?" He turns and storms off toward his den, his heavy feet stomping on the floor as he goes.

I let out a heavy exhale.

Jaz reaches out, grabbing my arm. "I can drive myself if you want to go with him. Honestly, babe, I'm okay to go on my own. I've been doing it all along."

"I don't want to let him walk all over me. I don't know what his problem has been with me the last couple of days, but I'm not going to let him just swoop in and pretend like we're fine. He needs to talk to me and tell me why he's been ghosting me. If I'm the problem, let me know what I am doing wrong so I can fix it, at least. But right now, demanding shit of me is *not* going to work."

Jasmine wraps her arm around my shoulders and leads me out of the clubhouse. "That's why everyone respects the shit out of you, Frankie. Because you're such a strong, independent woman, and even though you adore Raid, you won't let him push you around. Gotta give you props for that."

We walk toward Jasmine's car, and I exhale. "I do adore him, but you're right. I won't let him push me around." We jump inside her car, and I buckle up. "It's so hard because we both know we were headed somewhere, but it's all been put on hold because of Addi. And I'm not mad. I swear I'm not. I love Addi. It's just that the timing is off, and it's making us both frustrated. We can feel the connection and pull between us all the damn time, we just can't act on it, and it's so fucking hard."

Jasmine starts the car and pulls out of the lot to head for the college. "Maybe the best way to get past this is to move on to someone else. You know you can't be with Raid right now, so maybe a distraction with someone else in the meantime? I don't know if that's good advice or not. Probably not, but sometimes a distraction helps?"

Sinking into my seat, I don't reply.

But I can't help but wonder if maybe, just maybe, she might be right.

Captivate

***

It feels like class today is dragging.

Maybe it's because I am preoccupied thinking about the Cuban girls and how unlucky they were to fall into the hands of Frost and the Iron Chains. How in the blink of an eye, your world can change, and how that analogy is Raid and me right now.

Luckily, Novah was able to get the girls taken care of. With her contacts, she managed to get them sent back home to Cuba to be with their families. They were so grateful for our help.

But I can't stop my mind from wandering to Raid and how we seem off-kilter.

Like everything has fallen off its axis.

As Jaz sits next to me, chatting with Rose, another classmate, Dan, comes to my side with a bright smile. "Hey Frankie, looking lovely today as always."

The thing about Dan—he's nice.

He seems so genuine.

Like a safe bet.

Even though there's an air of bad boy about him with the leather jacket he wears, that devilish smirk he has going on is a warning sign. But the way he's always so happy to see me is in stark contrast to how Raid is treating me now.

"You find today's lecture interesting?" I ask.

He grins. "Seems Erin had to weave her thoughts on how Shakespeare could have done a better job on the syllabus again. She really has a lady boner for him. I think she has daddy issues if she loves a guy *that* old."

I burst out laughing and shake my head. "Oh, man, I don't even want to think about our lecturer with a daddy kink. Thank you!"

Dan smirks. "So, are you prepared for the new assignment?"

"Honestly? I don't even know where to begin. My expertise lies more in the romantic suspense genre. Writing ten thousand words set in a post-apocalyptic Sci-Fi universe seems way out of my depth."

Dan chuckles. "Don't they have alien porn in romance? Surely you could throw some of that in for good luck?"

I tilt my head, raising my brows. "Post-apocalyptic alien porn? Now that I can do. It's just the elements of Sci-Fi I'm not too familiar with. Think this is going to be a tough one for me."

"Well, you know this *is* my thing. Why don't you come over for that study session I've been trying to get you to do for a while, and I can run through some of the Sci-Fi elements with you. Teach you all the important factors to include in a Sci-Fi novella?"

I turn to Jasmine, who's watching my conversation eagerly with Dan, and she smiles, winking at me.

It's just a study session.

He's going to help me with schoolwork—*that's it.*

"Okay, I'll come to the study session after class. I need all the help I can get with this one."

Dan's lips turn up in a stunning smile, so much so his eyes twinkle. If I said I wasn't attracted, I would be lying.

He is gorgeous.

But he's not Raid.

And that's beside the point.

I'm only going to study with him.

The bell rings, and I glance at the clock on the wall.

"And look at that... class is over. You wanna follow me back, or do you want to come with me, and then I can drop you home?"

I turn to Jaz, and she smiles. "You go. I have to go back to the club to do some stuff. Have a good night. Take some time for you, okay?" she suggests, and I lean in to hug her.

"You sure?"

She pulls back, looking at me. "You deserve to be happy, Frankie. So let yourself be happy, okay?"

I weakly smile as she picks up her books and bag, then heads off for the door, leaving me with Dan. I turn to face him, and he places his hand out for me to take. "You ready to go?"

Placing my hand in his, I stand, then we walk out of the classroom for his car. The walk isn't far, and on the way, we talk about the class and the topics we covered today. When we get to his car, he opens the passenger side door for me, and I slide in with a smile.

What a gentleman.

Oh, God. My stomach twists and I'm overcome with nervousness. The fact that maybe I should take a chance on someone else is playing havoc with my emotions. I know that Raid and I can't go anywhere—he's made that abundantly clear—so what's the point in holding out for him? All that's doing is hurting us both. *Right?*

The problem is my chest hurts to even think about that and being with anyone else, for that matter.

Dan slides into the driver's side while I take a deep centering breath and decide to talk to him about Raid, just so he knows there's another guy in my life. "Have you seen the guy who sometimes drops me off for class?"

Dan starts the car. "The guy on the motorcycle?"

"Yeah… we kinda have this will-we won't-we thing going on. It's complicated."

Dan chuckles, taking off, but keeps his eyes ahead. "It always is."

"He has a kid, but she's only just come into his life."

"Oh, like a baby?" he asks, his eyes meeting mine for a moment, a look of shock registering on his face.

"No. She's fourteen. The mother just showed up and told him about her. They were together, and the mother found out she was pregnant and bailed on their relationship. Never told him anything about being pregnant and having a child."

Dan lets out a snort. "Fuck! Every guy's worst nightmare. A secret baby. Poor guy missed out on so many years of his kid's life."

"Yeah… it's hard on him. He's trying to get to know his kid, so that's why shit between us is so complicated."

"No room for a woman... makes sense, I guess. Unfortunately, sometimes our priorities don't line up with what we want. Doesn't make shit any easier, though."

Sinking into my seat, I sigh. "No... it doesn't."

Dan continues to drive and is quiet for a moment, obviously thinking about what to say. "But then I think that might be the universe's way of telling you that maybe what you think you want might not be the right thing for you. Everything happens for a reason, Frankie."

He is right.

Everything does happen for a reason.

And maybe Addi and Sophie showing up when they did was a sign. A glowing bright red neon sign that reads, 'Raid and Frankie are never meant to be together.'

Because we're not right for each other.

Because I am a club girl and he is a brother, the two never mesh well.

It's the way most biker clubs work.

Club girls and brothers are a no-no.

I turn to Dan and say, "I can't help but think you're right."

Dan chuckles. "Of course I am. I'm always right."

I snort out a laugh. "Typical male."

Dan chuckles. "So, you wanna grab some dinner while we study?"

Fuck it! Why the hell not?

"Yeah, sounds good."

We arrive not long later, pizza boxes in hand, at his upper-crust, unbelievably amazing condo.

As we take the elevator, my eyes widen at the state of the passageways in this place. "You live here?"

Dan smirks. "I come from money, so buying a condo was nothing for me."

Widening my eyes, I look him up and down. I would never have guessed he was stinking rich. The way he wears his jeans, tight white top, and leather jacket, I would have thought more of him as a struggling musician. But that's the thing, you should never judge a book by its cover. I should know that studying English.

"Well, I can't wait to see inside."

Finally, we reach his front door, and upon walking inside, I take it all in. It's like something from a reality design show on television with its all-black with gold accents. Pristine furniture with sleek lines. It's so masculine, but it has the feel of very dark and moody in a punk rock way. Again, I get that rocker vibe from him as I walk around his living room.

I turn to face him as he places the pizza boxes on the coffee table. "You into music?"

He smirks. "Father manages a few bands. So I grew up in the scene. How'd you know?"

"You have a vibe."

He chuckles, opening the pizza boxes and grabbing a slice. I sit on the floor in front of the sofa, making myself comfortable, and reach for a slice.

Dan smiles, joining me on the floor. "Just so you know, the fact you would rather sit on the floor than a perfectly comfortable sofa says a lot about you."

I chomp down on the cheesy pizza and raise my brow. "Mm... how so?" I ask with a full mouth.

He turns to face me. "Says you're comfortable around me. That you're being yourself. That you don't like to conform to the state of norms. You're a bit of a rebel and do things your way."

"You got all that from me sitting on the floor?"

"Honestly, I got most of that from watching you in class. But, you sitting on the floor confirmed it for me."

"You watch me in class a lot?"

Dan shrugs. "You're easy to look at, so why not."

I swallow the lump of pizza that suddenly becomes lodged in my throat. "Dan..."

He reaches out, grabbing my hand. "Look... I know you're going through something with the motorcycle guy, but I need you to know you have options."

My head begins to swirl.

My stomach clenches with nerves.

The thought of doing anything.

Of even *thinking* about another guy has me feeling all kinds of nausea.

"Can I use your bathroom?" I blurt out.

Dan's eyes drop, but he points to the other side of the room. "Through the hall, last door on your right."

"Thanks," I reply, then stand, dust off my skirt, and head for the bathroom.

My breathing is rushed as I quickly enter, closing and locking the door behind me. Leaning against the door, I slide down to the floor, releasing a long breath, suddenly feeling incredibly trapped.

"You're such an idiot, Frankie," I mumble to myself.

Dan's a nice guy, but he's not Raid.

Even if I can't be with Raid, I don't want to do anything to jeopardize a chance at possibly having a future with him. So, pulling my cell out from the inside of my bra, I send off a quick text to Jaz with Dan's address, then I dial Raid's number waiting patiently for him to answer. My foot taps nervously while it rings, and rings, and rings.

"C'mon Raid, where are you?" I mumble to myself.

But the call rings out.

"Fuck!" I grunt, feeling disappointment wash over me.

But I don't let it go and dial again.

I need him to answer.

While biting my bottom lip, my foot taps impatiently. I want to tell him that I know we can't be together, but it doesn't mean I don't feel things for him or that I need him to come and get me. I want to spend time with him and Addi, not anyone else.

It's *him*.

I choose *him*.

Always.

But the phone rings out again.

I let out a small groan as I shake my head. "C'mon, Raid, pick up!" I dial again, but on the third ring, knocking on the door startles me. My cell drops from my hand, clattering on the tiles, and the screen smashes.

"Frankie, you okay in there?"

"Jesus!" I blurt out, my hand shifting to my chest in fright. My heart hammers so hard I can hear the pulse in my ears while I try to calm my breathing. "Sorry, I'll be out in a minute," I yell, standing and bending over to retrieve my broken cell.

Scrunching up my face, I groan, shoving the phone back into my bra. There's no choice now—I have to play this out. Dan brought me here to study, and I need help. I have to stop freaking out and do the work. If he tries anything, I will put him in his place.

Simple, right?

Straightening my shoulders, I plaster a fake smile and open the door.

Dan is standing back with a concerned look on his face.

"Hey, everything okay?" I ask.

He looks me up and down. "You were taking a little while... I was starting to get concerned. You all right?"

I rest my hand on my stomach and grimace. "Dairy and I aren't the best of friends. All the cheese on the pizza... I'd give the bathroom a little while before you go in there." If I want Dan not to hit on me, what better way to do that than to make him think I have bowel issues and, for some reason, that thought makes me chuckle.

Dan nods in understanding. "See, this is what I was talking about. You're so comfortable around me. We work so well together that you feel you can share that information. Most women would be afraid to talk about bodily functions with guys. *This* is why I like you, Frankie. You're straight up. You tell it like it is, and you're not afraid to speak your mind. You're *so* fucking amazing."

Damn!

Shit!

Fuck!

That backfired.

I hum under my breath because I don't know what else to do. "Thanks, but ah… I think we need to keep things between us strictly about school. I don't want it to become awkward in class if things go bad between us."

Dan tilts his head, his left eye twitching just a little, but I don't miss it.

The movement makes me instantly nervous.

He's not happy.

Dan inhales deeply through his nose and lets out a small laugh. "This because of the biker?"

Rolling my shoulders, I nod. "I mean, a little… yeah. I don't want to mess things up with him. But I meant what I said. I don't want to ruin our friendship, Dan—"

"Friendzone? You're friend-zoning me?" His tone is harsh, his voice deeper. Dan takes a long stride closer, forcing me to move back until my back hits the bathroom door as he locks me in place.

My anxiety peaks and adrenaline instantly courses through me, making my body surge into high alert. I bring my hands up, place them on his chest and instinctively give a little push to ease him away, but I see it the instant the anger ignites inside of him. A low growl reverbs from deep in his chest, and he reaches out, grabs my wrists, and pushes them back beside my head against the door.

His eyes lock firmly on me as I swallow hard. "You like it rough then, do you?"

A soft whimper escapes my mouth as I shake my head, trying to pull my wrists free from Dan's grip. "Dan, stop it!" I cry out, trying to break his hold on me, but he shoves me harder against the door, his entire body pressing on me.

I feel his hard cock, and I internally cringe. His flinty eyes bore into mine, and mine begin to glisten. He snarls. "All I wanted was for you to be reciprocal, Frankie. I didn't want to have to do it this way."

"Do what?"

He leans in, sliding his nose up my face, sniffing as he goes. "Now that I have you here, and you smell so damn good, you don't think I can let you go without me having a taste, do you?"

Tears well in my eyes as I shake my head. "Fuck you, Dan! I'm not some whore you can just take what you want from."

He begins to chuckle. "I know what you are, Frankie. You're a motorcycle club slut. You give yourself over to the men of the club freely. So I don't see how giving yourself over to me is any different?" The words sound bitter coming from his mouth, and I close my eyes and sigh loudly.

I've never been ashamed to be a club girl, but the way he says it makes me feel all kinds of dirty.

Makes me feel regret.

Makes me rethink what direction my life is heading.

But my life choices are mine, and I am not about to let a man like Dan make me feel bad about myself. Not when he is holding me for ransom. So I do the only thing I can think of, I bring my knee up and plant it straight between his legs.

He yelps, hunching forward. His hands instantly let me go.

I shove him away from me and duck past him, rushing for the front door, but he reaches out, grabbing the hem of my skirt. It jolts me to a stop, pulling me back to him. I let out a squeal as he yanks me with so much force I lose my footing, falling onto the floor with such a thud that I know it's going to bruise my ass.

"Fuck!" I scream as I flail my hands around, trying to stop him from moving in, but he brings his closed fist forward and slams it straight into the side of my head.

My head jolts back, hitting the floor, my mind instantly

whirling, and a fog invading my brain. Nausea immediately overwhelms me as I dry wretch, my eyes blinking rapidly to help me focus attempting to stay in the moment.

"Why are you making me do this, Frankie? Just stop, lay still. Isn't this what you're good at?" Dan grunts.

And even though I am hurting, even though I feel like I can't possibly fight him off, I somehow find it in me to surge forward, using all my strength to shove him off me. He goes flying backward, hitting his head on the wall behind him. I take the small win and scurry on my hands and knees, trying to make my way to the living room. I am dizzy and try to keep focused, but it's hard when everything is spinning. I crawl on my hands and knees, but suddenly, my hair is yanked, pulling me backward.

I let out an ear-piercing scream when he pulls so hard I feel my scalp tearing and blood trickling down my face. The asshole throws me out into the living room onto my stomach. I pant heavily, barely holding down the bile threatening to escape while tears flood my face.

Dan moves over the top of me, and I hear his belt being unbuckled.

My thoughts move to Raid—I don't have any fight left.

All I can do now is go to a happy place.

Think of Raid.

Dan hoists my skirt over my ass and kneels over me from behind. "It didn't have to be like this, Frankie."

I close my eyes.

Picture Raid's face.

Go to a happy place.

CHAPTER 14

RAID

It's been a long evening, and I am glad it's over.

This parenting shit is hard, especially seeing as I am doing it solo at the moment.

I had a meeting with Principal Schneider today to go over how Addi is settling in, and honestly, doing that on my own was the most adult thing I think I have ever done in my life.

Sophie was too sick to attend, and according to Jasmine, Frankie was at a study session for class, so I had no choice but to go at it alone. But frankly, the way I've been treating Frankie the last couple of days, I wouldn't blame her if she's avoiding me. I've been a dick, but I don't know how to be around her.

That fucking dream was so vivid, it felt so real, and it has made me want her more, crave her more. So I've been trying to keep away so I don't give into temptation. But I think the problem with that is it's made her think I don't care, which is the complete fucking opposite.

After making sure Addi is settled in after our conference at school and that she is spending time with Soph, I try to find Frankie. I want to talk to her and be open. Tell her why I've been avoiding her, even if it means making a dick of myself.

Sometimes honesty is the best policy.

I make my way down to her room and tap on her door. Wait for a few seconds, but there is no reply. Furrowing my brows, I gently open the door to see she isn't inside.

I didn't see her out in the club.

Surely, she'd be home from her study group by now?

Walking back into the main club room, I step around the bar to Storm and Jaz. Jaz spots me, and I sit at the bar. "Hey Jaz, Frankie not back from study group yet?"

She exhales, wiping the bar down. "She must be having a good time."

I furrow my brows. "Why aren't *you* at the study group?"

She grimaces and places the cloth on the bar. "Okay… so maybe it's not a group as such. It's more of a one-on-one study session."

My muscles tense, and my pulse races as I stare at her and how cagey she's being with me. "Jaz, who's she with?"

She lets out a frustrated groan. "Look… don't shoot me, but she's with Dan from class. And yeah, he has a thing for her, so they're probably getting it on right now. But seriously, Raid, I know I have to respect you, but *you* need to respect Frankie. The relationship you guys have right now, you avoiding her, it's doing her head in. She needs someone who will make her feel appreciated and *wanted* most of all."

Oh, for fuck's sake! I yank my cell from my pocket, needing to call and tell her to come home—*right fucking now*. But as I swipe the screen, the call register lets me know she's already tried to call me, and I have missed *all* the calls because my phone was on silent from my meeting with Principal Schneider, and I forgot to switch it back on. That's a big no-no as I need to be contactable by the club at all times. *What was I thinking, even putting the damn thing on silent?* Goddammit! I sit taller, everything in me going on alert. The calls are from minutes ago, and I instantly swipe my screen to dial her back.

With my anxiety skyrocketing, I turn to Jasmine as it rings, and she watches me. "Where's this Dan live?"

Jasmine furrows her brows. "Not far from here. Frankie texted me the address. Maybe a couple of minutes. Why?"

Frankie's cell rings out, and I shake my head. "Come with me. We're going to get her."

Jaz tenses, her eyes widening. "You sure that's a good idea?"

"Something's not right. I have a heap of missed calls, and now she's not answering. She *always* picks up her cell…" My senses are going into overdrive just thinking about the consequences if I can't get to her. So I turn to Jasmine and, in a stern, gruff voice, say, "You're gonna show me where he lives? Fucking *now!* You got me?"

Jasmine nods and rounds the bar so fast that she almost falls over her feet. "You think she's in trouble?" she asks as we rush out the door.

"Yeah. I feel it in my gut. We'll take your car. We will need the extra seat to bring her home."

Jasmine pulls out her car keys and dangles them. "Of course, let's go. I'll drive. I know the way."

"Don't talk. Just drive fucking fast."

Jaz starts the car after we shoot into our seats, and before I have had time to buckle up, she pushes her foot so hard on the accelerator I slide forward in my seat. "For fuck's sake, Jasmine!"

"We gotta get there. Honestly, I don't know what I'll do if Frankie's in trouble. I pushed her to go tonight."

I turn to look at her, creasing my brow. "Why the fuck would you do that?"

Jaz slumps her shoulders. "Because she's miserable about you. She adores the ground you walk on, Raid, and you've been ghosting her. I wanted her to be happy and to find someone who could appreciate her for her. She's the most *amazing* person and she deserves to be loved. You *can't* give her that. At least not right now. So I thought maybe she should try to find someone who could help her forget about you for a while. And it's not exactly like I could come to you and ask if you could run a background on Dan to make sure he's clean so Frankie could date him, now could I?"

My hands ball into fists on my lap upon hearing all this.

I can't believe I pushed Frankie this much that she was thinking of dating other men to try to forget about me.

And now, she might be in trouble.

Because. Of. Me.

"Fuck! If he's hurting her, I won't be responsible for what happens. If he's touched her in any way, you'll get your first *real* introduction to club life, Jaz. You ready for that?"

Her fingers tighten on the steering wheel, and she nods. "If he's hurting her, then I will be there to watch. Because this is my fault, not yours."

"We can blame each other all we want. I just need you to put your damn foot on the damn gas and get to that damn condo!"

She accelerates faster, my skin tingling. I know, I just fucking know. I can sense that something isn't right.

I need to get to her.

We pull up at a lavish building—*fucking typical of the little upstart*—and I jump out as fast as I can, not closing the car door before taking off running.

Jaz is by my side in an instant, and we race inside the complex and hit the elevator button to head up with my anxiety through the roof. I pull out my cell again and try to call her one last time.

Nothing.

No answer.

Straight to voicemail.

Grunting out my frustration, I clench my eyes. "How fucking long does an elevator take?"

Jaz doesn't say anything in response, but I can tell she's as anxious as I am. Finally, the elevator comes to a stop, and the doors open. We take off for the condo door, and Jaz stops in front of his place.

I point to it. "This one?"

She nods. "Yeah, they should be inside."

I don't hesitate, banging loudly on the door. "Frankie! You in there?" I yell.

But there's no response.

I pull out my cell and turn on the locator app for Frankie's cell. Sure enough. She's inside. Even if she is fine and simply studying, the fact they're not answering the door is cause for me to be concerned. So I turn to Jaz and exhale. "I'm about to go full biker."

She nods. "I'm with you."

Backing up to the other side of the hall, I brace my shoulder, then run full force at the door, slamming into it, my shoulder taking the full brunt of the hit. The door breaks off its hinges, and I rush through the doorway. Stumbling a little, my shoulder aching like a bitch, I quickly right myself as I race into the living room to see Frankie on her stomach on the floor, with who I assume is Dan, unbuckling his belt while kneeling over the top of her.

Dan snaps his head up, clear shock evident, while bile rises in my throat so violently I cough a little to keep it down.

"Frankie!" Jaz calls out, rushing to her side.

Dan stands, raising his hands in surrender and backing away from her, but with Jaz helping a beaten Frankie on the floor, that leaves me to deal with this fucking *cunt* in front of me.

"You were going to rape her? Was that your plan, *big man?*" I grit the words out through my teeth.

Dan lets out a cocky laugh. "She's a club whore. Can you rape a *whore*, when fucking is her job?"

I tilt my head, my neck cracking as I crane it. The anger burning through me is so voraciously hot that I'm unsure I can contain my rage. "Wrong answer!" I reply.

My hands grip his throat then I shove him back against the wall. His eyes bulge out of his head as he gasps for breath, but his hand comes up, socking me in the ribs. I let out an "oomph" and let him go to take a step to the side.

The guy wants to fight?

Then I'll give him a damn fight!

One he won't soon forget.

Bringing my right fist up, I slam it into his cheek so hard his head snaps around to the side. He drops to one knee, spitting out a line of blood. Actually, there goes a tooth as well.

But I don't stop.

I bring up my knee, which hits him in his nose, and he jerks back, landing on the floor on his back, his arms stretched out as he lies on the tiles. Moving in, I kneel over him. "How do you like it when a man kneels over *you*, asshole?" Then I land another blow to his face. Then another. And another. Until his face is black and blue, and I can barely breathe because I'm in a flurry of adrenaline that won't allow me to stop giving him what he fucking deserves.

"Raid!" Jaz calls out, but I ignore her.

"Raid, Frankie needs you," she calls again, and this time, I stop.

I look down at the gutless prick beneath me.

He's still breathing—fucking pity.

But he's bloody and broken.

I shift off him and crawl across the floor to Jaz, who has Frankie cradled in her lap. I notice Frankie's skirt up around her waist, luckily, her panties are still on, and inwardly I thank whoever is listening that we got here in time. I lean over, pull her skirt down, and hoist Frankie into my arms. Her face is bloody, and so is her scalp.

"It's okay. I'm right here. I'm not going anywhere."

Tears stain Jasmine's cheeks as she holds onto Frankie's hand. "Raid, we need to get her to the hospital."

Her entire body shakes. She's dazing in and out while I stroke her bruised cheek. "Jaz, use my cell. Call Hurricane, put him on speaker."

Jaz reaches for my cell in my pocket and dials the number. It rings a few times then he answers, "Where you at? I was lookin' for you a min—"

"Pres, we got a situation. I need the club. Frankie's hurt, and I need a clean-up crew."

Hurricane grunts. "How bad?"

"I gotta take her to the hospital. I got Jaz with me. We're gonna head there now. We're at this guy, Dan's condo. I need this asshole brought back to the club. I want him dealt with. This place needs to be wiped clean."

"On it. Text me the address. I'll send some guys over asap..." There's a pause, then, "Raid, she gonna be okay?"

I hold onto Frankie looking down at her injuries. I think she'll be okay, but I have no idea the effect this might have on her mental health.

One thing about Frankie...

... she is strong.

She's one of the strongest women I know.

She'll get through this.

"She'll be okay. I need to get her taken care of and for this asshole to fucking pay."

"What do you wanna do with this guy?" Hurricane asks.

"I want him to meet La Fin, and I want it to be all kinds of painful."

Hurricane chuckles. "You wanna be there when that happens?"

I glance over at Dan. The asshole's still passed out. "That a trick question... yeah, of course."

"I'll see you when you get back. Take your time and look after Frankie."

"Will do. And Pres... Dan will be in the condo tied up. So come prepared."

"You got it." The call ends, and I look at Jaz.

"Can you hold her for a moment while I deal with that fucking prick?"

Jaz sniffles, wiping away her tears but pulls Frankie into her arms again. "Shove something in his ass while he's waiting for Hurricane. See how he likes it!"

I walk to the kitchen, finding cable ties and duct tape in the second drawer. I shouldn't be surprised as I take it out and walk over to him. He is starting to come to, so I grab his wrists and draw them together behind his back, tying them together. Then I attach him to a pipe on the wall. Grabbing a piece of pizza from the coffee table, I fold it up and shove it in his mouth. The piece is so big there's no way he can swallow it, then I place the duct tape over it.

He wakes fully, shaking his head from side to side like he's outraged. He struggles against the pipe, but it is holding perfectly fine.

I love the idea of shoving something up his ass, but I won't stoop to his level. But I am impressed that Jaz is adapting to the biker lifestyle so easily.

Walking back over to Frankie and Jaz, I bend down, hoisting a broken Frankie into my arms, and hers slowly wrap around my neck. She clings to me like she knows I'm here to help. "I got you, baby. I got you."

My chest feels heavy, with the weight of guilt flowing through me as I head for the elevator. I want to smother myself in her to make sure every inch of her is taken care of. I want to look at every mark he has tarnished on her skin and kiss them better.

But I need to get her to a damn hospital and make sure there's nothing seriously wrong with her.

We get to the car, and Jaz runs around, opening the back. I slide us in, then sit in the back with Frankie cradled to me. "Get us to that fucking hospital right now, Jaz."

She slips into the driver's side and takes off. My fingers trace the bruises along Frankie's arms where he'd obviously been holding her down.

Motherfucker.

Cradling her to me, I hate that I pushed her into this. That she felt like she had to give this guy the time of day because I didn't. All because I couldn't put my shit aside.

Now Frankie has paid the ultimate sacrifice and was almost raped.

Shaking my head, I lean down, kissing her forehead tenderly. "You're gonna be okay, Franks. He's never gonna hurt you again."

Her eyes slowly flutter open. They glisten with unshed tears, and I weakly smile at her. "Hey, it's okay. It's just me."

She clings to me as she comes to. "Raid, you're here?"

"I got you. We're taking you to the hospital to see Dr. Adams."

Frankie lets out a small whimper as she tries to sit up.

"Hey, hey... don't move. Just take it easy," I tell her.

"I'm okay, just a little shaken..." She grips her bleeding scalp and ignores me, sitting up. "I can't believe Dan did that to me."

"What happened? What can I do to help?" I ask.

Her hand moves to her head, where she touches her scalp, then instantly recoils with a small hiss. "I told him we were good as friends, and he went psycho... said because I am a club girl that I am nothing but a whore, and that meant I should behave like one with him."

I want to go back and smash him in the face some more.

"Then, when I wouldn't give in to him, he tried to take what he wanted. I blacked out. I am assuming you came at just the right time, a minute longer, and I don't even want to guess how far he would have gone."

My stomach churns, thinking of how different the situation could be right now if I didn't act on instinct. What I would have done if that fucker had hurt her like that. Even with what he has done to her, I am going to make his death as *painful* as fucking possible.

I lean in, caressing her cheek. "I'm so glad I got to you... I don't know what I would have done if he..." I trail off, not wanting to think about that scenario.

She smiles, and somehow, it's like she's the one giving me

comfort at this moment. *I should be comforting her.* But she's the strong one right now, and I know it.

"Honestly, I'm okay. A little banged up and bruised, but that will heal. Raid, I'll be fine. You got to me in time. You saved me. I don't know how to thank you."

My chest squeezes as I pull her to me. "You can thank me by getting yourself checked out at the hospital and by making sure you're okay."

She leans into the embrace and nods. "Deal."

CHAPTER 15

RAID
Hours Later

After spending the last few hours getting Frankie checked over at the hospital with Dr. Adams, she got the all-clear, plus a few sutures for her trouble. Dr. Adams says there are no breaks or fractures on all the scans they ran, so she was happy with Frankie returning to the clubhouse. And Frankie's more than glad to come home to rest.

As Jaz pulls the car up, I wrap my arm around Frankie to help her walk toward the clubhouse.

Jaz steps in front of us, her eyes glistening with unshed tears. "Frankie, I know it won't mean much now, but I am *so* sorry I encouraged you to go with Dan. I feel so fucking guilty. This is *all* my fault."

Frankie detaches herself from me and moves to Jaz, pulling her into a tight embrace. "Hey, no one forced me to go with Dan. We all thought he was fine. No one saw this coming. I should have seen the warning signs, and I should have fought harder. This is no one's fault, just a shitty incident that luckily had a good outcome."

Jaz exhales.

I can't help but feel the same guilt Jaz shares.

We have both let Frankie down.

The problem is the reason I let Frankie down hasn't gone away. My responsibilities haven't changed even though this incident happened.

This fucking situation I am in is near-on damn impossible.

What's the damn solution?

Why do I have to make a choice?

Why can't I have both—a daughter and a beautiful woman by my side?

I fucking hate this whole position I have been thrust into, with my life being torn in two.

Because all I want to do is spend every fucking second with Frankie.

Ensure she is okay.

Devote every second of my time to her and make sure she's safe, cared for, and adored in a way she has never felt before.

But it's not feasible.

Why? Because I have a kid to look after. One that will need a lot of my attention now that Sophie is getting weaker.

But tonight.

I *can* give Frankie tonight.

She needs this.

I fucking need this.

"C'mon, let's get you to bed," I tell her, and she nods.

We walk inside the clubhouse, everyone is waiting for us as we enter, but Addi is the first to run up to us. "Oh my God, Frankie, I was so worried when I heard. Are you okay? You look like shit."

I scrunch up my face, but Frankie chuckles, letting go of me, and pulls Addi into an embrace. "I'm totally fine. It looks worse than it is. I promise I'll be back to full strength in no time."

Addi steps back, biting her bottom lip. "Is there anything I can do? You help me so much. I want to do something for you."

I smile, liking this generous side of my daughter because, believe me, I don't see much of it. She's a brat most of the time around me, but for some reason, Frankie and Addi have an affiliation I can't quite decipher.

Frankie exhales, shaking her head. "Thanks, honey, but honestly, I'm fine. I need to rinse this dry blood off me and get some sleep. I'll be good as new tomorrow. You'll see. I'm tough. When I wake, we can have a long chat."

Addi sniffles, reaching out for Frankie's hand. "Frankie?"

She raises her brow. "Yeah?"

"I'm glad you're okay."

Frankie pulls Addi to her again in a tight embrace, but I don't miss the slight grimace of pain Frankie displays when Addi squeezes her tighter.

"Okay, let's get Frankie to bed. I'll take you to school in the morning, okay, kiddo? You better head off to bed yourself."

Addi smirks. "Look at you being all adult."

I narrow my eyes on her. "*Bed*, Addi."

"Okay, okay... night, everyone." She smiles.

Everyone replies, "Night, Addi," as she walks down the hall.

Hurricane steps up to us and dips his chin. "Glad you're okay. Just so you know, we got Dan in the Chamber. But that's tomorrow's job. Let him suffer panickin' about what we're gonna do to him."

Frankie inhales deeply through her nose. "I don't want to think about that right now. I just want to sleep."

"You got it. Whatever you need," Hurricane states.

"Okay, let's get you to bed." I wrap my arm around her again.

She nods, and Jaz smiles compassionately when we walk past her and down the hall toward her bedroom. Frankie is quiet. Like she's thinking. I know we've been in a weird place, and circumstances haven't changed, but I need Frankie to know it doesn't mean I don't care about her.

We open the door and step inside her room.

She turns to me and sighs. "I've got it from here, thank yo—"

"We might not be able to take shit further, Frankie, but tonight, of all nights... I'm not fucking leaving you."

Her bottom lip trembles, her glistening eyes water with one tear rolling down her cheek. "Raid—"

"Frankie, I know shit is complicated. Extenuating factors are at play, but we can put all that aside for one night. Please, let me be here to support you when you need—"

"I'm fin—"

"No, Frankie, you're not."

The tears threatening to fall finally break their hold and slide like a river down her cheeks. I step up, my thumb brushing them away, then I lean in tenderly, pressing a kiss to her forehead. This woman, this amazingly beautiful, strong woman, was almost sexually assaulted tonight. I want to be here for her.

So that is what I'm going to do.

Her arms slide up, wrapping around my back and pulling me into a tight embrace. I hold her to me, my nose buried deep into her red hair. She smells so good, even teamed with the aroma of the antiseptic Dr. Adams used on her wounds.

"I got you," I whisper against her ear, holding her tight while she softly cries in my arms.

Her body gently shakes with emotion.

She sniffles, pulling back, her glistening hazel eyes meet mine, and we stop, simply staring at each other.

Time pauses.

The world around us fades away.

Both our worlds could have changed irrevocably tonight.

I'm thankful that didn't happen.

And as I stare at her, seeing the gorgeous beauty that she holds, every part of me wants to devour her.

But tonight is *not* the night.

Tonight is about recovery.

Healing.

Captivate

A chance to restore her world to the way it should be.

My hand caresses her cheek, the dried blood grating against the palm of my thumb, and I sigh. "Let's go to the bathroom," I suggest.

She widens her eyes but doesn't say anything. Instead, Frankie simply lets me go and then takes my hand, leading me to the bathroom. As I walk in behind her, there's a clear tension between us. When she turns, there is curiosity in her expression.

So I reach over, grab the plug, place it in the bottom of the sink, and turn on the faucet. "Let's get some of this dried blood off you. Seeing as Doc said you can't get your sutures wet, a shower seems out of the question, so I'll take it off with a washcloth. That sound okay?"

"Sounds perfect."

I test the temperature of the water. Lukewarm. Just right. So I drop in the washcloth, squeeze it out, bring it up to Frankie's head, and begin dabbing at the congealed blood, trying to avoid the sutures.

She winces occasionally, but her hands slide up, sitting on my hips as she leans against the basin. I move between her legs to get closer, our hips almost touching, but I keep back enough so she can't feel my cock through my jeans.

She doesn't need that right now.

Being as gentle as I can, I ease the cloth over the bloody patches and remove the reminder of the violence from her body.

What that guy did to her was... fuck!

Her hands slide under my cut, her nails grazing along the skin on my back, making it so fucking hard to concentrate. But I keep going, removing the blood from the scrapes on her arms.

The fucking bastard did a real number on her.

My anger builds, but I know I have to pull back and stay calm and collected. This is all about Frankie, not about the revenge currently pulling at every fiber of my being to exact on that asshole in the Chamber.

I need to be intimate and caring, confident, and considerate of her feelings.

Mine do *not* matter.

My eyes lock with hers. Something unspoken is shared between us.

I know that Frankie knows I would be in this with her if I could. One hundred percent.

Swiping the last of the blood from her forehead, I rinse the cloth, the water instantly turning red. So I pull the plug, draining the memory down the drain.

"There... you look beautiful," I tell her, and she smirks.

"I look like I've done a round with Mike Tyson, but thank you for trying to make me feel better."

"You could be neon green with red spots, and I'd still think you're beautiful."

She chuckles. "That is oddly specific. Some weird fantasy of yours?"

"Thought it might be part of that alien porn stuff you authors are into." I smirk.

She widens her eyes, her smile genuine. "Not an author yet, but I like that you know about alien porn. You a closet romance reader, Raid?"

"I might have read about a certain '*red room.*'"

She bursts out laughing. "You did not!"

Grinning, I shrug. "I think it would surprise you what I read on my Kindle. In a year, I wanna be reading a book by Frankie Lambert."

She playfully shoves me. "A year? I don't think my book will be ready in a year. I've barely started writing it."

"I have faith in you, Franks."

She slumps her shoulders, then pulls me into a tight embrace. "You're the best... have I told you that?"

Warmth floods me.

We could spend all night in the bathroom, or I could get her to bed where she should be resting. I prefer the latter.

"If that were true, I would already have you in bed resting. So c'mon, let's get your feet up."

She nods, and I take her hand to walk back into the bedroom. "I need you to change into whatever you feel comfortable wearing for bed."

Frankie slides off her skirt, throwing it on the floor, and I have to remind myself there is nothing sexual in this.

Keep your damn self under control.

As she draws her shirt over her head, leaving her in her panties and bra, this woman is picture-perfect. Then she unhooks her bra, which falls to the floor, exposing her perfect breasts.

But I keep my eyes up, making sure not to look at her tits—well, I try not to. I am a man, after all—as she makes her way over to her bed.

She climbs in, and I bend to pull the covers over her, but her hand reaches out, grabbing mine. "Don't go."

Shaking my head, I gesture for the desk chair. "I'm not going anywhere. I'll be right there... all night."

She pulls the covers back and taps the bed. "Stay with me tonight... please. I want this Raid. I need the company. Someone I know who cares enough about me to want to be with me. I need this. Please," she begs.

Hesitating for just a moment, I stand.

Once I have my head in the right place, I begin to pull off my club cut, placing it on the desk. Then I kick off my boots and unhook my belt. I'm not entirely sure what she's asking for, but whatever she wants tonight, I will give her. Sliding my jeans down my legs, I pull them off, then draw my shirt over my head and drop it on the floor with the rest of my clothes, leaving me in my briefs.

Making my way back to the bed, she smiles up at me as I climb in beside her, and she rolls over, her back to me. This beautiful woman just wants me to hold her tonight, and I am going to do that for her. So I slide in behind her, wrapping my arms around her stunning body, pulling her tight to my front. She pushes back into me, and I nuzzle my nose into her hair.

This is the calmest I have felt in an incredibly long fucking time.

She needs me right now.

But maybe, I need her just as much.

So tonight, I am going to hold Frankie and sleep with her in my arms, even though we both know in the morning, nothing about our situation will change.

But tonight.

We will have tonight.

And I am going to savor every last second.

***

My night was fucking unreal, considering the evening I had.

Sleeping with Frankie in my arms was the most peaceful, relaxing sleep I have had, well, in, I think, ever.

It felt right.

Like I was finally home.

In the place I'm meant to be.

But then morning came crashing us back to reality.

I had to get up to take Addi to school.

Life took hold again full throttle.

Frankie was sore—taking into account everything she went through, that's not surprising—so I left her in bed and got on with my day. However, I haven't been able to get her out of my mind. She's burrowed in there constantly and so incredibly deeply, and now I am worried about her safety, her well-being, her damn everything.

I'm returning to the club after dropping Addi off, and I know there's a special package in the Chamber waiting for me.

One I can't wait to hand deliver to a certain club pet.

Pulling the pick-up into the parking space, I jump out with a pep in my step.

Dan thought he could hurt Frankie and get away with it.

Yeah, not on my watch, asshole.

Making my way into the clubhouse, I spot Bayou sitting with Novah and walk over to him as they cuddle together. "Brother."

He glances up at me. "You get Addi off to school, okay?"

"Yeah, I did. I assume you haven't fed La Fin today?"

Bayou smirks. 'I've been waiting for this."

Novah rolls her eyes. "You guys get off on this far too much. You know that?"

Bayou wraps his arms around his Old Lady and waggles his brows. "I thought you liked it when I got off?"

She grins. "I'd prefer it if I was the only one who got you there. Having to share you with an alligator is kinda strange."

I chuckle, nodding my head. "She's got a point, brother."

Bayou chuckles. "Admit it! Watching La Fin do his thing turns you on too, baby." He leans in, pressing his lips to Novah's neck.

She sighs. "Fine! Go on… *go*. Do your big, badass boy thing with La Fin."

Bayou presses his lips to Novah's, devouring her, not giving a fuck that I am watching. Considering where they were even a few months ago, they have come a long way in their relationship.

I am happy for them.

But they're taking far too fucking long.

I have a problem to solve with an alligator, and I can't wait to resolve that problem permanently.

I shove Bayou in the arm. "C'mon, asshole, I don't have all damn day."

Novah giggles against Bayou's lips, and they slowly break apart. "Have a good day at work," Bayou says to Novah.

She stands, and he slaps her on the ass as she leaves.

"See ya, Novah," I mock sarcastically.

She giggles again, waving as she struts off.

Bayou watches her ass the entire way, and I move my fingers in front of his eyes, clicking them twice. "Fucking focus!"

He snaps his eyes to me. "Right, yeah. She's so fucking hot. How can I not look."

I gesture for the back door. "La Fin?" I ask.

"Yes, yes. You think Frankie will want to be a part of this?"

"Yeah, I'll go get her."

My initial instinct was to say *no*.

But then I think about how strong Frankie is.

How resilient.

How tough.

She's capable of this and using it to grow.

Revenge is a powerful tool. It can rid all wrongs and make everything right.

So yeah, I think this will be good for her.

"I'll head to the Chamber and fetch the feast."

"Thanks, brother."

"See ya out there."

Taking off, I head for Frankie's room. I told her she was *not* to leave her room today. She was to rest and recover. So if she is following my orders, she should be there.

When I knock on the door lightly, her voice soon follows. "Come in."

Opening the door just a little, I stick my head through and spot Frankie sitting at her desk, typing on her laptop, so I scowl at her. "You're supposed to be resting."

She groans. "Laying in bed is not for me, Raid. I'm constantly running around this place doing something. It's impossible for me to just *lay in bed* all day. My mind won't keep still."

I open the door fully and step inside. "I hear you. If you're up for it, I have something for you to do?"

She stands abruptly and starts pulling on a pair of boots. "God, yes! Gimmie something to do. I'm dying of boredom."

I chuckle, then gesture for her to follow me. "C'mon then, let's go."

She rushes out the door, excited as I lead her out back.

"Where are we going?"

"Down to the bayou," I reply, and she instantly widens her eyes.

"To La Fin?" she asks with a raised brow, and I nod.

"You okay with that?"

A slow grin crosses her face. "Hell, yeah."

Wrapping my arm around her, I walk her down to the bayou fence. After entering the six-digit code, I flick the latch and walk us through, ensuring it closes behind us. The last thing we want is a rogue alligator wandering around the grounds of the clubhouse.

Spotting Bayou and Hoodoo standing on the rickety deck, Dan is in their arms, his one good eye wide in fear. The other is swollen shut from where I beat him senseless. *Not senseless enough, obviously.* Frankie and I slowly approach him.

"If at any time you feel uncomfortable, you let me know," I tell her, and she nods.

"I'm good. He deserves what is about to happen to him."

This woman!

We approach Hoodoo and Bayou while Dan struggles in their grip.

"Well, well... looks like all your bravado has left the building, Dan?" I say, not being able to keep the sarcasm from my tone.

"You can't possibly think you're going to get away with drowning me," he snaps.

Frankie snickers. "You think we're going to drown you?"

Dan stops struggling, focusing his attention firmly on Frankie. "I know I went a little far—"

"A *little* far, Dan? Would you like to rephrase that at all?" She puts her hand up to stop him when he goes to speak. "You fucking bastard. I have thirteen sutures in my scalp, bruises and grazes all over my body. You were going to *rape* me. If Raid and Jaz didn't turn up when they did... *a little far* doesn't begin to cover what you were going to do, right?"

"So, what? I deserve to die for that?" he snaps.

I curl up my lip. "You hurt the people we care about. In our books, yeah... that's a punishment paid by death."

He looks at me, and I see it, the second his bravado turns from arrogance to fear. His body begins to shake, and he thrashes about in Hoodoo and Bayou's arms again. *"Heeelp, somebody! Anybody! Help me!"* he screams like a baby.

We all chuckle. "No one is going to hear you. We're too far out from civilization. You're well and truly on your own," Hoodoo states with a smirk.

"But honestly, make as much noise as you can. It only makes La Fin arrive sooner," Bayou chimes.

Dan snaps his head to Bayou. "What the hell is La Fin?"

Out of the corner of my eye, I see his scales peeking up through the water, swerving and waving through the murky depths heading right for us. "You're in luck. He's headed right for us."

Bayou smiles wide. "Who's daddy's favorite boy?" Bayou coos making me shake my head.

Dan looks from Bayou to me to Frankie, trying to figure out what the hell is going on. "Frankie. *Frankie!*"

"Don't come crying to me, Dan. You had your chance... you blew it. You sealed your fate the second you called me a damn whore."

My fists ball at my side, anger igniting inside me. "Fuck, I am going to enjoy this."

"Enjoy what? What's going on?" Dan asks in a blind panic.

Frankie steps away from my side and over toward Bayou and Hoodoo. I don't walk with her. She needs to do this on her own.

"Payback!" Frankie grits through her teeth. Then she shoves Dan. Hard.

He yelps as he falls headfirst into the water with a splash. His hands are tied, so he's having trouble keeping himself upright, but it's not long before the huge waving body of La Fin creeps toward him through the ripples of the water.

Dan bobs up and down, trying to catch some breath, but before he has a chance to say anything else, La Fin's jaws open wide, and he slams them down right onto Dan's left shoulder. Dan screams, a blood-curdling shriek, while blood floods the bayou. Then, La

Fin starts his spinning maneuver, taking Dan under the water, his screams now muffled by the murky deeps of the bayou.

I walk over to Frankie and pull her to me as we watch La Fin rolling and causing havoc beneath the water. Blood bubbles to the surface, a random arm floats to the top, and we all widen our eyes.

"Are we gonna have to do something about th—" Then, before I can finish my sentence, La Fin bursts through the water, snapping the arm into his jaws and chomping down on it.

I chuckle while shaking my head.

Frankie lets out a long exhale like a weight has been lifted from her shoulders. "Thank you… all of you. This is exactly what I needed."

Bayou grips her shoulder and smiles. "Glad we could help. Now go, get some rest. Because this club needs you, Frankie."

She nods and smiles. "Thanks, guys. I appreciate you all backing me like this."

Hoodoo tilts his head. "You're family. We do *anything* for family."

We start walking back up the deck toward the exit, and I finish with, "Absolutely anything."

She smiles, her eyes glistening like she's holding back tears. "You know, I can't believe I was thinking about leaving the club."

I jerk my head back in shock, my heart stopping a beat as I stare at her. "What?"

"I'm not going to obviously, especially after all this. It's just… shit with us was strained. And I thought maybe it would be easier," she sighs, closing her eyes, "… for you, for me…" she opens them again and looks directly at me,"… if I didn't have to see you every day."

I stop walking and turn, taking her hands in mine. "Fuck! I never meant nor wanted what's happening between us to affect you like this, Frankie. I certainly never want you to doubt your place here at the club. If I thought for a second it would make you turn to another man, I would—"

"Raid, stop! This is all on me and my stupid decisions. I went home with Dan because I was hurting. I know your priority is Addi. I don't expect you to change that, nor do I want you to. I'm okay... we're okay. I promise. After you took care of me last night, I don't know... it changed things. I know you care. If things could be different, they would be, but for now, we both have to focus on Addi, and I am okay with that."

I look into her eyes, trying to figure out if she's being serious or not. Then it occurs to me that she is one hundred percent serious. I can tell by the confident stance and the look in her eyes. "You are the single most amazing person I know."

She grins wide but doesn't answer.

"C'mon, back to bed for you. You still need to rest."

She groans, rolling her eyes. "*Boooring.*"

"Don't be a brat when I can't punish you for it."

She widens her eyes with a smirk, then waggles her eyebrows.

We head for the back door of the clubhouse just as Hurricane is walking out with his head looking at the dark and dreary sky. "All good, down there?"

"Yeah, all done," I reply, my eyes following his up to the heavens, seeing the greenish tinge to the sky. "You okay, Pres?"

He rubs the back of his neck, seeming uncomfortable. "Don't like the look of this weather. They say there's a storm developin' off the coast. Just gonna keep my eye on the sky."

Great. Like we haven't had enough storms roll through here.

Enough with the turbulence.

CHAPTER 16

FRANKIE
Two Days Later

The girls and I are getting back from a supply run.

I'm still a little sore, but with the storm coming, I have to suck it up because it's all hands on deck. So as we walk back inside the clubhouse, the guys are boarding up the windows, locking down everything in the yard, and preparing for the storm that's due.

The hurricane has already made landfall at the small towns on the coastline and is headed our way. The wind has picked up significantly, and the sky shows an eerie shade of gray that sends a chill down my spine.

As the girls and I stock the soundproof shed full of canned goods, nonperishables, and so much bottled water, it's not funny, it's easy to see Hurricane, our president, is tenser than normal. Considering what he went through with his mother during Hurricane Katrina, it's no wonder he gets anxious whenever the threat of a hurricane strikes. Katrina is the reason his road name is Hurricane, and while we've had some pretty intense summer storms at the club before, this is the first real hurricane we've had to deal with.

We are as prepared as we can be.

Hurricane brought his stepmother, Ingrid, to the club to ensure her safety, while Raid has made sure we have plenty of backup generators. I've made sure we have copious amounts of food and water.

I know Raid is anxious because of Sophie. She can't get out of bed much, and we'll all have to head into the soundproof shed soon. So we're going to need to get her up. I just hope she can manage enough to cope with what's coming.

I make my way over to Raid as Hurricane starts signaling everyone to make their way from the clubhouse to the shed. We call it a shed, but it's the most secure building on the property. It's the best place to hunker down in a hurricane. The thick concrete walls make for good security from the harsh weather outside.

"You ready to get Sophie?" I ask, and Raid nods.

"Yeah, we need to get her over there. I might get Hoodoo to help me."

"Just let me know what I can do."

"Maybe grab anything she might need, extra blankets and her medications?"

"You got it."

Raid walks off to find Hoodoo, and I head for Sophie's room.

As I walk in, Addi is inside, holding her mother's hand. "It will be fine, Mom. You know Raid will make sure they take care of you."

"He's gone to get Hoodoo to help bring you to the shed now," I tell her.

"It's not me I am worried about. It's you, Addi."

I wrap my arm around Addi and pull her close. "You have nothing to worry about. She'll be safe. All you need to do is rest."

A gentle knock at the door makes us all turn to see Raid and Hoodoo step inside.

"Your escort is here, m'lady," Hoodoo offers.

Sophie smirks. "I'm sorry to be such a burden."

Addi snaps her head around to her mother. "You are *never* a burden."

Raid steps up to Sophie and reaches out for her hand. "Addi's right, Soph, definitely *not* a burden. We want to take care of you."

Sophie carefully positions herself to sit on the bed and says, "Then let's get me out into that shed before this hurricane hits."

"Good idea," I state, moving out of the way for Raid and Hoodoo to step in.

Hoodoo runs some medical checks over Sophie before Raid is permitted to move her. Once Hoodoo is done, he stands back and nods his head. "She's good to go."

Raid exhales like he's relieved and steps up to the bed. Sophie wraps her fragile arms around his neck, and he scoops her up. I move in, sliding a blanket over her as Addi takes off after him. I rush about the room, grabbing Sophie's medications and anything else I think she might need. Then, I run after them.

We all make our way for the shed, the wind whipping at us intensely, the clear howling whistling through the trees, making it sound like the song of chaos is near. When we enter the soundproof shed, mostly everyone's hunkering down and sitting on mattresses with blankets wrapped around them. Generators running keep the lighting on. Radios are tuned in for information on the storm while the chill in the air seeps into my bones.

Raid takes Sophie over to a mattress and lays her down. Instantly, I wrap her in ample amounts of blankets to try and keep her warm in this frigid place. I want to do my best to make sure Sophie is taken care of and as comfortable as she can be. But even though the walls are lined with insulation and lots of concrete for the extra soundproofing, I have to admit, even I am scared shitless.

But I have to be brave and keep control of this situation.

Storm, the second in charge, looks to me for guidance, and I need to ensure she is okay during this. As well as taking care of Addi and Soph. Plus, Jaz is new here too, and she's being locked in a room full of people she's just getting to know, and it's her job to make them feel safe and keep them calm.

That's the job of a club girl.

What a welcome.

As the howling and intense rain hammers down outside, I can't help but feel a shift in the air. That ominous groaning of the trees outside as we all sit and simply wait it out.

There's not a lot of talking going on. There's not much we can say. Hushed conversations can be heard, but everyone is pretty much trying to brave it out. Addi clings to her mother while Raid sits by their side. My eyes meet Raid's, and he gives me a silent head bob, a gesture to ask if I am okay.

I nod my head back at him.

A loud crash sounds on the roof of the shed. A small scream escapes Addi and Clover as the rest of us glance up, but luckily it is holding. The wind is picking up in intensity, and even though the walls are cement, they are vibrating with the fierceness of the gale force outside.

The pummeling of rain slams on the shed so loud it's hard to hear. I glance to my right to see Storm physically shaking, so I dart off to the side and wrap my arms around her. "Hey, we're going to be okay," I tell her, stroking her dark hair.

Another loud crash hits the side of the shed, only this time, part of the roof lifts, and a massive stream of water starts flooding the corner of the shed. City, Bayou, and Omen run to try and pull the lifted part of the roof back down.

Storm cuddles into me, she's a grown woman, but she is still my responsibility, so I hold on and comfort her as Jaz reaches out for Clover holding her tight. I glance over my shoulder to check on Addi and Raid. He's fine, making sure Addi is okay.

It's my duty to be the head club girl right now, so I need to let him handle his family while I care for everyone else. I glance down at Storm and grab either side of her face. "Storm, we're club girls. We need to do our jobs and make sure everyone is okay. You want to step up. Now is the time to prove you can shine, okay?"

She sniffles but nods as we stand and start racing around the shed, along with Jaz. The wind ravages everything outside while the guys continue to work on the leak. We rush to everyone near the leak, handing them blankets and grabbing whatever we can to try and stop the water from flowing too far into the shed.

From flowing anywhere near Sophie's mattress.

It's fucking chaos as more of the club comes to help. Storm seems to have calmed her nerves a little now that she has a job to do rather than focusing on the terrifying factor of what's happening around us. Jaz is stepping up to the plate—she's going to be damn fucking good at this.

Another slam into the side of the shed rocks the entire foundation. We all duck, waiting for some giant tree branch to break through the roof—but nothing. I have no idea what the hell that was, but shit is going on outside that we can't even see.

The sound of metal grating, and the howling of the intense wind, is like nothing I have ever experienced. The moisture in the air is sticking to my skin, and my heart races so frantically while trying to keep my head on straight when all I want to do is run to Raid and take shelter in his arms.

I want him to protect me.

I want to feel safe with him.

I want his arms around me.

I want to feel his warmth.

Compassion.

Concern.

But I know his main consideration is Addi and Sophie, and I still have a job to do. I can't just abandon my post because I'm terrified. I have to put on a brave performance and help my club.

Because that's my job.

The job of a club girl.

The wind swirls and howls, picking up momentum. The roofing shudders with force. The mood in the shed is electrified—

everyone on edge as the guys finally manage to mend the broken part of the ceiling, just in time for the door to swing open on its hinges. Hurricane jumps up, grabbing the door and pushing it closed, but the force of the wind is trying to slam it open again. Grit and Hoodoo run over to hold on with everything they have.

I grab Storm, and we make our way over to Kaia, who's holding onto her one-month-old. I want to make sure while Hurricane is tending to the door that she's okay. I sit beside Kaia and Storm on the other. Then I wrap my arm around her. "You okay?" I yell over the noise.

She nods, her hands cradling her baby. "This is intense, and we're not even getting the full force of the hurricane here."

"The guys made sure to lock everything down. They will make sure we're okay," I try to reassure her.

She glances over at Lani. "I just hope Lani doesn't have an episode. Her epilepsy can be triggered by stress, and I don't know about you, but this is pretty fucking stressful."

We all turn to look at Lani, but her eyes are fixated on Grit while he, Hurricane, and Hoodoo hold onto the door. "We'll keep an eye on her. You need to look after yourself right now and your baby."

Kaia exhales, holding her child closer to her chest. "We're okay. I need to make sure no one gets hurt in this god-awful storm."

"Storm and I are going around to everyone, doing the rounds and checking in. We can do that job for you. We'll ensure everyone is taken care of. You just take care of that beautiful baby, okay?"

"Frankie, are you sure? You should be with Raid and Addi," Kaia says, glancing over at them.

I follow her line of sight to see the three of them cuddled together.

My chest squeezes that I can't be with them, but I have a duty to the club, and I don't want Hurricane to think I can't do that duty in a time of crisis. So I turn back to Kaia. "I'm the head club girl, Kaia. This is the exact time I need to step up and help as much as possible. Raid can take care of Addi and Sophie. They will be there when all this is over."

Kaia grips my shoulder. "This is why you're so fucking good for this club, Frankie. You're so damn loyal, even at your own detriment. Thanks for helping. I do appreciate it."

"I need you to stay calm while this is happening. Let me and Storm do the rest."

Kaia nods, sinking back down, getting comfortable.

I grab Storm, and we jump up, ready to make the rounds.

Another piece of debris slams against the shed wall with a sickening cracking thud, making me instinctively duck. My heart rate is sky-high, and Storm is clearly freaking out, but I grab hold and force her to look at me. "We've gotta continue, make sure everyone is okay. We have to give off the impression we're not scared, so they can feel better about the situation as well. Do you think you can do that?"

Storm subtly nods her head.

"Do you think you can do that, Storm?" I reiterate.

She clears her throat. "Yes... yes, I can do that." She lacks conviction, but at least she's trying.

"Good, our first stop is Lani. Let's make sure she's okay. You with me?"

Storm straightens her shoulders and plants on the best stoic face she can muster, which still looks terrified, but she's at least reined in the tears. "I'm with you."

"Okay, let's go."

We take off, and even though I feel like I am completely faking the enthusiasm I am putting on right now, I need to pull up my big girl panties because I have to fight for this club, for the people in it who need me. And even though every ounce of me is screaming, 'run to Raid and jump into his arms,' I have to stand tall and be the strength that's needed for the others who are here.

And I'm going to fight for these people who are my family because I love them, not just because it's my duty, but because it's the right thing to do. Because I *want* to fight for them, to stand up for them, to be strong for them when they're scared and at their weakest. Because I know they would do the same for me.

Even if, at the end of all this, I want more for myself than the life I have, I am exactly where I want to be, right now.

Even if I am terrified to death.

CHAPTER 17

RAID

It's been hours, and the hurricane has been intense, but it feels like the worst of it is over as the wind dies down, the banging against the shed begins to slow, and the rain sounds like it's easing somewhat.

We made it through.

I have to admit, it was rough for a while there, but everyone kept their cool, and even though Addi is holding onto Soph, and I am holding onto Addi, it feels more like we're bonding than anything.

Frankie had to help the others when shit got bad. I couldn't check on her, and though I had to stay where I was, my mind was constantly on Frankie, hoping she was okay. I know she is as tough as they come, but I can't help the fact I still want to be the one to protect her.

Especially after what happened with Dan.

But my priority is Addi, then Sophie and I had to be present for them during all this fucking madness.

Now the dust is settling and the storm outside seems to have ebbed, I let Addi go. "You going to be okay if I go find Frankie?"

Addi smiles. "I'd be annoyed if you didn't go find her and make sure she's all right."

I smile at my kid and chuckle. "I'll be back soon, okay?"

"We're not going anywhere. Just make sure she's fine."

"You got it," I reply, then stand and make my way through the ankle-deep water to find Frankie.

She's with Storm and Jaz, who are getting ready to distribute fresh bottled water to everyone. I step up to the club girls and reach out, grabbing Frankie and pulling her to me into a tight embrace. Her eyes widen as I spin her to face me, but when she sees it's me, her arms slide up around my neck, and she clings to me tightly. My nose slides into her hair, and I just spend the moment drinking her in. I inhale, smelling her fruity perfume, and it just about does me in.

I didn't realize how fucking worried about her I was until now. "I'm so glad you're okay."

She pulls back, her eyes meeting mine, and she smiles. "You too. How's Addi? And Sophie?"

"They're fine. Scared, but fine."

Frankie takes a step back and hands me a water bottle. "We're just trying to get organized for the cleanup. We know you guys are going to need to keep hydrated."

"I should have known you would be onto looking after everyone else. You're fierce and strong, and that's what you do in shitty situations. Just look after everyone..." I sigh. "But I wasn't there for you during the storm."

She reaches out, caressing my arm. "You had important cargo to take care of. Naturally, Addi and Sophie come first, and I completely understand. I'm okay with that, Raid."

"Everyone, listen up," Hurricane calls out, gaining our attention, and we both glance over at him. "I'm pretty sure the storm is over. We're gonna check out the damage. Then we can start the cleanup. Y'all ready for this shit?"

"Yes, Pres," we all call back to him.

Then City and Hurricane walk out of the shed. Tree branches fall into the water onto the ground in front of them as they open the propped door. With frayed nerves, they jump back a little, and we all hesitate.

Hurricane raises his hand. "It's debris from the roof. We're good."

They venture out as Frankie and I make our way over to Addi. She spots Frankie and runs up, slamming her arms around her. "I'm so glad you're okay."

Frankie winces a little, still recovering from her injuries, but she cuddles Addi anyway. "I'm glad *you're* okay, honey. I was worried about you guys."

"We were fine. Raid kept us safe."

"He's good at doing that." Frankie grins at me. "We should take a look at how bad it is outside."

I nod but glance down at Sophie, who waves her hand through the air. "You three go and check it all out. I'll be okay here until you're ready to take me back inside. Honestly, go. I'll be fine. I'm comfortable, I'm warm, just go. Help clean up."

Addi, Frankie, and I look at each other, then nod. "Okay, I do need to get out there and help, but if you need us—"

"I won't. *Go!*"

We all smile and turn, heading out of the shed and into the lot. I glance over to check the clubhouse is still standing, and amazingly it's perfect. Maybe the roof needs a little love and care in some places, but other than that, it looks pretty damn good.

But outside, though, that is something else.

There are branches and debris everywhere, not to mention the fence that surrounds the back bayou is down. My eyes widen when I take in the sight, and I spin, looking over my shoulder. "Bayou!" I call out, graining his attention.

He's trying to shift some large portions of sheet metal. He looks at me when I point to the fence. His body tenses initially, and he starts madly looking around the back lot. "Where the fuck is he?"

Bayou calls out to me, and I shrug.

"Haven't seen him. Could still be in the water, but you need to get that fence back up, pronto."

Bayou grabs City and starts rushing for the bayou when a mad-as-a-cut snake, La Fin, comes crawling out from under some debris, heading for the back of the clubhouse.

Bayou and I spot La Fin simultaneously, and Bayou is on the hunt quicker than I can even get one word out. He picks up some rope, and he and City move into action.

"C'mon, baby boy, you gotta go back in the water while Daddy fixes the fence."

Addi reaches out for my arm, grabs hold and squeezes tightly. I smirk and wrap my arm around her for comfort. "It's okay. Bayou will get it under control. La Fin won't hurt you."

Addi swallows a lump in her throat. "It's a freaking alligator... and it's on the loose!"

I nod. "Yeah, he's normally behind that fence, down in the bayou. It'll be okay. I assure you that Bayou has it handled."

And without another word, Bayou jumps on the back of La Fin in a move like you would see the late, great Steve Irwin do from Australia. His hands clamp down around La Fin's jaw then he ties the rope around his mouth, and City sits on La Fin's tail, stopping him from thrashing about.

Addi is tense beside me, but I hold her as the two men wrangle the alligator. Eventually, they get control, tie La Fin up, then drag him back down to the bayou.

I start slow clapping with Frankie chuckling beside me while they puff and pant, completely out of breath. "Good job, guys."

"Fucking storms!" Bayou grunts as he drags his pet down what is left of the embankment.

I turn to Frankie and gesture for us to head inside the clubhouse, keeping Addi close to me.

Everyone starts the cleanup, and we pitch in and help.

Captivate

***

It feels like hours pass, and the clubhouse is slowly returning to somewhat of a normal state.

The power is still not on, but the generators are working well for now. We have plenty of food and water, which is good. Bayou and City have the fence back up, keeping La Fin out of the main areas, *thank God,* and outside has piles of debris and shit we'll need to get rid of. For now, that will have to wait until the city is back and functioning again. The water needs to recede, so it's all a waiting game.

Luckily the hurricane only hit us on the outskirts of town. It's why the damage was minimal. The main impact went to the east, pummeling Mississippi with the eye passing over Slidell. Luckily we were hit by its minimal wrath.

We've taken our time with some of the cleanups, and Addi wants Sophie to come back inside. She's been out in the shed on her own while we've been clearing everything. We need at least a path to the clubhouse. So I head back out there and grab a tired Sophie, hoisting her up and bringing her inside to her more comfortable bed. Sophie seems like she's struggling, though she is in good spirits as I lay her down.

Addi is by her side instantly, concern crossing her face. "I'm sorry I left you so long, Mom, I was trying to help clean, but I don't want to leave you alone when you're looking so pale. Are you cold? What do you need?"

Sophie shakes her head. "I'm fine. You should continue to help."

Addi glances up at me, sheer desperation in her eyes, and I know she needs this. She's asking my permission without saying anything, and she's been a great help, so I can give her this. "There's not much left to worry about right now. We got the rest of this, Addi. You stay here with your mom."

"You sure?"

"Yeah, I just have to check my den and ensure it's all good.

There's not much you can do in there, so you stay here and keep Soph company."

Addi's eyes glisten in thanks as she cuddles into her mother. "Okay, but if you need help, I'll be here. Just come get me."

"Will do. Rest up, Soph," I say, then turn and walk out the door for my den.

As I open the door, the ceiling has sprung a leak and is dripping down over my table, onto my keyboard, and over one of my monitors. "Fuck!" I blurt out. That keyboard and monitor will be fucked, but I need to check and see if anything else in the room, especially the servers, are impacted by the leak.

I get to work, plugging the hole in the ceiling—which will need a major repair later—then checking everything while avoiding as much damage as possible. The rest will have to be either new products or I might even have to wait for the power to come back on for a couple of other things to see how bad it is, especially in the server room.

I am a couple of hours into the mess of my den when there's a tap at the door. With the security feed down, I turn and simply pull the door back to see Frankie standing there with a sandwich and a huge glass of beer.

Fuck I could kiss her.

"You're the best!"

She smiles, handing me the tray. "Is there much damage?"

"It seems the servers are fine. Think it just might be the filing cabinets, my keyboard, and one monitor that took the brunt of the leak, but we should be good. I keep multiple backups of everything, so there shouldn't be any issues, just need to buy new shit."

Frankie sits on the edge of my desk and shakes her head while I grab my sandwich and take a bite. "That whole thing was so crazy. The noise, and to think we were only on the outskirts, what the hell must it have been like on the dirty side of the storm... crazy, just crazy."

I didn't realize how hungry I was until now, so I take a bite. *Damn, my woman makes a good sandwich.* "We're just fucking lucky. This could have been so much worse." I continue eating, almost scoffing the whole thing in a few bites.

Frankie smiles. "I should have fed you sooner. I'm sorry. I was trying to get around to everyone, and I didn't know you were in here. Normally the little light shines, but of course, it was out, so I didn't think you were in here."

Placing my sandwich down, I stand and move in front of her when she sits on the desk. She glances up at me while I move between her legs, my hands resting on either side of her. The gold in her eyes shines so brightly as she stares at me. A strand of her red hair falls onto her cheek, and I bring my hand up, swiping it back behind her ear. "You have dirt on your cheek."

She licks her bottom lip as I stare at it, my cock hardening from just looking at how vulnerable she is like this. She clears her throat, the air around us sizzling with our intense chemistry. "It's been a very messy afternoon."

I smirk, my thoughts running rampant right now, as I edge closer, my cock grinding against her pussy. "Sometimes messy is good."

Frankie's breathing hitches as she shakes her head. "Sometimes messy is bad, Raid."

I lean in, my chest heaving with the tension in the air. "But bad can be *so fucking good* if it's done right."

She whimpers, my cock straining so damn hard against my jeans it hurts. Her hands slide along my back, her nails digging in, while my nose glides along hers. Both of us are panting with the anticipation of the moment. My fingers clench in her hair. Teasing her. Tempting her. Her eyes boring into mine, begging me to kiss her. She bites that luscious bottom lip—*so fucking sexy.*

A low growl reverbs from my chest, my fingers gripping her hair so tight, her chest heaving as she folds under the weight of the moment. "Fuck! Kiss me, Raid," she begs.

It's all I need.

Without hesitation, our mouths collide, my tongue sliding in with hers. The second my lips touch hers, an intense tingling erupts in my balls.

It feels like I'm coming alive.

Every part of me is on fire but shuddering like I'm frozen at the same time.

It's earth-shattering and so fucking hot I can't stop.

I need more.

I need to feel her.

I need to make her feel good.

I've waited so fucking long to have a single damn taste of her—to have *any* part of her, I can't stop at just a kiss.

My hands slide down between us, and I hoist her skirt up. She doesn't stop me as I grab her panties and yank, tearing them on one side. She shuffles her ass, helping me to get them down and off. Then I toss them to the other side of the room with a slight chuckle. My eyes meet hers again, a moment passing between us as we stare at each other, but I quickly move back in, my lips to hers, needing her, wanting her. My hand slides under her skirt, my finger gently easing up between her legs to find what I desire most—her hot wet pussy.

She whimpers at my touch as I press against her already slickened folds. "Good girl, you're so wet for me," I murmur against her mouth and don't hesitate to slide two fingers up inside her.

Her grip on my back tightens when her head throws back, and her hips thrust forward, seeking more. "Fuck, Raid, yes!" She moans as I press my thumb on her clit. I push my fingers deeper, scissoring them to get the right reaction. Frankie whimpers, her hips rocking against my hand.

"That's it! Fuck my hand. Ride it, Frankie," I demand.

I feel her pussy tightening around my fingers, and it's great that I have this effect on her. Feeling her insides spasming because of me is so fucking electrifying, beads of precum form on my cock.

Her body begins to shudder, and I can tell she's close. "Come for me, baby. Come *now*, Frankie!" I demand as I thrust into her deeper, hitting her G-spot at the same time I flick her clit.

Her eyes clench, her muscles tense, her breath hitches, then she lets out a guttural moan. Her entire body shakes, her pussy clamping and clenching around my fingers as she comes so hard I think I see her eyes roll into the back of her head.

"Raaaid," she screams.

That's when I slam my lips to hers to capture her moans. My tongue dances with hers as I slowly bring her down from her high, rocking my fingers in and out of her. Then I pull my fingers from her completely and shove them in my mouth with a salacious grin. She chuckles, her eyes lazy with lust-fueled desire. "You taste too fucking good."

"Raid, you in there?" Addi's voice calls out from the other side of the door.

My eyes widen as the door begins to open. Rapidly, I pull my fingers from my mouth and take a dramatic step back from Frankie. She quickly yanks her dress down to hide the fact that she isn't wearing panties, but as I step back, I trip over something and fall into the wall as Addi walks inside.

"Fuck!" I grunt, trying to straighten myself out.

I pull myself up into a standing position and try not to look guilty as hell while Frankie sits on the desk, her cheeks flushed as shit while trying to catch her breath.

We both look guilty as sin.

There's no denying it.

Addi looks from me to Frankie and back to me. "*Okaaay*... so you guys are acting weird."

I snort out a laugh trying to brush it off while also attempting to hide the fact I have a raging fucking boner. "Nah, you're imagining things."

Frankie jumps down from the desk and wraps her arm around

Addi, trying to stop me from acting like a damn idiot. "How can we help, honey?"

"New mop heads for the mops?"

Frankie smiles. "That I can help with. Follow me..." Frankie glances over her shoulder at me with a smirk, and I wink as she walks out of the den with my daughter.

They exit the room, and I exhale heavily, running my fingers through my hair.

I thought it was parents who were supposed to walk in on their kids?

But fuck me if that wasn't the best first kiss I have ever fucking had.

I never knew kissing a woman could feel that intense.

That electric.

That world fucking shifting.

I knew Frankie and I had a connection.

I knew it was something worth exploring.

I knew we were biding our time.

Well, I am sick of waiting.

Sick of holding off.

Because that—that was everything I ever thought it would be and more.

And I don't want to let another day go by where Frankie isn't a huge part of my life.

Because she is worth *everything.*

Every. Damn. Thing.

Now I need to let her know that.

CHAPTER 18

RAID
A Couple of Days Later

The cleanup from the hurricane has taken us a couple of solid days.

The clubhouse is returning to a normal state, with minimal damage to the property being not as bad as first predicted. It appears New Orleans managed to get out of it lightly compared to other areas.

We received calls from Houston, Chicago, and LA asking if we needed a helping hand after the storm. Each club was more than willing to make their way over to assist in any way they could, but honestly, there wasn't a lot. Some roof replacement, some ceiling repairs, and moving the massive amount of debris were about all that was required. It was great to have support from our brother charters.

Sitting in my den, the alert pings for someone at the door. When I glance at the security feed, it's Hoodoo. I knew he was going to assess Sophie, so I quickly press the release button on the door with anxiety creeping through me. "Hey man, how's she doing?"

He closes the door behind him and scrubs at his face. "It's not looking good, brother... she's deteriorating. I hate to say this, but if you're considering putting her into hospice, now is perfect. Otherwise... it's only a matter of time. Days at this point. I'm so sorry, but there's not much more I can do for her." My stomach tightens, feeling like I want to throw up as I hunch over with my elbows on my knees. Hoodoo rests his hand on my back as I clench my eyes shut so tight I see stars while trying to fight the tears threatening to fall.

"We could get Dr. Adams to come over and give Sophie some stronger drugs for her pain, though," Hoodoo states.

With a heavy sigh, I glance up and nod. "Thanks, brother. For everything you've done. You've been a fucking godsend."

He weakly smiles—it's packed full of sympathy, knowing we're nearing the end. "If there is anything else I can do, let me know. I'm here for you and Addi too. The whole club has your back through this, brother."

Clearing my throat from the baseball-sized lump that is firmly lodged inside it, I nod. "I better call Dr. Adams then."

"Good idea. Remember, if you need me?"

"I'll let you know, thanks."

He grips my shoulder supportively, then turns, walking out of my den. As he closes the door, I let out a long exhale, slumping back in my chair.

Days.

My heart breaks for Addi.

She's just starting to find her feet here.

You can't tell me this isn't going to set her back.

I know I have to be strong when the inevitable happens because I have a daughter to protect. To look after. And she will need me more than ever, so even though this is killing me right now, I've got to pick my shit up and deal with it.

Nodding my head to give me the extra courage boost I need, I pull out my cell and dial Aubree Adams' number. It rings for so long that I think it will ring out, but eventually, she answers, "Dr. Adams."

"Hey, it's Raid from NOLA Defiance. I know you don't generally do house calls, and I know technically I shouldn't have your private cell number, but I have a terminal cancer patient here. A woman. She's in her final days, and I could do with some help to make her comfortable."

Aubree is quiet for a moment, then exhales. "You're their tech guy, right?"

"Yeah?"

She hums under her breath. "So I'm going to assume that's how you got my number, and you're right, I don't do house calls, but... I don't like the idea of a person suffering at end of life. The problem right now is I am swamped with victims from the hurricane. Let me tackle the rest of my patients today, and I will stop by with what will help at the end of my shift tonight. Will that work?"

A wave of relief washes over me. "That will be perfect. Thank you, Aubree. You don't know how much I appreciate this."

"I'll see you tonight." She ends the call, and I can't help but hope she brings something that will help ease Sophie's pain. Because even though she doesn't say she is suffering, I can see it in her eyes, and I don't want her to hurt anymore.

But now I have a task I didn't think I would ever have to do in my lifetime. I have to find Addi and prepare her. I feel she should know and not be kept in the dark about all this.

Getting up from my chair, I take in a deep breath, then head out into the main clubroom. Addi is sitting with Frankie. They're laughing and giggling over something, looking like they're having a real good time.

It only makes what I have to do all that much harder. I don't want to be the one to have to tell her, but I know it's all part of being a parent, of being the one who's going to have to take care of Addi when this is all said and done.

Sometimes you just have to deal with hard shit.

As I approach the two of them, Addi glances up at me. Then, her adorable smiling face falls, and she stands abruptly like something is wrong. "Is Mom okay?"

Here we go.

I glance at Frankie and move in front of Addi, taking her hand in mine. "She's all right for now, but Addi, I need you to know I've spoken with Hoodoo, and he says she's fading fast." I take a deep breath. "It won't be long now. Days at best."

Addi rips her hand from mine, her eyes brimming with tears. "No, not yet. I'm not ready."

Frankie stands moving for Addi, but she begins to pace while shaking her head like she is in disbelief. "It can't be days. There's still so much I need to tell her, so much we need to do. She's my mom. I... I need her!" She bursts into tears, and Frankie rushes to her, cradling her in her arms.

My chest squeezes tight, watching my daughter completely break down in front of me, and I feel like there is nothing I can do to help her. I want to be there for her, but she obviously doesn't feel connected enough to me yet to lean on. It's why she's leaning on Frankie right now.

Frankie cuddles into her, smoothing her hair and whispering something in her ear.

More than anything, I want to be that kind of father for her.

So I move forward, reaching out to take her from Frankie. "Addi, I'm here for yo—"

But as I try to embrace her, she shoves me back, letting out a massive sob, and takes off, running as fast as she can for her room.

Defeat and unworthiness hit me like a tidal wave of despair and failure. I flop into a nearby seat, feeling completely shattered.

Frankie squats in front of me, her hands sliding out onto my thighs supportively as she looks up into my eyes. "Hey! Look at me," she urges. My eyes slowly lift to look at her hopeful gaze. "You need to give her time. She's going through a lot, and I know you're hurting too, but the bond between a mother and daughter is incredibly strong. Addi's losing her too young…" Frankie takes a deep centering breath. "I should know, Raid, I lost my mom when I was Addi's age, so I can relate to her. I know how she is feeling. The pain is unfathomable. Watching your mother fade like this, plus everything else Addi is going through…" she trails off, shaking her head, her eyes glistening with unshed tears.

Letting out a long, stuttered breath, I nod. "I know. I just want to be the one Addi turns to. Who she can rely on."

"You will be… *one day*. She doesn't know you well enough yet. But she will."

"I fucking hope so."

My chest tightens with anxiety as I reflect on how she shoved me aside, and I close my eyes to take a deep breath.

CHAPTER 19

FRANKIE
Two Days Later

For the last couple of days, Addi has been home from school to be with her Mom. Now that the clubhouse is completely fixed, I have decided I want to do something to bring Raid and Addi closer.

I make my way over to Hoodoo and Grit, who are sitting at the bar having a drink. When I slide in next to them, they both smile at me.

"Frankie, normally you're behind the bar serving us drinks. You taking on different roles in the club these days?" Hoodoo asks.

I chuckle. "Generally, I would, but I have an idea I want to run past you. You too, Grit, if you're up for the challenge?"

They both raise their brows like they're intrigued.

"Okay, hit me," Hoodoo states.

"My idea is to set up the projector outside. It's going to be a nice evening, by the forecast, and I want to do something for Addi, Raid, and Sophie. A movie night for them. I want to make some lasting memories for Addi that involve Raid as well."

Hoodoo rolls his shoulders. "I think if we can manage to get Sophie comfortable enough, it will be a very good thing for Addi.

To have this memory with her Mom."

"That's what I thought, and it will give Raid and Addi some bonding time too. So what do you think? Sophie has the approval to be outside if we set it up right?"

Hoodoo nods. "Yeah, we'll make it happen."

I turn to Grit. "And you can help me set up the projector and everything else I need?"

"Absolutely. Whatever you need to make this happen, I'm your guy. I'll get Lani to make food, so you have plenty of snacks and great things to eat as well."

My heart is full.

"Amazing. Thank you, guys. I think this is exactly what they all need."

We get to work, and I don't tell Raid what's happening. Grit and I just go to work setting the scene out the back of the clubhouse. The projector is being set up near the bayou fence, and a ton of cushions, mattresses, and blankets are being spread out on the ground for us to lie on. We set it up to look like a Moroccan outdoor experience. It's gorgeous as I put on the finishing touches, ensuring that Sophie is going to be as comfortable as possible.

A fire pit sits to the side for warmth if the night turns chilly, and Grit stands back, handing me the remote for the projector. "You're all set. The speakers are behind you, so the sound quality should be good, but if you have any problems, just let me know, and I'll tend to it. But knowing Raid, he'll have it fixed before I get out here."

I let out a small laugh and nod. "You're so right, but thanks for your help, Grit. You've been amazing."

"Now you need to go and tell Raid where you've been for most of the day."

Smiling, I nod, place the remote on a cushion, and turn to walk back inside the clubhouse with a pep in my step. I see Raid sitting with Hurricane, so I make my way over to them and slowly ease my way to his side.

Hurricane spots me first. "Frankie! Was wonderin' what you've been doin' outside, neglectin' your duties inside. Kaia and Lani are working in the kitchen, and I found out. I am assuming you'll be takin' Raid off my hands now?"

Raid furrows his brows, looking confused. "Off your hands? The fuck are you talking about?"

I smirk as Hurricane slaps his back. "You think I wanted to talk to you about the fuckin' system reboot? I don't give a flyin' fuck about all that crap, brother. As long as you have our shit under control, it's all good. Was keepin' you distracted."

I smile wide. "Thanks, Pres."

"Keeping me distracted? What for?" Raid asks, but Hurricane ignores him.

"You're welcome, Frankie. Now go make some memories. Have a good night." Hurricane stands, slaps Raid on the back with a chuckle, then walks off, shaking his head.

Raid turns to me, seeming completely confused, and I smile at him. "So I might have done something," I tell him.

He stands, his eyes focused on me. "And what exactly have you done?"

I take his hand and start leading him toward Sophie's bedroom. "C'mon, we need to get Sophie and Addi."

He stops. Confusion crosses his features. "Sophie? She has to stay in bed. She's too sick."

"I have approval from Hoodoo. Trust me. It'll be worth it."

He tilts his head like he's skeptical, but he starts walking with me toward their room. We knock on the door, and Addi calls for us to come in. She is working on some homework at her desk, and Sophie's resting in bed.

Addi glances up and smiles. "Is it dinner time?" she asks.

"Better. I have a surprise for you," I tell her.

"For me?" she asks, looking to Raid.

Raid shrugs. "Apparently, for all of us."

Addi glances over to Sophie, who is awake and weakly smiling now. "Mom too?"

"Mom, too," I confirm.

Sophie widens her eyes. "Well, this *is* exciting."

Raid turns to me. "So, what are we doing?"

Beaming with excitement, I gesture to Sophie. "We need Sophie, so if you don't mind?"

Sophie widens her eyes, moving slowly to sit up a little as Raid chuckles. "I don't mind at all." He walks over to the bed and gently lifts her from the mattress. She wraps her frail arms around his neck, and Addi stands from her chair.

"So, Miss Secretive, where to now?" Raid questions.

"Out the back of the clubhouse," I tell them.

All three of them furrow their brows in confusion, and I lightly laugh. "I promise you'll love it."

We make our way through the clubhouse, and Hoodoo and Grit smile wide at us as we go. I subtly thank them with my eyes when we walk out the back door. Addi's eyes light up the second she sees the setting. She runs, leaving the rest of us behind. I turn to Raid.

A slow smile crosses his face. "You did all this?"

"I had a little help from some of the guys, plus Lani and Kaia made the food."

He shakes his head as he moves Sophie to the mattress and lays her down. We all fuss about her plumping up her pillows and getting her comfortable.

She chuckles. "I've never had so many people fuss over me. I should be sick more often."

We all swallow hard, not knowing what to reply.

She snorts. "Oh, relax, you guys. It was a joke."

Raid wraps her in a big plush blanket to keep her warm while Addi cuddles into her side. "I'm so happy. Thank you, Frankie."

Raid sits next to Addi, and I take a step back, handing Raid the remote. "Okay, so here is the remote. The choice of movies is in that box, just there. You can pick whatever you want and spend as long as you want out here. Food will be coming short—"

"Wait! You're not staying?" Addi asks, her eyes sullen.

I drop my shoulders. "I thought this would be a good chance for you all to spend quality time together."

Raid smiles, but Addi stands, grabs my hand, and pulls me to sit. "No, Frankie, you're a part of our group, and you did all this. You have to stay. Right, Mom?"

Sophie beams from ear to ear. "I can't thank you enough for doing this for us, Frankie. So let me try by you staying and enjoying this night with us?"

I turn to Raid.

This is *his* family.

I don't want to intrude.

This wasn't why I did this.

This isn't what I wanted.

He nods. "Stay, Frankie... please?"

I can tell he wants this.

It seems they all do.

It wasn't my intention to gatecrash, but how can I say no?

"Okay, I'll stay, but on one condition?"

Addi bobs her head. "Anything..."

I grin, my eyes shifting straight to Raid. "That we watch a ridiculously girly movie, one that Raid is going to hate but us three girls are going to love."

Sophie and Addi both laugh loudly.

Raid groans.

"Yes!" Addi giggles, racing for the movie box and flipping through the selection. "I know just the one!"

***

As we watch chick flick after chick flick, we eat, laugh, and joke, and I watch as the bond between Raid and Addi grows a little tighter.

It is so nice to see.

Sophie seems to have found some strength tonight. Maybe it's because we're all here keeping her entertained. She's keeping up as best she can as she tells us stories of her past.

"Remember when we went to that bar, and you were trying to defend my honor to that guy who was hitting on me in front of you?" she asks.

Raid bursts out laughing, nodding his head. "I was gonna smack him down, but you turned and whacked him one before I could land anything. The guy had a broken nose and said that I was a little bitch for not being able to defend my girl."

Sophie chuckles. "Then you said, 'Why do I need to defend her when she can do it herself? Saves arthritis in my knuckles later in my life.' We walked off, and you carried my handbag for good measure."

Addi and I burst out laughing.

Raid shakes his head. "You know I'd forgotten about that. Fuck, we got up to some trouble, you and me."

Sophie sniffles with a smile. "Yeah, we had some damn good times. And even though I went and fucked it all up, at least we did one *real* good thing." Her eyes fall on Addi, and she smiles.

"Mom, stop!" Addi whines.

But Sophie lifts her hand, stroking Addi's face. "You're the best thing that ever happened to me, Addilyn. Have I ever told you that?"

Addi chuckles. "Only every day of my life."

Sophie sighs. "Good, because I need you to believe it. Yes, I made some mistakes along the way, but Addi, you were *never* one of them."

Addi's bottom lip trembles as she rushes in, embracing her mom.

Sophie blinks away the tears forming in her eyes. "I never meant for it to end this way, Jay."

Raid places his hand on her thigh supportively. "It's not ending,

Soph. You'll always be with us."

She nods, pulling Addi off her and wiping away her tears. "No more crying. This is a happy night."

Addi clears her throat and stands. "How about some more popcorn?"

Raid stands next to Addi and bumps into her side. "And we need more cocoa. C'mon, the quicker we go grab it, the quicker we can get the next chick flick over with."

We all chuckle as father and daughter walk off together, leaving me with Sophie. I stretch for the movie box to find our next movie when Sophie reaches out, grabbing my arm. "Frankie?"

I glance up, raising my brow. "Yeah?"

"You should go for it with Jay. You make him happy, and you're so good for Addi… you're the missing puzzle piece connecting them. Nothing would make me happier than for you to be the glue holding the three of you together."

I smile, wishing it could be the case, but since our moment in his den the other day, there's been no further indication from Raid that anything else is likely to happen. "The timing just isn't right for us, Sophie."

She scrunches up her face, shaking her head. "I did that. I thought the timing wasn't right for Jay and me when I got pregnant, and look how that turned out. *Don't wait,* Frankie! Waiting is a fool's errand. Don't put off to tomorrow what you can do today. Live for now because tomorrow isn't promised. So promise *me,* you and Jay are going to be okay. Promise *me* you're going to act on your feelings?"

Smiling, I nod. "I promise."

Raid and Addi casually step back to us, carrying copious amounts of popcorn and cocoa.

"What are we promising?" Raid asks.

"Secret women's business, never you mind, Jay," Sophie states, and I smile at Raid as we all get back to our movie night.

Sophie sure has given me a lot to think about.

CHAPTER 20

RAID
The Next Morning

Slowly waking, my back aches from practically sleeping on the ground. But as the sunlight slowly makes its way into my eyes, a soft smile hits my face.

Last night was fucking magical.

Frankie outdid herself to make sure we had a night we could all remember so fucking fondly. It was great to be together and have a moment of pure joy.

I move to sit, seeing Addi snuggled into Sophie, and I turn to Frankie. She's awake, too, and she sits with a yawn. "Morning."

"Morning, how'd you sleep?" I ask.

She grins. "Considering we're sleeping on the ground, really fucking well."

"Me too..." I chuckle. "I just want to say... you're amazing for doing this."

Her lips turn up into a warm smile. Her face radiates happiness. This woman is so damn beautiful inside and out.

"I'd do anything to make you happy, Raid."

I believe her.

Addi lets out a long yawn as she stretches, slowly sitting up. "Morning, guys. How early is it?"

I glance over, seeing the sun rising over the horizon. "It's dawn."

Addi groans. "Urgh, too early. We should go back to sleep, right, Mom?" Addi states, and we all turn to look at Sophie. Her eyes are open, but she's pale, and her breathing is labored.

"Mom?" Addi repeats, but there's clear panic in her tone.

I stand, rushing over to Sophie's side, and I press down on her pulse to see if she's okay.

It's weak as hell.

My heart begins to race fast. "We need to get you back inside, Sophie—"

Her hand comes up, pressing on my chest to stop me. "No... I had the b-best night with my f-family. I-I want to stay o-out here. See the sunrise, one l-last time."

My stomach somersaults and ends up three blocks over.

Addi bursts into tears, clinging to her mother.

My breathing increases as I pull Sophie into my lap. "Hoodoo!" I scream at the top of my lungs to see if I can get him out here.

Frankie sits back, tears streaming down her face, her hand to her mouth as Sophie's shaking fingers slide out, caressing Addi's cheek. "I l-love you, m-my sweet, sweet g-girl."

"Mom, d-don't g-go." Addi croaks out, the sound breaking my heart in two.

"I'll always be with y—" Sophie's hand falls from Addi's face, and she lets out a long exhale, her body goes limp in my arms, her eyes softly close.

And with the breath of wind, Sophie is gone.

We all stop still, just staring.

Addi shakes her head rapidly. "Mom? *Mom!*" Addi lets out a half-scream, half-wail as she flops onto her mother's body. Gut-wrenching sobs wrack through her as Frankie runs over and kneels by her side, wrapping her arms around her while I stare down at Sophie.

She looks so calm.

So peaceful.

No pain.

Finally at rest.

But my heart is thudding so hard it feels like I can barely breathe as I move my hand out and softly rest it on an inconsolable Addi.

The sound of thunderous footsteps to the side makes me slowly turn my head to see Hurricane and Hoodoo running toward us.

"We heard a commotion. What's goin' o—" Hurricane stops, staring at the scene in front of him, and he bows his head as a mark of respect.

Hoodoo quietly kneels, placing his hand on Sophie's wrist to check for her pulse, and he shakes his head. "I'm so sorry for your loss."

Addi screams, the pain clearly full of agony as she stands and takes off, running toward the clubhouse.

My heart breaks.

It completely shatters.

Seeing her so broken.

I knew it was going to happen.

But watching it happen is a whole other world of hurt.

I'm completely numb as I gently ease Sophie off my lap and onto the mattress. I lean down, planting a tender kiss on her forehead. Then stand and turn to Hurricane, needing his help now more than ever.

He grips my shoulder and nods. "I got this, brother. You look after your girl."

I glance over my shoulder at Frankie, and she gestures for me to go, so I take off running to find Addi. I head to the one place I know she feels connected to Sophie—their bedroom.

Walking up to the door, I take a long deep breath, hearing her sobs on the other side, and don't bother to knock. Instead, I simply walk in, closing the door behind me to see her cradling Sophie's pillow while she sobs into it.

I don't say anything. Instead, I simply walk over to her and lift her into my arms as I sit on the edge of the bed, holding her. She pushes against me, her hands coming out and slapping at me to get away, but I only hold her tighter. "I'm not going anywhere. I got you. I'm never letting go."

She sobs harder, all her energy spent as she collapses into my arms, wrapping herself into me, finally seeking my comfort.

I run my fingers through her hair, trying to soothe some of her pain, trying to soothe me. Right now, we need each other. And we sit for what seems like hours like this, her fingers clenching onto my leather cut. "It's okay, Addi. I got you. I will always have you."

And as of now, it's just her and me against the world, so I will always have her back.

Because I am all she has.

It's taken a lot for us to truly feel connected, and I wish it didn't take losing Sophie for us to come together, but all I know is that I have spent fourteen years without her.

I'm not letting Addi go now.

Not after this.

Not for a single fucking thing.

Nothing else matters but her.

CHAPTER 21

RAID
A Week Later

The service was lovely, simple, and elegant, just like Sophie.

Surprisingly, Addi kept herself together for the most part until the coffin was lowered, then she gave herself permission to fall apart.

Addi has done her fair share of crying the past week, but I have made sure to be there for her, letting her talk to me whenever she needed. Letting her cry on my shoulder as often as she wanted. We've been a rock for each other in this time of grief.

I had no idea it would hit as hard as it did.

But as I wrap my arm around Addi and we walk away from the funeral home, she sniffles, and I grip her tighter. "You ready to go back for the wake?"

She glances up at me, biting down on her bottom lip. "Actually... do you think you could take me for a ride on your bike?"

I stop walking and stare at her, a little shocked. She hasn't shown any interest in my bike since she arrived. Actually, she seemed kind of anti-club, especially that first day at school—so this is a huge step forward. My chest floods with pride, and I try to hide my smile. "Sure, let's get out of here."

I glance over my shoulder at Frankie and mouth, "Taking her for a ride."

Frankie widens her eyes with a small smile and nods, walking with the rest of the group back to their rides. I take Addi to my bike, and she glances over it when I hand her a helmet.

She narrows her eyes on me. "You don't wear one, so why should I?"

I let out a small laugh. "Because I'm allowed to be reckless. You, however, are *not*. Not on my watch, young lady."

"Figures." She slams it down over her head, and I move in, doing up the straps for her.

It's weird. A month ago, I never dreamed I would be standing here in awe of how brave my daughter is and being so fucking proud to be taking her on a ride for the first time.

A month ago, I didn't know I had a daughter.

It's crazy how fast your life can change.

In the blink of an eye, my life is forever different.

In that short amount of time, I've gotten to know Addi, and nothing in this world could ever make me give her up. She is my flesh and blood, my child, my everything.

Turning, I slide my leg over my ride and grip the handlebars. I glance over my shoulder and tilt my head, gesturing for her to hop on. "C'mon, kid, time for you to become a real biker brat."

She lets out a giggle, the first since her mother passed, and I have to admit it's fucking good to hear. Her arms slide around my waist, and warmth floods me as she holds me tight. "Move with me. Don't lean in too far. Just get a feel for it. It's in your blood. You'll know what to do."

She exhales. "You sound so sure."

Glancing over my shoulder at her, I smile. "You got this, Addi."

She nods, and I turn back, starting my bike. It roars to life, and instantly I feel her relax behind me.

Yeah, it's in her blood.

Duck walking back from the curb, I turn the bike toward the road, then take off, leaving the rest of the club behind. The vibration from the engine soars through my soul, somehow making all the turmoil we've been through today start to ease. Knowing Addi is with me and beginning to accept me into her life makes this bearable in some small fraction of a way.

I hammer down. If she wants to see what riding a bike is like, I will give her the full experience. She lets out a small squeal, but I know it's not from fear but excitement, and I can't help but smile as I ride, probably faster than a father should with his kid on the back. But I want Addi to experience something good today, even if only for a brief moment of happiness after this shitty day.

I take her for a ride along the Mississippi, the current moving slowly in the steady breeze. The murky depths show our emotions—bleak, but there is movement forward. The slight glistening on the top of the water from the sun shining down from above grabs my attention as a row of bulkhead edging leads a path to the water's edge.

I slow the bike and turn in, pulling to a stop at the bulkhead. Turning off the engine, I glance over my shoulder at Addi, and she widens her eyes at me. "Why'd we stop?" she asks.

I tap her hand, and she lets go of my waist and moves to get off the bike. "I think here is a nice place to get out and take a beat."

She nods, climbing off, and I follow her to the water's edge. It sparkles in the sunlight, the sun breaking through the clouds. It shines right in front of us, onto the Mississippi, lighting it up like a beacon.

It's like Sophie is here with us.

Telling us we're going to be okay.

We simply stare out at the sunlight on the water.

"It's like she's here," Addi whispers.

I reach out, grabbing her hand and holding her tight. A single tear slides down her cheek, and we just stare, a slow smile crossing my face, and when I glance down at Addi, she's smiling too.

I don't know why, but we're both feeling it.

The moment.

The energy.

The connection.

We're going through this grieving process together, and we might both be imagining it, but it feels like Sophie is watching over us.

Addi lets my hand go and slides her arms around my waist, cuddling into me. I hold on tight as she sighs. "How am I going to survive without my mom?"

Exhaling, I tighten my arm around her further. "You have me… and Frankie. We're going to give you everything you need. I know it's not the same. How could it ever be? But Addi, I'm going to be the best dad you could want. I'm gonna be here for you every step of the way."

She nods. "Thank you… for stepping up." Addi sniffles and then murmurs, "Raid?"

I glance down at her. "Mmm…"

"I'm glad you're my dad."

My heart stops for a moment, then thumps back twice as hard, making my breath catch in my throat. I try to hide my smile by leaning down and kissing Addi gently on the hair. "Well, I'm fucking glad you're my kid."

She clears her throat as she slowly pulls away from me. "We better head back. Everyone will get worried."

Nodding, I turn, and we start to walk back to the bike. She doesn't take the compliments any further, but fuck, I will take all of that as a huge damn win.

We jump on the bike and ride back to the clubhouse, taking it a bit slower and enjoying the scenery on the way back. Addi points at things, and I nod. There are a lot of places I need to take my daughter. NOLA is a fun city, and she has to experience it all. So many life experiences for her to explore, and I'm going to be right by her side for every single one of them.

Finally, we pull in, and Frankie is standing there waiting for us. She must have been worried. I should have told her we were okay. Pulling up my ride, Addi hops off, and I follow. We walk over to Frankie, who looks like she is bursting at the seams to talk to us, but she's holding herself back. As we approach, her face shows clear concern. "Are you both okay? I was worried."

I reach out, placing my hand on her arm. "We're good. Just needed a moment to decompress."

She lets out a long breath, and her shoulders visibly relax. "Okay... well, Addi, Clover is waiting for you if you want to hang out?"

Addi turns to me, raising her brow. "Can I?"

Furrowing my brow, I nod. "Of course." Because I would let her do anything she wanted to right now.

Addi dips her head, smiles at Frankie, then walks off to find Clover.

I turn to Frankie and slump my shoulders, finally finding some respite in Frankie's kind eyes. "What a day."

She links her arm with mine and sighs. "Wanna talk about it?"

I nod because it's the best I can do right now.

We head inside and make our way to my bedroom. I close the door behind me and step over to my bed. Frankie sits next to me, and I reach out for her hand. She smiles when I let out a long exhale.

"Addi wanted to go for a bike ride, so I took her along the Mississippi. We pulled off somewhere along the way. I don't know why I stopped where I did. Something told me to. So I pulled over, and the sun broke through the clouds right where we were and shone on the river. I know this sounds corny, but it was like Sophie was with us... Addi felt it too."

Frankie tightens her hand in mine. "It doesn't sound corny at all. I am so glad you both had that time together."

"She told me she's glad I'm her dad." I turn to her, trying to keep my shit contained.

Frankie gasps, her eyes flooding with tears. "She did?" she chimes excitedly.

I nod, and she wraps her arms around me. "Oh, Raid, that's so good to hear."

My arms slide up her back, holding her to me. My nose slides into her fruity-smelling hair. It's intoxicating, and as I slowly pull back, my eyes meet hers. A silence falls between us as we stare at each other, the chemistry exploding through the air.

My hand slides up, caressing her cheek as I lean in and slam my lips to hers. My heart skips a beat when I kiss her. Every part of me wants this, wants this incredible woman.

My tongue slides into her mouth, caressing her, needing her. I deepen the kiss, just wanting a little more from her before I have to stop. She whimpers into my mouth while her fingers tug my hair.

Fuck.

A low growl is pushed from my chest. I want to take this further, so much further, but instead, I slowly pull back. My breathing is fast and frantic as my eyes meet hers. She's smiling, her expression hopeful.

But I can't be what she needs of me right now.

And I fucking hate it.

Reaching out, my hand caresses her cheek, and I shake my head. "While I want to take this further, I need to prioritize Addi right now."

Frankie doesn't even bat an eyelash. She already understands and is so fucking accepting of Addi. "Of course. She's your main priority. Our time will come… or it won't. Either way, I am here for you. The both of you, in whatever capacity you need me."

I pull her to me in a tight embrace. "I appreciate all that. I love how great you're being with Addi. I honestly don't know how I would get through this without your help."

"We'll be okay… sometimes a slow burn makes it even more enticing at the end."

I smile. "A slow burn, huh?"

She grins. "Sorry, that's my inner author coming out."

"Have I told you how proud I am of you? You run this place, go to damn school, and keep up with all my bullshit?"

She shrugs. "It's not easy, sometimes."

"I know you've been putting my needs above your own. If there is anything I can do to help you—"

"I'll let you know, but my focus is on ensuring Addi is taken care of. Everything else seems too trivial."

I sigh. "Yeah… life is so short, right?"

"You gotta look after those you care about."

I feel like there's a double meaning behind her words, but I know Frankie's main priority is Addi, just like mine.

She is right—our time will come.

We have to be patient.

Ride out the *slow burn*.

But fuck does this relationship burn hurt.

CHAPTER 22

FRANKIE
A Couple of Weeks Later

In the last couple of weeks, life at the club has been all about us trying to get into a rhythm.

Before, we were all about making Sophie comfortable and spending as much time with her as possible.

Then, we focused on her funeral and ensuring Addi's needs were addressed.

Now there's just…

… *after.*

And we have to try and get ourselves into step.

With each other.

Finding a balance that suits everyone.

Especially Addi as she navigates this new version of her life.

She is slowly coming out of her shell, but with the loss of her mother, she spends a lot of time with Clover and some with me when she needs a womanly ear. Actually, Addi and I are growing quite close, and I love the bond we're forming.

I still have a job to uphold here at the club and my studies to maintain. It's not easy wearing all these hats, but I'm managing.

Somehow.

As I wipe down the bar, I glance at Raid while he talks to Hurricane. My lips tingle, remembering our kiss in the den, the way he finger-fucked me on his desk. The way he kissed me again in his bedroom—how fucking hot both times were.

I wish we could act on our feelings a little more, especially because I promised Sophie I would, but there seems to be so much standing in our way.

Maybe we are a lost cause?

Maybe I just need to keep us in the friend zone?

We're so good as friends, and I don't want to jeopardize my relationship with Addi.

But damn, his arms look so fucking delicious today.

Shaking my head to rid the clit-tingling thought, I clench my thighs together, and as I do, Addi steps into my line of sight, looking a little out of sorts. It's enough to stop me from fawning over Raid and put me straight into protection mode. "Addi? You okay?"

"Can I talk to you?" she whispers, leaning in so no one else can hear.

My brows pull together, and I move around the bar. "Of course, honey. You can always talk to me. What's going on?"

Addi gnaws on her bottom lip, a certain tell there is something very wrong. "Can we talk in private?"

I glance over my shoulder seeing Jaz standing at the bar. She can take over for a while so I can deal with whatever the problem is with Addi. Taking her by the arm, I walk us toward the kitchen. "Are those kids at school being cunts again?"

Addi bursts out laughing. "Frankie, language! And no, nothing like that. But aah... I need to go to the store, um... for some... *products.*"

I squish my eyebrows together, wondering where she is heading with this. *Is she being sexually active?* "What kind of products?"

The grimace shows not only on her face but in her body language. "I have my period, but I don't have anything for it. Mom always got me everything for that, and now... well, she's gone."

My heart sinks and then shatters. *Why didn't I think about this?* Of course, Addi will need help with this kind of stuff. I reach out, pulling her to me in a tight embrace. "Okay, let me get you something for now, and then we'll go straight to the store to grab whatever you need."

Addi's eyes glisten, and I grip her hands tight. "I got you, okay?"

She nods, and we take off to my bedroom for supplies. Once I grab everything I think she might need, she heads to the bathroom, and I say, "I'll be out here if you need me."

Addi moves to close the door, then hesitates. "Thanks, Frankie. Honestly, I don't know how I would cope if you weren't here."

"I'm not going anywhere. I'll always have your back." I give her a warm smile.

She ducks into the bathroom, closing the door.

Letting out a long exhale, I move over to my bed and sit, just taking a second. The amount of sadness washing through me is insurmountable. I hate that Sophie isn't here to help Addi—that can't be helped—but I am glad Addi feels comfortable enough to come to me for help. I'm thankful I can be that person for her, and I am more than honored to fill that void in her life. Because she is filling a void in my life I didn't know was missing. While it's so damn hard seeing her go through the motions of grieving, I'm grateful to play a small part in her healing process.

After a few minutes, Addi returns, and I smile up at her. "You all good?"

"Yeah, thanks so much."

I stand and slap my legs. "Then off to the store, we shall go."

We walk together out to my car and hop in without saying anything to anyone about where we're going. As I drive off, I hand Addi my cell. "Okay, passenger picks. What are we listening to?"

She swipes through the playlist and giggles. "How old *are* you?"

I turn and fake glare at her. "I'm thirty. Why?"

"Ke$ha, Shakira, Eminem? These artists are like... totally ancient."

I burst out laughing. "Oh, the youth of today..." I glance at her. "Eminem, I'll have you know, was my first real crush. He's still around, maybe not as big as he was back in 2010, but *giiirrrl*... that guy can slay."

Addi giggles, holding onto her stomach as she laughs. "Did you just say he slays? Oh my God, Frankie, you *kill* me. Okay, I need to hear one of his songs."

"What? You've never heard an Eminem song?"

She shrugs. "I mean... I probably have, but it's not really my thing."

"Jesus, Addi, you need educating. Okay, put on "Lose Yourself" and listen to the lyrics."

"Okay." She swipes, and as the soft intro kicks in, so does my excited eighteen-year-old self, as a faint smile crosses my face waiting for the beat to commence.

Addi groans. "This sounds like a girly song."

I chuckle. "Just wait, and listen... the message in this song is a good one."

Then the beat drops, and Eminem starts talking about seizing the moment. I can't help but mime the words, lyric for lyric, exactly as they are when he starts rapping. Addi giggles, watching me while I tune into my inner teenager with hand movements waving through the air and everything as I drive.

The chorus kicks in, and I grin. "Now listen to these lyrics, Addi!" I mouth along with Eminem as he raps about losing yourself, only having one shot, and taking every opportunity.

Her eyes widen as I see it clicking in place for her.

Smiling wide as the song continues, I keep driving to the store, completely in my element, rocking along to the music.

As the song is winding down and Eminem says the last line, I say it with him, turning my head to Addi. "You can do anything you set your mind to, Addi."

The song fades, and Addi smirks at me. "You enjoyed that, didn't you?"

"Did you get something out of it?"

She shrugs. "I mean… other than being thoroughly entertained by your miming and dancing antics. Yeah, I guess there's a message in those lyrics—"

"You guess? *You guess!* Damn, Addi, we need a deep dive into my music history. But right now, the store is calling. Though mark my words, this debate isn't over, young lady."

She giggles, handing me my cell as we slide out and walk toward the convenience store. I grab a cart as we head in—if we're here, we will make it worth our while.

"Okay, first aisle, sanitary pads, then we get all the good stuff," I tell her.

"The good stuff?" she asks.

"All the junk food we can muster to take our minds off the cramps."

Addi grins. "Have I told you you're my favorite person?"

Warmth radiates through me as I bump into her shoulder. "No, but I'll take it. C'mon, let's get shopping."

We walk in, go straight to the essentials then head for the chocolate. Addi is looking at two candies, trying to decide which one to get, and I smirk at her. "Addi, we don't have to choose. We can have both."

She widens her eyes. "Really? I don't want to be greedy."

"Honey, we're here with the club's credit card. Girl, go nuts!"

She hesitantly places both bars into the cart, then turns back, eyeing another. I let out a laugh and move over to the row that she's studying, knowing she wants one of everything, so I simply swipe my arm along the entire row pushing everything into the cart. Addi gasps, her eyes bulging out of her face as she laughs loudly. The old lady across the aisle from us is scowling like we're being disorderly.

"Addi, if you want something, you get it."

"You're a little bit crazy, you know that?" She grins so wide.

I shrug and walk with her out of the chocolate aisle. "Oh yeah, I know. Just wait till you get me in the ice cream freezer."

Addi giggles and suddenly wraps her arms around me tight. I sink into her embrace and hold her back. "Thank you for making me forget about my pain for a little while. Both physical and mental."

"That's what I am here for…" I lean down and kiss the top of her head. "For you to lean on me as much as you need."

She pulls back, that gorgeous smile still firmly on her face. "Shall we cause some chaos in the ice cream aisle?"

I grin, tightening my hands on the cart, ready to run. "Let's see if we can irritate some more old grannies."

Addi laughs, and we take off running through the store.

***

After hopping out of the car, we step around to my trunk and start unloading the bags of groceries. I smirk at Addi while she quietly hums the words to "Tik Tok" by Ke$ha.

I'll convert her to my ways before she knows it. I quietly giggle to myself.

As we walk inside the clubhouse, each loaded with a ridiculous amount of grocery bags, Raid rushes over to help. "What on earth have you girls been up to?"

Addi instantly flushes bright red, like she is embarrassed. I guess telling the father, who you've only just started a relationship with, about having your period is not high on your agenda.

So I take the lead. "What? Like us girls aren't allowed to binge on chocolate and ice cream every now and then?" I narrow my eyes on him, trying to get the message across that there is far more to this than simply craving junk food without spitting it out, and Raid widens his eyes like he has figured it out without me even really trying.

"Oh, well, yeah... I think you deserve some extra calories. Let me know if you need anything," he replies.

Addi starts walking off with the bags.

"We're gonna sit in my room and eat and binge reruns of *The Vampire Diaries* because... Damon," I tell him.

Raid stares at me blankly. "I don't know what you just said."

I can't help but giggle. "Damon to females is what Selene from *Underworld* is to males."

Raid widens his eyes. "*Riiight*, super-hot vampire."

"Now you get it."

"Frankie, you coming? The ice cream is melting," Addi yells.

"I'll be right there. Go to my room and get the TV ready."

"You got it," she calls back and is gone in a flash.

I turn back to Raid, who's smirking. "Thanks for being the woman she needs in her life right now. I don't know how to thank you."

"Honestly, it's bringing me as much happiness as it is her." I give him a peck on the cheek. "I better go, don't want to waste perfectly good ice cream."

He reaches out, taking my hand. Sparks of electricity flick straight up, slamming into my chest as I look at this incredible man before me. He simply nods, and I smile, then turn and walk off.

When I enter my room, there are candies, chocolate, and ice cream tubs all over my bed. I can't help but smile wide as Addi sits in the middle, my duvet curled around her, television remote in hand.

It's only been a few weeks since Sophie's passing, so it is good that she feels comfortable with me, and I am glad I can be here for her and do something to ease her pain. And maybe me doing this with her is helping to ease my pain as well.

If I get to have an amazing relationship with Raid's daughter as a consolation prize, then maybe that is the perfect reward.

The problem is those damn butterflies won't stop when I'm around him, and I know it doesn't do me any good.

CHAPTER 23

RAID
A Couple of Days Later

We've had to start getting business back to normal, and the only way to do that is to get on with tasks that we would usually carry out.

It doesn't lessen any pain Addi might be feeling.

It just means we have to keep going.

It's the only way to survive.

So while Addi is back at school today, the club and I have come out to The Plantation to do a routine check to ensure everything is running smoothly. Maxxy is going through the figures with Hurricane while the rest of us stand back.

"So what you're sayin' is that we're good… right?" Hurricane asks, placing the pen down.

Maxxy juts her hip to the side, placing her pen on top of her ear. "We're better than good. Seeing as we got the drugs back from the cult Maddie was involved with, everything has been running like clockwork again. But the fact remains, Hurricane, you're leaving me without a set of hands that needs fixing. Felix is out, and I need someone to pick up his slack. I can't do all the work around here and still be able to function at full capacity."

Hurricane runs his hand over his beard and grumbles under his breath. "Fine... Hoodoo will help."

Hoodoo snaps his head around. "Huh?"

"You're in charge of findin' Maxxy someone permanent. I trust your judg—"

"I don't know the first thing about recruiting people, Pres. I'm a damn medic."

Hurricane flares his nostrils. "No! But you get along with Maxxy. So you know what kinda person to fuckin' hire. They gotta be one hundred percent right. Only the best for our Maxxy."

"Aww... thanks, Pres," Maxxy chimes.

Hoodoo rolls his shoulders, his eyes lingering on her. "You're right. It *will* have to be a certain type of person to put up with Maxxy and her demanding ways," Hoodoo teases.

Maxxy scoffs, folding her tattooed arms over her chest. "Oh, c'mon now. If I wasn't so demanding and straightforward with everything I do, shit around here wouldn't get done now, would it?"

"Or as modestly either." Hoodoo snickers.

Maxxy chuckles. "You're just pissy because you have to spend time with me when you know I'm gonna boss you around." She leans in, lowering her voice to a whisper, "And you're gonna like it."

We all chuckle.

Hoodoo leans in, narrowing his eyes. "The thing is, Maxxy, you're gonna have to put up with me now too. This goes both ways because I get to help choose who's working with you next. So I wouldn't be so smug if I were you."

The chemistry between them is clear.

It's fucking explosive.

Fiery.

Damn well combustible.

They eye fuck each other with the rest of us watching.

Hurricane steps in. "All right, I've seen about enough of this shit. Hoodoo, I need you on top of thi—"

"Oh, he'll be on top, all right." Bayou chuckles, high-fiving City.

The rest of us snicker while Hoodoo glares at Bayou.

"Just do what you're here for, Hoodoo. Find someone to work with Maxxy. Stop fuckin' foolin' around. In the meantime, we're gonna talk to Dominic at the docks. Check on our Mississippi shipments and make sure they're goin' to schedule. Boys, let's ride."

Maxxy flirtatiously waves at us, or should I say Hoodoo, before we leave.

I poke my elbow into Hoodoo's ribs. "You got your work cut out for you with that one."

He groans. "Hurricane is punking me or something. He's gotta be?"

Chuckling, I shake my head. "He chose you because you and Maxxy have this banter. Because you gel with her. You're gonna pick the right person who's going to be able to work with her. To deal with her damn attitude."

"I fucking hope so."

"C'mon, let's head to the docks. You can think about *your* Maxxy problem later."

He exhales as we walk to our rides and head for the docks.

The wind in my hair and the breeze on my face tells me I am alive. Life's been challenging for the last month or so, and it's still not easy. Raising a kid I'm getting to know is far from a walk in the damn park, but we're settling into a groove. It's helpful having an entire club at my back. And for some reason, riding my bike right now, feeling like we are getting back to some semblance of normality, has my soul feeling good.

At ease.

At peace.

It's fucking all kinds of pleasant.

Then we approach the dock, and that feeling disappears and is replaced with irritation. The flashing of red and blue lights gains my attention at the same time as it does for the rest of my brothers. Then, almost in unison, we drop our gears and slow the fuck down, pulling off into a side road, far enough back so the heat can't see us. We park our rides, jump off, and gather together in a tight circle.

"What the fuck?" I ask.

Hurricane scrubs at his face. "I have no damn clue. I haven't had a call from Dom, so I don't know what's goin' on. We can approach on foot. Sneak up, keepin' to the shadows. Try to get as close as possible to see if we can figure out what's happenin'?"

Bayou tilts his head. "The parking lot across the street. We can make our way over there and hide in the bushes facing the docks."

"Solid plan, let's do it," Hurricane orders.

We walk silently to the parking lot, rush in behind the bushes, crouch down, lie on the hot concrete, and watch the cops swarm the place.

"Is that Cain?" I whisper, seeing Detective Tyler Cain and his men searching the dock, looking like they're seizing *every-fucking-thing*.

"What the fuck? How in the hell did Cain find out about these shipments?" Hurricane grunts.

I shake my head. "No one is supposed to know about this dock. We pay Dom and his team to keep quiet. No one knows what runs through here."

"The club will be fine as long as Dom and his men stay the course, stick to the story and what to say if this ever happened. They know the damn drill. Product, the paper trail, none of it leads back to Defiance. Dom has to deny knowin' what's in the shipments. They just load and ship. There's no doubtin' Cain'll seize the product. So that should be that."

"Let's hope Dominic and his crew stick to the damn plan then," Grit states.

"In the meantime, we go dark on the dock. No more shipments

in or out. This is gonna be a massive disruption to our supply chain. We're gonna have to go old school, back to runnin' them via transit. It's more dangerous, carries more risk, especially with the heat on our tail, but it's our only option. Godammit!" Hurricane snaps.

While shaking my head slowly, my mind goes into overdrive.

This feels wrong.

Something is off.

"There's a reason they searched here. Someone tipped them off. Let's go back to the clubhouse, and I'll do some digging. There's gotta be a reason this is happening now," I suggest.

Hurricane exhales heavily through his nose. "There's nothing we can do here anyway. Watchin' this shit unfold won't do us any good. Let's head back. Do some diggin', see what you can find out. I wanna know the second you find anythin', Raid."

"You got it, Pres."

CHAPTER 24

RAID

As I sit in my den, typing furiously on my keyboard, trying to figure this dock situation out, I look through all my computer logs and come across something suspicious—a login attempt was made twenty-four hours ago. It's so inconspicuous my detection programs didn't pick it up.

Fuck my life!

Someone has hacked into our servers and definitely got a whole bunch of data.

"Jesus fucking Chris!" I groan loudly as I try to track and pinpoint precisely what they were looking for and what they took.

After a few minutes of checking and double-checking, it dawns on me.

"Well, fuck me into the middle of next week!" I say, knowing no one can hear me.

Anger surges like adrenaline through my system when I realize the extent of what has happened.

The damn data they pulled is the location and information about where our product is shipped from, which just so happens to be the fucking docks with Dominic. *What a coincidence!*

Whoever came for this information obviously sent it to Detective Cain so they would find evidence to frame us, so the heat could bring us in. The problem is, we know how to be untraceable—there won't be anything linking those drugs to us at the dock.

Cain won't have collected anything but a stash of unmarked drugs, none of which tie them to us, and a lead that goes ice cold.

Cain won't be happy.

But neither will Hurricane.

He's going to reem me a new asshole for letting this slip by me.

We already had an altercation not that long ago about him thinking I'm not doing my job properly, and this will probably cement it for him.

Letting out a long breath, I shake my head. I've been fucking preoccupied recently with Addi, Frankie, and of course, Sophie passing away. Unfortunately, my head hasn't been completely in the game, and I have now let some asshole break through our firewalls and gain access to sensitive information. I don't care *why* it happened. I want to know *how* it happened. How could this asshole slip through my defenses?

Any product lost is on me.

Any problems are on me.

This is *all* on me.

And I know I'm going to pay for this gigantic clusterfuck.

I get up from my chair and pace, not knowing what to do.

Don't be a dickhead—it's obvious what you have to do.

I've got to find Hurricane and fast.

Once I finally build the courage to face the music, I locate Hurricane and Kaia playing with baby Imogen. He's the epitome of a doting father. I've missed all the pivotal years with Addi, which makes my chest hurt, but I can't focus on that fact right now. Hurricane needs to know what's going down.

"Pres," I call out.

He turns to face me, hands Immy over to Kaia, then makes his way to my den.

"You found somethin'?" he asks.

I gesture for him to enter, and he closes the door behind him.

Nodding, I sink into my chair. "I found something, and you're not gonna like it."

Hurricane says nothing, simply folds his arms over his chest, and sits his ass on my desk. "Okay... hit me?"

Scrubbing at my beard, I let out a long exhale, knowing what happened at the dock was firmly on me.

This shit is *not* going to go down well.

But I have to tell him.

"There was a breach..." I pause to gain the courage to go on. "Someone hacked our systems and knew what they were looking for. They took data about precisely where we ship our product from at the docks. They then sent that information to Cain. I am assuming to set us up for a fall. Fuck, Pres, I've been so distracted with Sophie and Addi and Frankie, to some extent, that I missed the hack. If I was paying closer attention and I hadn't been so intently focused on whether Addi was coping okay, I might have seen them infiltrate the system. I failed you... I failed the club. I fucked up, and I've cost the club a stash of product. I'll dip into my savings and pay the club back. It just might take some time with me having to pay for Addi's private school and—"

Hurricane grips my shoulder, cutting me off mid-sentence. "Addi's been goin' through a lot. She's needed you. Don't forget, brother. You've been goin' through a fuckin' lot too. Before having Immy, I mighta been the type of guy to accept what you just said. To make you pay for the loss of our product. To make you work off the error. But now... after lookin' into my baby girl's eyes, I know family comes first. I know Addi comes first. If the club burns to the ground because we gotta save our families, then so be it, Raid. Family first... always. Just tell me you fuckin' know who's behind tryin' to set us up?"

My eyes widen, not believing what I am hearing. Before Addi

showed up, I wouldn't have believed Hurricane was capable of changing this much. But after feeling the emotional switch being flipped inside me when I heard Addilyn was mine, I totally relate to how Hurricane is a changed man.

Spinning in my chair, I start typing. "Let me ping the IP address and see where it lands."

I start typing frantically, my fingers barely keeping up with how fast my mind races. The IP is bouncing around, but I'm finally able to land it back to what appears to be the clubhouse of the Iron-fucking-Chains MC.

"You've got to be fucking me." I let out a shocked laugh come mocking sound.

Hurricane leans down, looking at my screen, even though I know he can't read the code before him. "What? What's it sayin'?"

"Pres, if I'm reading this right, the hack came from Frost at the Iron Chains."

Hurricane growls while standing back up, and he starts pacing. "That motherfuckin' asshole!"

"Why the fuck would Frost come at us like this?" I ask.

Hurricane shakes his head. "Because he's pissed we're assertin' our dominance over him. He wants to be the top dog. Well, we're not gonna allow this shit to go down. Can you hack into *their* systems?"

I crack my knuckles and tilt my neck to the side. "Abso-fuckin'-lutely."

"Get in there and find anythin' valuable. Save that shit, then come get me. I'm gonna call church."

"You got it!"

Hurricane slaps my back as I put on my noise-canceling headphones, and he turns, walking out the door and leaving me to it. I have some making up to do, and right now, I'm going to hack the shit out of their damn systems, but unlike them, they're not gonna know I've been there because I don't leave any trace. I am too good at what I do to leave any damn evidence behind.

Captivate

Time to fuck some shit up!

***

After making sure to cover my tracks, so no one will ever know I was in their system, I leave my den hours later to find Hurricane.

He raises his brow when he spots me, a slow grin forming. "How'd ya go?"

I hold up a flash drive and chuckle. "Got it! I got it all."

Hurricane punches me in the shoulder with a huge grin as he stands. "Good fuckin' work," he states, then sends a whistle through the clubhouse. "Brothers, church. *Now.*"

Everyone appears confused. They obviously had no idea I was working on something.

We all head into the chapel. Taking my seat, I pull out my laptop, ready if Hurricane needs me, as everyone else sits down.

Hurricane bangs his gavel, gaining everyone's attention, and cranes his neck. "Right! Some information was brought to light about the strike on Dom's docks. Raid came to me and told me our computer systems were hacked and the information stolen was details of where our product was being shipped from. We're sure that information was leaked to Cain and his men, *especially* to target us. To get us in the shit with the heat. To wipe us off the damn map."

Bayou sits forward, his fists on the table. "We know who hacked us?"

"The IP address filtered back eventually to the Iron Chains MC," I tell him, and everyone sinks back into their chairs with arms folded across their chest in some sort of defiant stance.

They all know the consequences of this information.

They know what it means—*betrayal of the worst kind.*

Defiance and the Iron Chains MC are supposed to be allies.

But they came at us.

Tried to take us out.

Right under our noses.

It was a deliberate attack on us to try and take over New Orleans.

This means we're going to war.

City is the first to speak, "So what's the plan? How are we going to fire back?"

Hurricane lifts his chin at me to take the lead on this one, so I hold up the flash drive. "Pres told me to hit them back where it hurts. They aren't good enough to cover their tracks when they hacked into our servers, but I sure as fuck am good enough to cover my ass. So I went in and found as much dirt as possible on their systems... I have shit on how they traffic women and how they have another shipment coming in tonight. I'll send an anonymous tip to Cain so when their men go to pick up the women that they're intercepted as payback..." I pause, knowing the next words to come from my mouth mean everyone's lives will be in danger. "Just know, brothers, this will probably incite a war between our clubs. We have to be prepared for that."

Everyone nods in agreement.

"Fuck that and fuck them. They had no hesitation in takin' our income stream. We know we can work around that, but still, we gotta fight back. We're not gonna go nuclear, just enough to let 'em know we know it's them targetin' us. We'll send this information to Cain. A few of their brothers get arrested and sent to the can for being dicks. We specifically told them to stop traffickin' women, but they ignored us, so it's a win-win in my books. Will it escalate? *Maybe.* But maybe it'll show 'em we're capable of playin' hardball too." Hurricane grunts.

I place the flash drive into the USB on the laptop and open the email program to type up an encrypted email. "Okay, it's ready to go. Brothers, you all sure we wanna do this?" I ask, looking around the room.

Everyone dips their heads in agreement, but my eyes shift to Hurricane.

"Execute," he demands, and I press enter, watching the email drift off into cyberspace.

"Done. Now, we wait for the fallout."

Hurricane's lips turn up in a mischievous smile. "I have a better idea. Do you know where the Iron Chains are doin' the handover?"

I raise my brow. "I do."

"When's it happening?"

I glance at my watch. "In about two hours."

Hurricane chuckles. "Then we'll have a quick bite, and we're ridin' out to watch this all go down. We gotta ensure those Iron cunts go down for this."

A round of cheering erupts through the Chapel.

We need this.

A damn win.

Something for us to fight for.

And seeing those bastard Iron Chains assholes get what's coming to them is exactly what everyone needs right now.

***

The moon shines so brightly in the clear onyx sky, and the stars are twinkling, making it look like the Milky Way is on steroids tonight. It's fucking dazzling, and immediately my mind goes to Frankie and what it would be like to spend a night under the stars with her. But instead, I'm nestled next to Ghoul as he lets out a long, drawn-out fart.

I turn to him, and the bastard has the audacity to damn-well smirk. The rest of the guys chuckle as we lay on the ground opposite the truck stop.

"Jesus, man... did something crawl up your ass and fucking die?" I whisper.

He shrugs. "Too many burritos at dinner."

"If you need to go take a dump or something, we'll all still be here waiting when you get back," I tease.

"And miss all the fun. I'd rather hold it and let it out when needed. Seeing you squirm? Yeah... fucking priceless."

Everyone chuckles as I shove Ghoul in the side. "Fucker! Keep your gas to yourself. Your noxious green smog cloud will give us away."

"All this fuckin' yammerin' will give us away. Shut the fuck up, you assholes." Hurricane grunts making us both shut up.

Then out of nowhere, a truck pulls to a stop to do the handover.

"I think we're up. It's got the right number plate," I say.

"Look, there's the Iron Chains. I don't see Frost, but I do see Dirty, his VP, and three other guys," Hurricane states. "Where's Cain?"

"They're here. See that red light in the bush over there?" I keep my voice low and point.

Everyone turns to look through the bushes, and Hurricane chuckles. "What are they waitin' for?"

"They need to see the girls in Dirty's hands. They have to witness the transfer happen before they can storm in. Once the Iron Chains have the girls in their possession, don't worry, Cain will swoop in."

Payback's a bitch, or in this case, payback is so damn satisfying.

We all lay back, watching this play out with our binoculars.

Dirty steps up to the back of the truck, talking to some guy. They shake hands, and then the truck opens, and four girls slowly and hesitantly hop out, their hands bound, bags over their heads, and the other Iron Chains brothers grab hold and start leading them to their van.

"Here we go," I whisper.

Dirty hands the guy an envelope and another handshake.

Within seconds, lights blast, illuminating the entire truck stop. Police cars drive in, swooping on the section blocking the guys in as the driver goes running, but some pigs take off after him.

Dirty raises his hands, and Cain walks straight up to him, striding with his usual cocky stance.

Captivate

We can't hear what is being said, but we know Dirty is in deep shit. He is shoved to his knees, along with the other three Iron Chains brothers then cuffs are placed around their wrists.

Hurricane nods his head. "Okay... let's quietly fuck off. We don't wanna be here any longer than necessary. We know they're gonna be processed. Our job here is done, boys."

We're all careful as we get up and make our way down the road a couple of miles, then jump on our rides and return to the clubhouse in full celebration mode.

Our mission—a success.

Jumping off my ride, I start walking.

The guys are all hyped up, knowing we won this round.

Hurricane slaps my back. "Good job, Raid."

I dip my head as we enter the clubhouse, my eyes instinctively searching for Frankie and Addi, thinking back to what Hurricane said about family.

Family comes first.

My eyes fall on Frankie, her smile lighting up the room like it always does. There's something about her that makes me feel whole. More of a man—if that's possible. And it's at this moment that I realize that Frankie *is* family. Even though shit is going at a snail's pace with us, or a *slow burn*, as she calls it, I want her to be a part of *my* family.

I might have had hang-ups about her being a club girl. I might have had some illogical thoughts about my brothers never finding love with a club girl. She is a club girl, but she's a distinctly different breed from the others. Frankie is amazing at the club, around my brothers, supportive of me, and incredible with Addi.

She was there at my beginning.

She has been there through the toughest of times in the middle.

And right now, I can see she is my end.

My everything.

No one at this club cares that she is a club girl—*so why should I?*

Turning, I make my way to Hurricane and pull him aside.

He raises his brow. "Somethin' else happenin'?"

I clear my throat. "No. Nothing to do with those fuckers, and everything to do with me."

He nods. "Okay, what's goin' on?"

Swallowing hard, I take a deep breath. "I know Frankie is the head club girl, and it's her job to perform those duties to the best of her ability, but brother, I'm asking…" I hesitate because I don't know how he's going to take this.

"Just ask, Raid," he urges.

"I want you to make Frankie unavailable to our brothers… so she can concentrate her time on Addi."

Hurricane smirks. He's not stupid. He knows this is *not* about Addi but about what *I* want for myself.

He grips my shoulder. "Yeah, brother… she's all yours."

Inhaling sharply through my nose and then out again, relief floods through me. A warm smile lights my face, and for the first time, I finally feel like I'm making the right choice.

For Addi.

For me.

For my family.

And it feels so fucking good.

CHAPTER 25

FRANKIE

It's been a long day, and I know the guys were on club business tonight. I don't know what it was, but something seemed to go down. Either way, they all looked happy when they got home, which can only be a good thing.

As I walk back inside from the mailbox, I flick through the mail and smile, seeing one of the love letters Hoodoo gets every so often that we like to tease him about. Making my way through the clubhouse, I find and approach him as he's drinking a beer. Handing him the letter, he glances up at me.

"Another one from your pen pal."

Hoodoo smirks. "Don't call her that. She's a good friend."

"One you've never actually met nor talked to in person."

"Goodnight, Frankie."

I smirk. "Night, Hoodoo." I take off, walking over to Addi, who looks like she is about to head off for the night. "You heading to bed?" I ask.

She yawns, stretching her arms out. "Yeah, had a busy day at school today. I'm wiped."

"Okay, let me walk with you to your bed," I say as Raid

approaches us.

"You going to bed, kiddo?" he asks while the three of us walk down the hall.

"Yeah. At least I don't have to go to school tomorrow and can sleep in."

Raid smiles. "Weekends... God's gift to humans."

I chuckle as we reach Addi's room. When she steps in, Raid and I follow her, then she turns to give me a tight hug. "Night, Frankie."

"Sleep well, honey."

She then turns to Raid and embraces him too. "Night, Raid."

"Night, Addi. See you in the morning."

She's already in her pajamas, so she jumps straight into bed.

We took Sophie's bed out of Addi's room a couple of weeks ago so she could make the room more about her. I think she feels more comfortable now the room has a more 'teenager' feel about it.

"Have a good night, you two," she says while snuggling under the blankets.

Raid and I turn and walk out, I flick the light, and Raid closes her door behind us with a gentle click.

As soon as he closes the door, he reaches for my wrist and starts dragging me.

I let out a small laugh. "Raid, what are you—"

"Shh..." he replies while pulling me down the hall.

I race along, and when he gets to his room, he spins us, forcing me against his door with a thud. I let out a breath as he pushes his body against mine. His eyes connect, and my clit instantly begins to throb. With one hand on my face, the other holding my wrist up next to my head, he says, "I'm sick of fighting this."

Everything tingles, excitement bubbling inside me as I glance back down toward Addi's room. "What about Addi?"

"She adores you. *I* adore you. I told Hurricane to make you off-limits to all brothers."

My eyes widen as a gasp leaves my lips. "You did?"

"Hurricane told me today that he would burn this whole place down for family. That put some shit into perspective."

"Yeah? What shit?"

"You are *my* family, Frankie. You and Addi. And I would burn *everything* down for you."

His words send a shiver up my spine, and it settles in my heart. "Raid," I whimper, and I'm unsure if it comes out as a question or a plea. The idea that we are finally taking this to the next level puts me on edge.

He leans in, his breath heavy and laced with desire. "You need to understand something, Frankie," he says against my ear in a low, commanding tone, one I haven't heard from him before.

My eyes widen, and I try to pull back to look at him, but I'm pressed too firmly against the door to move. So I shift my arms up, wrapping them around his neck, my fingers playing in his hair.

Raid shifts, his green eyes alight with hunger as he gazes at me. "You enter this room… there's no going back. *This* is *mine*," he demands, the growl emanating from his throat, letting me know he means business when he slides his hand down and cups my pussy.

My breath catches.

Instead of replying right away, my arms drop, and I reach for the door handle, giving it a twist. "Are you sure it's not *you* who's *mine*?" Then I step back through the door, smiling as he stumbles from my abrupt movement.

"That's it, you belong to *me*," he declares, grabbing hold. I'm not quick enough to step back, and he wraps his arm around my waist, pulling me to him.

His lips meet mine in a punishing kiss, stopping briefly, biting and sucking on my lower lip. I let out a whine, but it's not out of pain. I need his lips desperately, so I wrap my hands in his hair and devour his mouth.

All the time we wasted with our bullshit push and pull, fighting what was brewing was for nothing. Not willing to waste another second, my hands drop to his jeans, undoing his belt. Raid growls, releasing me and giving me a slight push that has me taking a step back. Instantly, my brows furrow in confusion, making me wonder if I have misread what's happening.

"Tsk tsk tsk... you *will* take everything I give. I warned you... there is no going back." His eyes remain focused on me, all while he removes his belt in one fluid motion that has my panties soaked. "Turn around," he commands.

He is right, though.

I am his.

I have been for years.

It's just neither of us was willing to take the risk.

My breaths are coming fast with anticipation, and I have no choice but to do what he says. As soon as I'm turned, he's behind me, his firm length pressed against me, and I can't help but wiggle my ass. The growl he releases has a satisfied smile spreading across my face, but it quickly falls when he steps back.

Slap!

The sting on my ass from his belt makes my breath catch in my throat, followed quickly by a moan.

"Baby, we are just getting started." He steps in behind me again and rubs my ass cheek through my jeans. Raid grabs the hem of my tank top, pulling it up and over my head, the cool air a sharp contrast to the heat building between us. Once my shirt is discarded on the floor, his hands slide up my sides and take hold of my breasts, squeezing to the point of pain.

His touch is punishing, but I'm here for it.

"Do you know what I went through every time you stepped out with a brother? Knowing what you were doing. Knowing what was happening with what's *mine*? It's why you were on a dry spell, I made sure those assholes stopped coming to you. You are *mine*!" He slides a hand up, holding my throat. The move possessive but gentle. "Never. Again." Releasing me, he breaks the front clasp of my bra, discarding it with my shirt somewhere on the floor.

"Raid, please," I beg, needing more.

I need him to touch me.

I need to touch him.

"Soon." He reaches for my jeans, quickly undoing and sliding them with my black lace panties down my legs, letting them pool around my ankles. "Frankie, I want you to cross your ankles and bend over. You are not to move until I say so. Got it?"

"Yes." I pant, doing exactly as he commands.

Fuck, he needs to just touch me already!

With my legs crossed, I at least find some relief as I squeeze my legs together.

"Fuck, you're gorgeous. You are goddamn stunning like this."

"Just fuck me already," I demand, knowing how desperate I sound.

But I don't care.

Raid chuckles, then he's on his knees, his face buried in my wet pussy, and I moan out with pleasure. "Shit, you're dripping. I wanted to make this last, but I can't wait any longer. Not with how sweet you taste." His words are followed by his tongue buried deep in my pussy and his thumb on my clit.

It feels so damn good.

I'm no stranger to someone giving me head, but with Raid, this feels different. Maybe because I feel a connection with him and am so desperate for him.

His tongue slides up my pussy in intricate patterns, making me tingle in ways I never knew I could. At the same time, his thumb circles my clit.

It's too much.

The pleasure is too much.

Lights flash behind my eyes, heat invades my skin, and I shake all over. "*Raid,*" I scream out as my orgasm, combined with being bent over, has me swaying.

Slap!

He smacks my ass again, but he doesn't bother to rub the sting away this time, and I'm left whimpering. Instead, he helps me slide off my boots and jeans from around my ankles, leaving me completely naked and him still fully dressed.

I stand slowly, coming down from the sensations reeling through my body. When I turn to finally face him, his chin glistens with my arousal, and it's so fucking hot. Pressing my lips to his, I carefully slide his cut off and gently lay it on the bed.

"Woman, did I say you could move?" he questions as he pulls away to remove his shirt.

"Just shut up and fuck me already."

He chuckles and turns to the side table, grabbing a condom and sliding it on after undoing his pants. "Safety first," he says, the same words he used when doing up the straps on my helmet.

I smirk when he faces me again and warns, "This is going to be hard and fast. Fuck, I have wanted this for too long. To wait any—"

"What did I say? Fuck me already," I interrupt, pulling him to me.

Without another word, he bends slightly, lifting me by my legs which wrap around his waist, lining his cock up with my pussy. Our eyes lock, an intense moment passing between us, knowing we've waited so long for this moment.

We're finally here.

Then without a second more, he slams me onto his cock. I can't help but squeal at the sudden fullness as my body stretches around him.

"Fuck!" Raid hollers, using his hold on my ass to slide me on and off. "So fucking good."

His lips are on mine, our tongues fighting for control as he walks us to the door or a wall, I'm not sure, in my lust-driven haze, and he slams me against it. Then, with the extra support, he wraps a hand around my throat, forcing me to look at him. "This. Pussy. Is. Mine." Each word is reinforced with his relentless thrusts.

"Yours," I scream out, my pussy clenching around him. The pressure is building so intensely that I see stars.

Captivate

He thrusts harder while my fingers grip his long hair, tugging and pulling. His teeth clamp down on my collarbone, then glide along my skin, nipping and biting, making a wave of adrenaline surge through me.

I moan as I ride him, thrust after insatiable thrust. A low grunt growls from his chest as he continually slams me against the wall. This isn't intimate—there are no hearts and flowers—this is us getting years of pent-up sexual frustrations out in a few minutes.

We've been friends for so long.

Friends who have held back their sexual desires from each other out of fear. A fear that it would ruin what we have. If only we had acted on it sooner, we would have seen that we are an inferno together. He has captivated my entire soul. It burns for him.

As I rock against him, every inch of me is alive and tingling.

I let out a moan as goose bumps pebble on my skin. The heat flushes over me as lights dance behind my eyes.

I'm close.

So fucking close.

Raid tightens his hand on my throat so tight my skin begins to prickle, my head pulls back, and he leans in, biting my shoulder, which pulls a whimper from me. He's sure to leave a mark, but the sensation sends a jolt straight to my clit, at the same time as he thrusts up inside me. My body shudders, and I let out a scream as he murmurs against my shoulder, "Come *now*, gorgeous." Raid releases my throat, slipping his hand between us and using his thumb to rub circles around my clit. He presses his forehead to mine, and when my orgasm is close, I squeeze my eyes shut. "Uh-uh, eyes on me. I want you to see that it's me making you come," he states, holding my gaze.

"Fuck, only you, Raid," I say as the sensations hit me like a tidal wave. My eyes meet his, and all I see is him, those bright green eyes staring back at me, and I am done for. He thrusts one more time, and the orgasm hits me with a force that steals my breath.

I gasp when Raid's throbbing cock stills, his mouth agape as a low groan escapes him when he slams into me one last time before his cock jolts with his release.

Oh God!

Fuck, yes!

Both our bodies relax while we pant coming down from the high. My forehead rests on his as I stare lazily into his eyes.

"Holy shit, that was worth waiting for," I somehow manage to mumble.

He smiles, gently caressing my throat, his hand sliding up, stroking my cheek. "Fuck, yeah, it was. Gimmie five, and we can go again. We gotta make up for so much lost time."

I giggle, leaning in to kiss him.

Our lips connect, and it's like coming home.

And finally, it feels like we're on the right track.

CHAPTER 26

RAID
Halloween

Everyone is excited because we're on Bourbon Street for the Halloween parade.

Well, most of us.

Lani and Grit stayed back because they can't risk all the lighting effects with Lani's epilepsy, so they're babysitting Imogen for Hurricane and Kaia. This is their first night out without their daughter.

It's easy to see Kaia is already missing Immy, and I think Hurricane is too. But we're all trying to be in the moment and enjoy the festivities.

Addi is beyond excited. She and Clover decided to dress up for the occasion in Disney characters. She said her mom would have loved all this.

As I stand back with my arms wrapped around Frankie and the parade in full swing, I can't help but watch Addi, loving that this is our first Halloween together. I lean down to her ear and smirk. "So, do you want to go trick or treating after the parade?"

Addi furrows her brows and snorts out a laugh. "Like,

seriously? I'm fourteen."

I chuckle, raising my hands in surrender. "Sorry, I wasn't sure what age that all stopped."

Addi slumps her shoulders, her eyes turning kind. "I'm sorry you missed all those years."

I weakly smile. "Me too."

Then Addi turns as Clover grabs her attention, and they face back to the parade, cheering and watching the floats pass by. They mingle further into the crowd getting closer to the front to gain a better view, and I smile at how happy Addi finally looks.

I wrap my arms back around Frankie, who's standing in front of me, and nuzzle my nose into her hair. She presses her ass into my cock, and instantly, it reacts, starting to harden. I let out a low growl into her ear. "Frankie, we're in public, don't start something unless you want me to finish it."

She glances over her shoulder, her hooded eyes narrowing on me, and I know she won't stop. Frankie has taken that on as a dare. In support of the girls, she dressed as a slutty Tinkerbell, and it wouldn't take much to slip under her skirt.

Fuck.

Her hand slides between us, pressing on my cock through my jeans.

My eyes roll into the back of my head at the friction.

It feels so damn good.

But I have to play it cool because people surround us, and my kid is nearby.

"Dammit, Frankie!" I growl against her and can't help but risk sliding my hand under the short green skirt.

Wait! She's not wearing underwear?

"What the fuck?" I ask because it definitely doesn't feel like she has any on.

In response, she pushes harder against my cock, making me ache for her.

"I need you, Raid," she whimpers.

That is all I need to hear.

Spinning her around, I reach for her hand that's on my cock, and I grab it, pulling her with me through the crowd. She giggles as I push through the throngs of people, trying to find somewhere less *crowded*.

Making my way down a side alley—it's only small, so we'll have to be quiet because people are walking past constantly. Right now, I have an itch that needs scratching, and Frankie's lit a fire in me that only she can put out.

Tugging her back from the opening of the tight alley, I firmly push her down on her shoulders. "Gonna need you to wrap those gorgeous lips around my cock, beautiful."

Like the good girl she is, she opens her mouth and sticks her tongue out, waiting for my cock. I make quick work of my belt and pop open my jeans, pulling my aching cock out. "Damn, gorgeous. If only we had time for everything I want to do to you right now."

Her eyes are wide as drool begins to drip from her tongue. Grabbing the back of her head, tight around her glittery bun, I stroke my cock, guiding it to her ready mouth. Before sliding it through her lips, I slap her tongue with the head making us both groan in anticipation. Frankie doesn't need any direction as she tightens her lips around my shaft, breathing deep through her nose.

I'm lost in her.

The fact there's a crowd only feet away is irrelevant.

It's only us.

Her soft lips tighten around my cock, making me let out a feral growl. The feeling of her wet mouth surrounding my dick almost has me coming on the spot.

She feels too damn good.

So damn right.

I push my hips, forcing myself deeper while picking up the pace. Frankie slides a hand up my leg, gripping my ass, and draws me closer. I watch as she slides her other hand between her legs, and the sight does me in.

I forcefully thrust my cock, hitting the back of her throat, and she gags. "Come on, take it," I push.

She peers up through her heavy lashes with a spark of determination. Frankie stops rubbing her clit to grab me by my hips with both hands and forces the rest of my cock down her throat. The tightness wraps around the tip of my cock, and it feels like the damn heavens have opened up and swallowed me whole. I groan as all breath leaves me for a second. With a quick shake of my head, I step back, my cock slipping from her mouth, saliva coating my cock, leaving a trail stuck to her lips.

Reaching out, I gather all the spit, stroking my cock with one hand while helping her to her feet with the other.

"Turn around and put your palms flat on the wall," I tell her, using my foot to spread her legs wider. Then I press down gently on her back, getting her in position.

I flip up her tiny green Tinkerbell skirt, and sure enough, she's sans panties. "What the fuck is this?"

"I wanted you to have easy access tonight. I knew I wouldn't be able to wait until we got back to the clubhouse."

"That so?" I smirk as I line my cock up and slam it into her pussy, knowing she is already so wet for me. She moans at the intrusion, and as I thrust into her again, she pushes back, meeting me.

"Dammit, Raid! I need more."

"So fucking needy tonight." Pulling out, I turn her completely, forcing her back against the ally wall and bringing her leg over my hip. Driving into her again, she wraps her arms around my neck, holding me close like she can't get enough.

"Yes! Exactly. Like That."

My lips cover hers, needing to silence her cries of pleasure before someone hears us.

Each time I slam into her, she slides up the wall from the force, but she is far from hurting as I pull back, gazing into her sparkling hazel eyes. Her pussy clenches around my cock, and I have to brace myself against the wall.

"You gotta get there. You feel so damn good." I grunt the words out before claiming her lips again.

Shifting slightly, I thrust into her, then grind my hips against hers, creating friction. Frankie grabs my hair in both hands, tugging tightly as her breath hitches. "Shit, Raid," she whimpers against my lips, and with one more thrust, I can't hold it back any longer.

Her pussy contracts with her orgasm, squeezing my cock.

My balls pull up, and the familiar tingle builds, traveling up my spine. The pressure ignites inside me, my balls tightening, my muscles constricting as I let out a guttural groan releasing deep inside her.

"Fuck, the things you do to me, woman," I whisper against her neck, nipping at it slightly.

She drops her leg with a satisfied hum and a drunk-like smirk. I step back, my cock slipping out of her, and I freeze, my entire body going completely numb, staring at the bare skin. "Shit."

"What?" she asks, and when I look up, her gaze settles on my cock.

"I got carried away and didn't put a condom on. Fuck!"

Frankie laughs. Not a giggle or a light chuckle but an all-out laugh as I am tucking my dick back in my jeans. "What the fuck is so funny?"

"You should see your face right now. It's not a big deal. I have an implant. Perks of being a club girl," she states matter-of-factly and steps toward me. Holding my face in her hands, she kisses my lips, and when she pulls back, her smile is contagious.

I grimace at the reminder, but the fact she is looking so happy soon wipes away my angst. "What has you smiling so cheeky like?" I question, curious as to how she can be so happy after that mishap. Because deep down, I'm shitting myself. It has been years, well fourteen to be exact, since I last had sex bareback. And we all know how that turned out.

"I'm just thinking about how I now get to feel you between my legs for the rest of the night," she says, and now *I'm* the one with a shit-eating grin.

As nerve-wracking as this is, I do love that idea.

Without another word, she goes to step out of the ally ahead of me, but I stop her. "Uh... not sure you can wear those wings now. They got chewed up by that wall."

She glances over her shoulder, looking at the metal-framed wings now bent and hanging off her. She snickers, turning her back to me. "Can you detach them for me?"

I move in, unclipping the bent fairy wings, then hand them to her. "Looks like this fairy lost her... *wings*."

She snorts, rolling her eyes. "Lame Dad joke right there. But it's okay. You're still a DILF to me."

I chuckle, reaching out, grabbing her bun, and yanking her face right in front of mine. "Don't you forget who the daddy is in this relationship."

She licks her lips and nods. "Yes, sir."

I slam my lips to hers, kissing her strongly, before pulling back with a shit-eating grin, then I straighten out her costume.

"Now, Tinkerbell, shall we get back to the festivities?"

She tightens my belt putting everything back into place, and nods. "I think we shall."

We turn and walk back out into the crowd of people, who are all none the wiser about what Frankie and I just did in the alley, and I have a pep in my step. I swear nothing could ruin this good mood.

It's Halloween.

Everyone is having a ball, and the club is having a great time together.

What's not to enjoy about tonight?

My arm slides around Frankie's shoulders, pulling her to me, and I kiss her temple as we make our way back out onto the street.

People are running past, screaming at the ghouls and witches chasing them. Frankie and I laugh, feeling happy as we slowly wander back to find Addi.

Then suddenly, Clover comes frantically running toward us, a terrified expression crossing her features as I reach out and grab her. She's panting and gasping for air. It's almost impossible for her to talk as I try to calm her down. "Clover! *Clover*, what's wrong?" I force her to look at me, her eyes flooding with tears. Her bottom lip trembles, and she shakes her head. "Clover... where's Addi?" I grit the words out through my teeth.

Her entire body shakes, and she bursts into a loud sob before saying the words that make my blood run cold, "They took her!"

CHAPTER 27

RAID

An enormous wave of panic washes over me.

The world is spinning so fast, but I can't move, getting caught up in the gravitational pull of something much stronger than me. I feel fucking nauseous. I got swept up in my own shit and became distracted, not keeping my full attention on Addi.

Guilt wracks through me as I turn to Clover. *"Who* took her?" I practically yell in her face.

She shrugs. "Some guys. They shoved me to the ground so hard I grazed my knees and hands."

She places out her palms showing all the scrapes and blood which is dripping onto the ground.

Frankie takes Clover's hands in hers comfortingly.

But anger only surfaces inside me.

If Frankie hadn't seduced me, this wouldn't be fucking happening.

"I shouldn't have let you distract me like that. Why *the fuck* would you let me take my eyes off my kid, Frankie?"

She snaps her head around while raising her brow. "Excuse me? You're blaming this on me? You were a willing participant in being distracted, Raid. It takes two to tango. Don't put this on me."

"Except for the fact I wouldn't have been distracted in the first place if it weren't for *you*. Addilyn would still be here. Some assholes wouldn't have taken her. And now I have to try to find her. We're wasting time talking. I *need* to find her!"

Frankie glares at me as I go to walk off, not knowing entirely where I'm going or what my brain is thinking. Everything is a mash of 'save Addi at all costs' and 'playing the blame game' to someone who just so happens to be the closest to me for my mistakes.

Hurricane and the rest of my brothers step up to us. "The fuck is goin' on. I can hear you guys screamin' over the music and the fuckin' crowd."

I turn to my president.

I need his help.

Now more than ever.

"Hurricane, someone has Addi. Could be the Novikovs, could be the Iron Chains, could fucking be anyone at this point."

Hurricane widens his eyes, his nostrils flaring. "Well, do your thing. Get your tech gear out and search for her like you would anyone else. Get your head on straight and think logically, Raid."

Think logically.

I'm so fucking worked up.

I'm the guy the club goes to when there's a missing person.

I'm the guy who finds people.

Building some inner strength, I pull out my device and start hacking all the security cameras in the street, but before I manage to find anything, a message comes through on my cell from an unknown number.

> **Unknown:** *In exchange for Addilyn, we want compensation for the women the heat took from us. Pay us, or we hurt her. For every fifteen minutes you're late, we hurt her a little more.*

Time starts now.
Tick tock!

A clock appears on my cell, counting down from fifteen minutes.

A wave of voracious heat ravages my body. My hands clench into tight fists as I grit my teeth so hard they begin to squeak. "Motherfuckers!" I growl.

Hurricane glances over my shoulder at the message.

He exhales, shaking his head. "We're not payin' them, Raid. You find their location and fast."

My mind buzzes, flicking from one scenario to another. Wanting to pay the ransom and be done with it, but also knowing that when you pay, generally they hold the cards and will kill anyway. Frost is showing us all his cards. The asshole is unhinged and totally untrustworthy.

We can't believe a word he says.

The best thing I can do for my daughter is to get my tech hat on and try to find her.

"I need somewhere quiet to work. I can't do this with that parade going on behind us."

Hurricane nods. "Let's head back to the parkin' lot. See if you can triangulate the signal from the cell there."

I nod, and we take off.

We run.

This isn't something we can take our time with.

I have fifteen minutes to find my daughter.

I can't risk them hurting her.

Not when it's *on me* that they had a chance to take her.

I should have been watching.

I should have been taking better care of her.

That's what a father does.

I've let her down.

I've let Sophie down.

If Sophie knew I'd let Addi be kidnapped under my watch, she'd have me castrated.

And I'd fucking deserve it.

Fuck!

"Raid? Raid! You with us?" Hurricane asks as we approach our rides.

Nodding, I run for my bike and pull out whatever tech gear I have in my saddle bags. Getting to work instantly, I put in the cell number and attempt to triangulate where it came from, but I cannot trace where the message came from. I try to ping the number off cell towers, but they have the fucking thing turned off.

Everyone stands around while I work frantically, sweat beading on my forehead, trying with everything I fucking have in me to get an angle on this. Unfortunately, the cell tracing isn't working, so I return to the security cameras to focus on *who* took Addi. See if we can find where they took her from and follow their escape path.

But this will take time—*time I don't fucking have.*

"Ahhh!" I slam my hand down on the side of my bike in frustration seeing the countdown timer ticking down. "It's taking too damn long."

Everyone stands around anxiously, waiting for me to make some kind of discovery like I always do. *I always come through for the club, so why the fuck can't I find* my *daughter?*

The countdown timer clicks off, and my heart lurches into my throat, my breathing rapid while I keep trying as fast as I can. "Hold on, Addi, I'm coming," I whisper more as a reassurance to myself than anyone.

Then my phone buzzes, and I hesitate.

Hurricane grips my shoulder. "Brother, try to keep focused."

I ignore him.

Swipe it open.

There's a video of Addi with tears streaming down her face as they hold onto her arm. She's begging and pleading with them.

I grip my bearded chin, trying to stop the bile from rising in my throat.

"Please, I didn't do anything. I promise I won't tell anyone you took me. Please, no, stop! No, *aaahhh....*" She screams the most ear-piercing sound that sends a chill to my soul. My stomach churns as I watch who I can only assume is Frost slamming a sledgehammer down onto the middle of her forearm, clearly breaking the bones.

The video ends.

My entire body shakes with the adrenaline as I turn, pacing with so much force I'm not sure if I want to hurl, holler, or murder the closest person to me.

Maybe all of the above.

But I do the only thing I can think of to make the pain stop right now. I walk over to the brick wall, slamming my fist into it repeatedly. My knuckles split apart as I shout my frustration.

Bayou and City are on me, instantly pulling me away from the wall. I try to resist, but Hurricane steps in front of me, resting his hand on my shoulder. "Calm your fuckin' ass down. What you just saw was horrific... agreed. But she needs your head screwed on, now more than ever. Pull your shit together and do the fuckin' work. Find her, Raid. *Find. Her.*"

Letting out a stuttered breath, I find the inner strength I never knew I had. Seeing my baby girl in pain like that has only lit a fire inside me.

I need to get to her.

I won't let them hurt her again.

I can't.

Even though my knuckles are dripping with blood, I reach into my pocket and pull out her baby photograph. Looking at her cute little face only makes me more determined. Running my finger across the picture, my jaw clenches as a line of blood smears across the image. "I'm gonna find you, Addi."

I turn, racing for my tech gear, and get to work, pushing myself harder as the countdown timer starts again.

I focus with every ounce of energy I have.

Following the car that took her, it leads to a location, and I triangulate that location to a building not that far from here. "Got it! They're at an abandoned hotel. I can get us there in about seven minutes."

Hurricane turns to Kaia. "Call Lani, tell her and Grit to get the van to come pick up the rest of the women and Clover. We gotta take off."

Kaia nods. "Of course. You get Addi back, and you make Frost fucking hurt for this, Raid."

I narrow my eyes, the taste of vengeance already on my tongue. "Oh, you have no idea what I'm going to do to that fucking cunt."

Frankie approaches me as I pack my tech gear away, ready to ride out. "Make it *really* fucking hurt."

I look up at her. "I will."

She hesitates but then leans in, kissing me quickly on the cheek, the tension from before seeming to have ebbed between us a little. "You get *our* girl back in one piece."

"That, you can count on." Our eyes stay locked, a moment passing between us.

Addi means so much to us both.

And I know that no matter what, I need to put all my energy and effort into this. Because the one thing I know for sure is that I spent the first fourteen years not being there for Addi, and there is no way in hell I'm going to fuck up on her now.

Frankie nods her head like she understands exactly what I'm thinking.

She gets it.

She gets me.

And I know I was angry at her a moment ago, but right now, she is the only person who understands, and that sends a wave through me that I can't control. My hand rushes into the back of her hair, my fingers gripping tight as I draw her lips to mine and kiss her quickly.

Letting her know that we're okay as far as I am concerned.

That I am going to get Addi back.

For *us*.

She whimpers as I dramatically pull back but says nothing as I turn to rush for my bike. Then, throwing my leg over my ride, I take off with my brothers.

I *need* to get to Addi.

She is *all* that matters right now.

My bike takes off faster than I should probably push it, especially with everyone on the streets right now. But I don't give a shit about them. We ride as a group, me leading the way to the abandoned hotel with a fire burning through me so damn hot, I feel the vengeance coursing through my soul.

Frost isn't going to know what fucking hit him when I finally get my hands on him.

The hotel is on the city's outskirts, but civilians could be around, so we must play this carefully.

We pull up our rides a few streets back so we don't alert Frost and his men that we're here. While jumping off my bike, my trigger finger is itching to find this asshole and unload the entire clip into him.

I just have to find him first.

Hurricane steps up to my side as we walk up to the hotel. "You gonna keep your head on straight while we do this?"

"My priority is Addi... then Frost. If I have to let you guys deal with that asshole so I can get Addi, then so be it. I just need my daughter to be safe, Pres."

He nods in understanding. "Totally understand, brother. You get Addi. Leave the rest to us."

Nodding my head, an overwhelming sense of strength flows through me. "Got it! Let's do this."

We make our way quietly with guns drawn to the hotel entrance. We have no clue where they're holding her inside, it could be anywhere, so we slowly make our way in.

As we enter, there's plastic sheeting draped from the ceilings. It's like they've been doing renovation or construction work, making it harder for us to gauge where they could be holding her. The floor is covered in white powder, which seems to be debris from where they have pulled walls down on the interior, and they haven't cleaned up the fibers of the fallen plasterboard.

It makes the floor less stable.

We hear a commotion up the grand staircase, so we slowly ease our way through the plastic sheeting and gradually make our way up the stairs, trying not to make the wooden floorboards creak under our mutual weight.

Hurricane leads us in formation to a long hall, where rooms are stationed on either side. It's a typical hotel hallway, just completely rundown. The thing is, we have no idea what room they're in.

As we slowly ease down the hall, the floor beneath my feet lets out an almighty creak. I stop dead still, everyone turning their heads to look at me, and we all freeze.

Suddenly, the door two rooms ahead of us snaps open, and Salt sticks his head out. "Shit!" he calls as we raise our guns. He ducks back into the room, and we take off running. The asshole slams the door shut, locking it behind him, but I don't hesitate and slam my shoulder into it, breaking the door down, almost falling over with the force as I ram through the wood.

We all rush into the hotel room, which is a bare shell, and instantly gunfire rains down on us. We separate, filing off in different directions and ducking behind the builder's materials that are scattered around, causing all sorts of damn hazards. I weave in, falling behind some scaffolding, pushing the tray off the ledge to shield myself from the incoming bullets. I crouch down, my heart rapid firing as I turn to see Bayou and Hoodoo using an oversized toolbox as a shield and pushing it with them while they move forward.

I duck my head around the corner, risk getting shot, to see if I can find Addi in this mayhem and chaos.

But I can't see her.

So I take the risk.

I turn to make eye contact with Hoodoo and gain his attention. "Cover me!" I call out.

He and Bayou widen their eyes as I duck out from behind the scaffolding and run for it. Bullets whizz past my body as I duck and weave while trying to locate my kid. The Iron Chains MC are scattered throughout this place, which seems to have the wall into the next room partly taken down, and they're spread out in there too.

It's fucking chaos as I bring my gun up, aiming for Salt, and unload a couple of rounds. They slam straight into his chest, hitting my mark. He recoils as blood splatters across the fresh white wall in the most glorious pattern. He groans and falls, slumping on the floor. The floorboards turn red with his blood as I keep running, trying to make my way into the next room. It's what they seem to be protecting.

But suddenly, an Iron Chains brother slams into me so hard, I lose my balance, and we crash into the wall, bursting through it and landing in the other room on the floor in a scuffle. My gun clatters and slides across the cement as he brings his fist up, slamming it into my face. My head snaps to the side, and I spit out a line of blood, my eyes blurring from the blunt force.

But it's when I hear Addi scream that everything clicks into place.

I find my strength.

My eyes focus.

My blood pumps with new energy.

There's a hammer on the floor next to me, and my eyes shoot to it. The Iron Chains asshole comes for me again, but I'm too quick, picking up the hammer and slamming it into the side of his head when he reaches me. His temple disintegrates, his eyes roll into the back of his head, and he falls directly on me.

I groan, shoving him away. "Fucking bastard," I grumble and move rapidly but then come to a grinding halt.

That's when I see it.

Frost holding Addi.

In his arms.

With a gun to her head.

I spot my gun on the floor, then rush for it. Frost lets off a round right near my hand as I go to pick it up, but I am too quick as I swing my gun up and aim it directly at Frost. "Let her go, you *fucking* asshole!"

He presses the tip of his gun to Addi's temple. My poor baby is crying so hard it physically makes me hurt.

"It was never meant to be this way, Raid. Defiance came at us first. You tell us how to run *our club*? How the fuck do you expect us to react? You think you can get away with the shit you're doing in New Orleans? It's gonna catch up to you eventually. You can't hide your tracks all the time."

"You get that gun off my daughter's head. Or, so help me God, I will do things to you that will make you wish you were *never* fucking born."

Frost simply chuckles. It's like he doesn't give a single shit about what I say.

The fuckhead is deranged.

His eyes have an unhinged look to them.

Addi cries, clearly in immense pain from her broken arm.

"What, Raid? I've got the upper hand here. You give me what I want, or—"

"Or what?"

"Or I'll kill her right here, right now."

Addi sobs as my eyes meet hers. I try to let her know that it's going to be okay, but the utter fear in her expression tells me she is far from okay right now as her eyes squeeze shut, her body trembling, the shock taking over her body.

"You kill her. I kill you. There's no winning scenario for you here, Frost."

Addi tries to pull her head away from the gun, but Frost draws her closer and yanks on her broken arm causing her to whimper. "Uh, uh, uh, little one. Maybe there's no winning for me, but if I *do* kill her, I will have a brief moment of pleasure seeing *you* suffer. It's the least I can do for you assholes screwing us over."

"You're fucking delusional. We let you have your club here out of respect for the patch you used to wear. You were Defiance once, Frost, but you've lost your damn way. There's no coming back from this."

He grips Addi's broken arm, yanking her toward him more. She cries out in pain this time, the scream tearing through my soul as he presses the gun into her temple more forcefully. "Pay us for the girls you stole, or... *she dies!* I *won't* tell you again."

Hurricane and the other guys are standing at the hotel room's edge. It's only now I notice the gunfire has dwindled. Defiance has taken out the Iron Chains MC.

The time to do this is now.

My eyes meet Addi's—hers are filled with tears—but I give her a single head bob. Her bottom lip trembles and I wink at her. "Addi, duck!" I yell.

She doesn't hesitate, letting out a loud whimper when her arm wrenches against Frost, but she rips herself down with everything she has, giving me the briefest of margins.

But I take it.

The bullet shoots straight and lands right between Frost's eyes. The back of his head bursts open and brain matter sprays as Addi drops to her knees and Frost slides to the floor in a heap beside her.

Addi begins to scream—an unholy noise that would wake the dead.

I don't hesitate, running as fast as possible to reach her.

I slide across the floor, grab her with both arms, and lift, being careful of her arm. She holds onto me as tight as she can with her one good arm.

"I got you. I got you, baby girl," I tell her. Then moving at super speed, I get her out of the room, away from the blood bath and carnage surrounding her. I make my way out into the hall, my breathing frantic. Finally, I stop at the top of the stairs. Hoodoo's by my side in an instant as I take a second to simply relish that I have her.

She's in my arms.

She's safe.

She might be covered in blood.

She might be badly injured.

But I have her.

Hoodoo, steps in. "Raid, I need to look at her. You're gonna need to let me get closer."

I hadn't realized I was holding Addi so tight Hoodoo couldn't check her over. "Right, yes. Go for it, brother," I tell him as I gently ease her away from my body.

Addi's shaking so much that it kills my soul.

Hoodoo checks her vitals and assesses her arm.

Addi grimaces with the pain of him just touching her ever so gently.

He shakes his head. "It's broken. We need to get her to the hospital."

"Please don't leave me," Addi whimpers.

The rest of my Defiance brothers step up to us.

"I'm not leaving your side ever again, Addi. You're stuck with me."

Hurricane bobs his head once. "You gotta see Dr. Adams."

"Yeah, I'm gonna take her there right now. You okay if I leave this mess with you guys?"

Hurricane swipes at his sweaty brow. "Go! Take Hoodoo with you. We got this. We'll come to the hospital when we're done here."

"Thanks, Pres." Hoodoo and I take off down the stairs, and I get to my bike, then realize Addi won't be able to hold onto me.

She grimaces, tears falling down her face. "I'm so sorry—"

"This is *not* your fault. I should have been watching you. This is on *me*. I should be apologizing. I'm your father. I should have taken better care of you. Well, that starts right now." Keeping hold of her, I throw my leg over my bike and sit her in front of me. "I'm gonna ride slow, but I'm gonna need you to hold on with your good arm."

She nods and wraps her arm around me. I glance over at Hoodoo, who gestures that he's ready to ride. I start my engine, and we take off for the hospital.

I need to make sure she is okay.

Whatever Addi needs right now, she is going to get.

***

After spending hours at the hospital, Addi's forearm was put into a cast. She needs to wear a sling to keep it elevated.

The poor girl is exhausted.

She's inside resting while I make my way to the guys out by the bayou. Where I know they're waiting for me.

My body feels wrecked as I carefully open the gate. I'm mentally and physically drained, but as I step down the walkway to Bayou and Hurricane, they are standing with a couple of buckets in hand. I smile, feeling a flood of relief wash over me. Making my way over to them, I stand, looking out over the murky depths of the bayou water, and exhale heavily. "So Frost is all taken care of then?"

Bayou glances down at the dismembered pieces in the buckets and smirks. "La Fin can already smell his dinner. I've seen him circling. We thought we'd wait for you to make the first sacrifice seeing as Frost caused you the most pain."

I lean down, seeing Frost's hand in the bucket. I can tell it's his because of the tattoos across his knuckles. Smirking, I grab the hand and let out a chuckle. "Vengeance never tasted so damn sweet." I toss the hand up into the air, and before it can hit the water, La Fin jumps out, grabs it midflight, rolls over onto his back, and slams down into the water before disappearing below the murky surface.

I let out another chuckle while shaking my head. I don't know why, but there is something so cathartic in destroying evidence like this. In making those who hurt you pay in such a vile way.

"Fuck you, Frost," I murmur as I throw his foot in next. La Fin takes the hunk of meat and gulps it down without a second thought.

"You're gonna get fat with all this food, La Fin," I jest.

"He appreciates it." Bayou smirks.

I stay, feeding the entire two buckets of Frost chum to La Fin until I've made sure that Frost is well and truly taken care of.

That fucker will *never* hurt Addi again.

Then, I wipe my hands clean, and Hurricane, Bayou, and I head back inside for a beer to celebrate.

We purged the world of the Iron Chains MC.

Yes, there was some collateral damage.

Addi was hurt.

I know physically she will be okay.

But mentally? We may have to get her some help.

Addi's not used to this biker shit. She's had a life where she's never been in danger. Now, thanks to me, she may be in constant fucking danger, but I'm not willing for her to be anywhere other than at the club with me.

She belongs with me.

In the place where I can protect her the best.

And the only way I know how.

By being here for her.

By being the dad I am supposed to be.

By being the dad I want to be.

She may still be calling me Raid, but in my eyes, I'm her father. Nothing is going to change that fact.

Frankie is there when we step up to the bar, and she smiles as Hurricane, Bayou, and I sit.

"Hey…" I say.

"All taken care of?" she asks.

"La Fin is completely full," I reply.

Frankie lets out a relieved exhale. "So what happens now?"

"Beer. We celebrate with beer." Hurricane chuckles.

Frankie beams from ear to ear. "That I can do." She starts pouring, and I reach out, grabbing her hand. "Can I have a word?" I ask.

Frankie wipes her hands on the cloth she's holding, smiles, and then shifts out from behind the bar. We walk away, and I lead her to my bedroom, where we can talk in private.

As I walk through the door, I grab Frankie's hand, pull her inside, push her firmly against the bedroom wall, then kick the door closed. I go to kiss her, but she pushes on my chest.

"We need to talk first."

I step back, knowing exactly where this is heading. She's angry at how I spoke to her after Addi's disappearance, and if I'm any sort of honest with myself here, I completely understand. My outburst was unforgivable, but I hope she will remember it was a heat-of-the-moment thing, a time when I was vulnerable and shit-scared.

"Honestly, Raid…" she takes a deep breath, "… the way you spoke hurt me. To blame me for something out of my control and say it in such a cruel, undeniably brutal, and vicious way made me rethink our relationship."

I go to speak, but she puts up her hand to stop me.

"Now I have had more time to reassess your words… and remember exactly what they were… I do understand that you were under incredible stress. I understand that your daughter

Captivate

being in the hands of an enemy is your worst nightmare. But..." a tear falls over her eyelid and runs down her cheek, "... I have always been there for you and Addi. Addi means the world to me, and playing the blame game when you know I always had her best interests at heart was hard for me to swallow. I am still trying to absorb what that means for us as a couple."

Okay, so I have fucked this up between us. But have I made it so I am unredeemable to her?

"Frankie..." I sigh heavily, knowing my next words will be the most important words I have ever spoken. "There was no excuse for the shit I said. I know that. I know how much Addi means to you and that we got caught up in a *moment* together in the alley. We haven't had many *moments together,* but the one we shared was fucking incredible. I never *ever* meant to hurt you. Yes, my words were callous and cruel, but in my defense, I was battling an inner demon to protect my blood at all costs. So all I can say is I'm fucking sorry, I hope you'll forgive me, and I will do whatever it takes to make it up to you."

She sighs, her eyes still looking somber. "Raid, I know you were stressed. Hell, we all were. What happened to Addi was beyond terrifying. But if you ever, *ever* treat me with such disrespect again, I won't stand for it. I may be a simple club girl, but I still deserve respect—"

"I don't care if you're a club girl, Frankie. That don't mean shit to me. You're right. You deserve nothing but the best treatment and for me to fall at your feet. And I will do that if you want me to. I will drop to my knees right fucking now and kiss every one of your toes if it proves how damn sorry I am."

Her lips finally turn up into a hint of a smile. "All right... we're good. But you ever speak to me like that again, I'm gonna break your dick in two and serve it on a silver platter to La Finn. You get me?"

"I got ya." I chuckle and lean in, giving her a quick kiss before I drop to my knees.

This woman, she needs to understand just how much I value her.

That I need her.

Frankie is right to put me in my place. Something I have no doubt she will do every time I fuck up, which I hope isn't often, but knowing me, it will happen more than I like.

Right now, my place is showing her how much she means to me.

"Raid, what are you doing?" she questions, trying to get me to stand.

"I told you, Franks. I want to prove just how sorry I am," I explain, tapping her ankle to lift her foot.

She obliges but cautiously. "Uh... Raid? I'm not into any foot fetishes, so don't go getting any crazy ideas of putting your mouth anywhere near my toes," she warns, but there is a lightness to her voice.

When my eyes meet hers, that familiar spark between us reflects, and I can tell the anger has dissipated.

"Woman, would you just let me have my moment?"

She laughs and leans into the wall, giving in and letting me have control. I slip her shoe off and repeat the same thing with the other. Shifting my focus, I keep my eyes locked on hers as I unbutton her jeans and slide them down her silky legs. Her breath hitches when my lips follow, gently kissing and nipping my way down.

After tugging her jeans off, I toss them aside, then continue to nip and kiss my way, but this time, I start at her ankle, making my way up. "Frankie," I whisper, nuzzling my nose against her lace panty-clad pussy. She's wet, and I can't wait to taste her as I pull her panties to the side and slip my tongue out, licking her slit. "Fuuck!"

My cock is aching, but this isn't about me. This is me showing her how much she means to me. Showing her how she needs to be taken care of. Worshipped. Not me getting my dick wet. Although, *he* would say otherwise.

Frankie moans, threading her fingers into my hair and yanking me to her. "If you're truly sorry, Raid, you will stop fucking around," she says, grinding firmly against my face.

I let out a deep growl, then tear the delicate lace with my teeth. She squeaks, but it quickly becomes a loud moan when I bury my tongue in her pussy.

Fuck! I can't get enough of her.

She's my own personal nirvana.

I shift and tap each side of her thighs, wanting her to balance on my shoulders as I devour her. Then with my hands gripping her ass, I switch between circling her clit and sinking my tongue inside her, relishing in the way she tastes. Flicking her clit, I chance a glance at her. She's lost in the moment, giving in to me completely. Her eyes are closed as she rotates her hips, chasing her orgasm.

"Frankie, open those beautiful eyes. I want you to remember who brings you this kind of pleasure."

Her eyes snap open, a new fire burning. "I told you to stop fucking talking." She grabs a fistful of hair, yanking me into her to the point I can't breathe. She slips down the wall from the force. Now only her shoulders are supported against the plasterboard, and my firm grip on her ass.

I groan, loving this about her that she's not afraid to take what she wants. When I take her clit between my teeth and gently pull back, my teeth grazing her, she explodes. Her body tenses, her hips jerking erratically.

As she comes down from her orgasm, I slide my tongue inside her one last time, tasting her bliss. "S-s-stop. T-too m-m... uch," Frankie stutters.

Grinning, I help her to her feet and stand, using the back of my hand to wipe my face. I step into her space, bracing my forearms on the wall above her. She's still trying to catch her breath and her gorgeous tits are rubbing against my chest. My cock painfully throbs against the zipper of my jeans, precum no doubt making a mess.

This is about her!

With that thought, I step back and brace on my hands instead, giving us some breathing room.

She glances up at me, and I stare at her for a few seconds. Then, needing to touch her, I caress her face, sliding my thumb over her cheek before saying, "Thank you. For being here… for me, for Addi. We couldn't do any of this without you."

Later That Day

It's always felt like there's been something keeping Frankie and me apart, a reason for us not to be together, but for the life of me, I can't find that reason now.

As I stare at her, her gorgeous hazel eyes locked onto mine, full of so much hope and desire, it all seems so fucking clear to me.

Standing, I round the bar to Frankie, her smile so wide as I approach, my hands grab either side of her face, and I slam my lips to hers, kissing her in front of the entire clubhouse with everything I have inside me.

She whimpers while a round of cheering erupts around us. Her tense body finally relaxes as her hands slide up my back, her fingers digging into my skin while she holds me to her. Our tongues collide in a flurry of excitement. Every inch of me tingles like it's the damn Fourth of July, and fireworks explode through my body, making my dick instantly hard.

Kissing Frankie with no hesitation, no regrets, no concern for the consequences, and finally letting go is so fucking gratifying that it's like coming home.

Frankie has managed to captivate me without even trying. Everything about her makes me want more and more, and honestly, I've been fighting this for so damn long I don't want to fight anymore.

I want to give in.

Wholeheartedly.

I want to surrender to this woman, this incredible, amazing woman, completely.

Because when I allow myself to feel for her, when I allow myself to enjoy this sensation, everything is perfect.

Like my world is spinning correctly.

I should have given in to this long ago.

This woman is perfect for me.

This woman is perfect for Addi.

Fuck it! She's goddamn perfect in every way.

Breathless as hell, hard as a rock, my eyes lock onto hers, my fingers caressing her cheeks as I stare at her in unrelenting fucking awe. "Frankie... I love you."

Her breath catches in her throat, her eyes glistening with unshed tears, and she blinks away her emotion. "I love you too... so fucking much. Have for as long as I can remember."

Suddenly, an alert sounds around the clubhouse.

The one that lets us know the heat is approaching.

I let Frankie go, pull out my device and glance at the security feed. "Fuck! Hurricane, Detective Cain is at the gate."

Hurricane growls under his breath as Addi rushes over, cuddling into Frankie.

"You make sure Addi is taken care of during whatever this is, okay?" I instruct Frankie.

"Always," she replies.

The rest of us move to the middle of the clubhouse, ready to be raided.

We open the gates so they don't break the damn things down, and we prepare for Cain and his merry band of assholes to enter the clubhouse in a flurry of bullshit. But as they enter, there's no mad rush, just a gentle approach. There's no yelling and screaming, telling us to get on the ground.

So we don't.

We stay standing, waiting for instructions as Cain approaches us, looking like he wants to talk.

"Hurricane," he offers.

"Cain. Somethin' we can help you with?" Hurricane asks.

His eyes fall on me, looking me up and down, then he moves back to Hurricane. "I heard there was an issue with the Iron Chains and Defiance at the street fair?"

Hurricane shrugs. "Don't know what you're talkin' about?"

Cain glances around the room, his eyes lingering on Addi as she stands with her arm in the sling. The rest of the club obviously seems a little defensive. "My guys can't reach the Iron Chains members. Frost is missing. I can't prove you had anything to do with that." He takes a deep breath and continues, "The Iron Chains were into trafficking and a whole myriad of much worse shit than I know Defiance is into. So on a scale of 'am I going to push for conviction' to 'am I going to leave this alone,' I'm going for the latter. Because having one set of evil shit off the streets is better than nothing."

We're all silent, wondering if he is being serious or not.

We never thought Cain was *that* type of cop.

But I have to agree that having the Iron Chains off the streets is about as good as it gets.

Hurricane steps forward. "I don't know what you're after here, Cain. I have no clue what happened to Frost and his men, but if they're off the streets of New Awlins, then that's gotta be a win for us all."

Cain dips his chin. "Couldn't agree more. I'd just like to extend my thanks to whoever got the Iron Chains off the streets. It's not in any official capacity, just my own personal view."

Hurricane raises his brow. "Well, if I hear anythin' out there in the streets, I'll be sure to let whoever is responsible know your best wishes."

"Excellent... in the meantime, try to keep your noses clean. I wouldn't want to have to come down hard on you."

"Understood. We will keep the snot off our noses."

I smirk as Cain scrunches his face. "I'll see you around."

"Don't be in a hurry to come back now, Detective," Hurricane states.

Cain smirks and turns, walking out of the clubhouse with his posse in tow.

We all look at each other and shake our heads.

"The fuck was that?" I ask.

Hurricane rolls his shoulders. "His way of makin' us try to relax around him, to make us think he's on our side. It don't wash with me. I'm gonna treat him with the contempt I normally do."

"Yeah, he's still got his eye on us for sure."

I glance over at Frankie, who's trying to comfort Addi, and instantly have my hackles rise. I head over and step up to Addi, who has tears in her eyes, and Frankie's consoling her, so I kneel in front of her. "Hey, what's going on?"

She tenses, shaking her head, and looks to Frankie for support. I turn to Frankie, needing her to help me out here. "Having Cain come in like that brought back memories of Frost coming to take her. It scared her. She's feeling vulnerable at the moment."

She's fucking traumatized.

The club has done that to her.

I have to think about what I can do to help her.

Frankie, Addi, and I are a family now.

And families make shit work.

So I have an idea.

I reach out, grab Addi's good hand, and smile. "Addi, there's gonna be times when people show up at the clubhouse unannounced. Sometimes, bad people come to the clubhouse and make a scene. But I don't want you feeling like you're not safe here. I will always protect you, and so will Frankie. Everyone here will protect you. But I need you to feel and know that you're safe. And if you can't feel that here, how about you, Frankie, and I get a house outside the club? We can live in our own place, just the three of us? So you're not constantly worried about who is showing up?"

Frankie widens her eyes. *Dammit!* I didn't run this by her, but she doesn't say anything to the contrary, and I know she understands this is what's needed for Addi's sanity right now.

Addi glances around and shakes her head. "I understand why you'd want to do that, and thank you. But there are memories of my mom here. I feel close to her here, and I have Clover. This is where I feel comfortable. Sure, it might not be as safe as a house with just the three of us, but to be honest, I feel safer knowing that everyone would fight to protect me like they did at the hotel. I know I have some work to do on my mental health, but that will come with some therapy or something, I don't know. But I don't want to leave."

"Are you sure?" I ask.

Her glistening eyes meet mine, and she moves closer. "Yes. I was scared, but I know you'll take care of me. I know because of the way you protect me. The way you care about me. The way you have stepped up since you met me. You've been amazing, and I couldn't have asked for anyone better than you... Dad." She moves to hug me, and I hug her right back.

This is the first time she's called me Dad.

And not in a sarcastic, mocking tone like when I first met her.

She meant it this time.

It was completely, one hundred percent, an emotional from-the-heart gesture. And I couldn't feel prouder and more thrilled.

I am going to take the win.

While being careful of her broken arm, I hold her tight. "I couldn't have asked for a better daughter than you, Addilyn."

We embrace, and Frankie wipes a tear from under her eye and joins us.

The three of us.

Together.

As a family.
And I couldn't ask for anything more precious than this.

EPILOGUE

RAID
Two Months Later

The last two months have been a slow progression.

Frankie and I have been great, and together, we've been making progress with Addi to gain some emotional stability in her life and to help her be where she needs to be. She's not used to club life, but she's becoming more accustomed to it now. And she's fitting into clubhouse life like she has been here all along. She's part of the furniture now.

Her arm is healed, and we're preparing for Christmas—the first without her mom. Needless to say, Addi is finding it a struggle. Still, Frankie has been talking with her constantly, trying to help ease the void of not having Sophie around, but also doing everything we can to honor Sophie and her memory. The traditions Addi and Sophie used to have over Christmas, we're trying to keep alive for her, so she doesn't feel like there is such a huge difference.

We want Addi to try and enjoy this Christmas, even though it will be her hardest yet.

Stepping up to Addi, I wrap my arm around her and chuckle

Captivate

against her ear. "So, am I getting you Barbie dolls for Christmas, or are you too old for those?"

Addi rolls her eyes and shoves me to the side. "Wow! You're *really* getting the hang of these dad jokes now, Dad."

Chuckling, I nudge her back. "Kidding... how about an iWatch instead?"

"What! Really?" Addi widens her eyes.

Frankie giggles, shaking her head. "You know that's just so he can track you, right?"

Addi smiles wide, shrugging dismissively. "I don't even care. That actually makes me feel safer."

Frankie smirks. "Okay, well... we're gonna decorate the clubhouse today. You wanna help me, Addi?"

"Hell yeah, let me just go get Clover so she can help too." She runs off, and I pull Frankie to me, looking her in the eyes. "You know we couldn't do any of this without you?"

"What decorating? It's tradition for the head club girl to decorate."

I shake my head. "Not what I meant. You, me, Addi... we're a team. So how about we make this official?"

Her eyes widen as she stares at me. "What do you mean?"

I signal to Hurricane, and he walks over with a property patch. "Welcome to the club officially, Frankie."

I gesture to Frankie, and she slides it on, tears dripping down her face.

"I need you to be mine. To be my Old Lady. To walk through this life with me and Addi officially. Because I won't spend another minute without you as mine."

Frankie turns around as Addi walks over with a huge bunch of flowers.

Frankie chuckles. "You were in on this?"

"Absolutely. You and Dad are perfect for each other, and I can't imagine having anyone else in my life but you."

Frankie is almost sobbing as she takes the flowers from Addi

259

and embraces her so tight. "I love you, Addilyn." Frankie blubbers out the words.

"Right back at ya."

Then Frankie turns to me, and I smile while bringing my hand up and caressing her cheek. "And I love you, Francesca."

"I fucking love you, Raid."

Leaning in, I press my lips to hers.

This woman is mine.

Finally!

After everything we've been through.

After how long it has taken us to get here.

She. Is. Mine.

And the three of us can officially be a family.

I'm lost in Frankie when I hear a loud whistle.

"Wow, this seems like a lot of emotion right now." Maxxy chuckles while walking into the clubhouse.

Everyone turns, and we raise our brows.

I'm not sure Maxxy has ever been here before, but we all smile and approach her.

"Hey, Maxxy, what's goin' on? You don't venture out this way often?" Hurricane states.

"I wouldn't need to if Hoodoo was doing his damn job."

Hoodoo stands taller and scowls. "I'm trying, okay? But, finding someone to work at The Plantation who has the right skill set, and is willing to take on the confidentiality clauses, takes fucking time."

"Time I don't have, Hoodoo. Look... I'm gonna put it to you straight... either you find me some help, or I'm gonna walk. I can't do it all on my own anymore."

Everyone widens their eyes at her out-and-out threat.

Hurricane stiffens his posture. "Don't go sayin' shit like that, Maxxy. You know we need you. Hoodoo *will* pick up his fuckin' act. But, in the meantime, seein' as he's havin' such a hard time findin' someone, Hoodoo himself will come down to The Plantation and help you."

Hoodoo snaps his head around at Hurricane with his mouth agape. *"What?"*

"What?" Maxxy mimics.

"Max, you need help! Hoodoo has some biology experience with his medical background. I'm sure he'll be useful for somethin'. If not, he can be your errand boy."

Maxxy smirks and Hoodoo scowls. "Pres, you need me here as the medic."

"If we need you for an emergency, you're not that far away. We'll call you. This is happenin', Hoodoo. You're gonna work at The Plantation with Maxxy. No arguments."

Maxxy chuckles. "I hope you're ready to get down and dirty."

Hoodoo widens his eyes at the pun. "I don't think I'm ready for this shit... *at all.*"

I smirk at Frankie, and she giggles.

Hoodoo might not be ready, but we're all waiting with bated breath to see how this will turn out.

Because Hoodoo and Maxxy are heading for an explosion, and when it happens, it will be worth pulling up a chair and dragging out the popcorn.

TO BE CONTINUED

NEXT FOR K E OSBORN
Fixate
The NOLA Defiance Series Book Six
A Pen Pal Romance

K E Osborn

If you liked this book you may also like:

THE HOUSTON DEFIANCE MC SERIES
Books 1-8 – The Complete Set

THE CHICAGO DEFIANCE MC SERIES
Books 1-9 – The Complete Set

THE SATAN'S SAVAGES MC SERIES
Books 1-6 – The Complete Set

ACKNOWLEDGMENTS

First and foremost, I would like to thank my mother, Kaylene Osborn. Thank you for helping me, as always, with the process of editing this book and for always being a sounding board. I couldn't do any of this without you.

To Chantell – Thank you so much for all your help. You honestly make my author journey so much easier! Thank you from the bottom of my heart. I am so glad I have you on my team. My books shine brighter because of your input.

To Cindy, Diana, and Kim – Thank you for always helping my books shine. You find all the little idiosyncrasies I miss and show me how to improve. I am so glad to have you on my team.

To all of my awesome beta readers – Thank you for once again putting your thoughts into this book. I appreciate all of your energy and ideas, and together we make a great team. So thank you.

To Jane – I get to see you soon and am counting down the days. That damn ocean between us is the bane of my existence. I love you to the moon and back. Thank you for being my sidekick through all of this.

To Dana – This cover is pure fire! I love the way you managed to capture the emotion in his eyes. I don't know how you keep topping these covers. You're a wizard, Dana. lol <3

To Reggie and Ryan Harmon – This gorgeous cover wouldn't be as amazing as it is without the two of you. Reggie, you always deliver the most amazing photographs to bring my characters to life. Doing this photoshoot with you was so much fun. And Ryan, we have worked together on several books, but I think this is my favorite. Thank you for continuously being my muse.

Thank you to The Hatters PR and Chaotic Creatives for helping me promote Captivate and for the provision of PA services. You all work tirelessly to support me, and I am honored to have you as part of my team.

To my playful, adorable, crazy, and chaotic pups—Bella and Harley—what a whirlwind it has been since you came into our lives Harley Bear, but my gosh, I wouldn't change it for anything. The interrupted nights, the constantly having to pick up all the sticks you bring in from outside that you like to chew, not to mention all the barking between you and Bella. But you have lightened up our lives, not just mine and Mama Kay's, but I have also seen a change in Bella. She seems happier now you're here, more social. Harley, you're a pain in the ass, but we all adore you. And Bella, you've had some eye issues and needed surgery, but you are the most kind, loving, and loyal dog I have ever known. You have been with me since the beginning of my writing journey, and now I have two puppies in my office, helping me with my inspiration. I adore you guys—I swear, I will be a dog mum for life.

Last of all, I want to thank YOU, the reader. Your continued support of my writing career is both humbling and heartwarming. I adore my readers so much; honestly, I couldn't keep going without the love and support you all show me daily. Again, thank you for believing in me, and I hope I can keep you entertained for many years to come.

Much love,
K E Osborn

On a more serious note:

This book is a work of fiction, but some situations discussed are of a sensitive nature.

If you or anyone you know is in emotional distress, suffers from any sort of abuse, including violence, or is suffering from a terminal illness, please seek help or assist them in obtaining help.

Crisis hotlines exist everywhere, so please don't hesitate.

If you live in:
USA call RAINN - 1-800-656-HOPE
Canada call 1.888.407.4747 for help
UK call The Samaritans 116 123
Australia call Lifeline Australia 13 11 14
For general matters.

USA call American Cancer Society 1 800 227 2345
Canada call Canadian Cancer Society 1 888 939 333
UK call Cancer Support UK 020 3983 7616
Australia call CANCER SUPPORT 131120
For cancer matters.

CONNECT WITH ME ONLINE

Check these links for more books from Author K E OSBORN.

READER GROUP

Want access to fun, prizes and sneak peeks?
Join my Facebook Reader Group.
https://goo.gl/wu2trc

NEWSLETTER

Want to see what's next?
Sign up for my Newsletter.
http://eepurl.com/beIMc1

BOOKBUB

Connect with me on Bookbub.
https://www.goodreads.com/author/show/7203933.K_E_Osborn

GOODREADS

Add my books to your TBR list on my Goodreads profile.
https://goo.gl/35tIWV

AMAZON

Click to buy my books from my Amazon profile.
https://goo.gl/ZNecEH

WEBSITE

www.keosbornauthor.com

TWITTER

http://twitter.com/KEOsbornAuthor

INSTAGRAM

@keosbornauthor

EMAIL

keosborn.author@hotmail.com

FACEBOOK

http://facebook.com/KEOsborn

ABOUT THE AUTHOR

With a flair for all things creative, *USA Today* Bestselling **Author K E Osborn**, is drawn to the written word. Exciting worlds and characters flow through her veins, coming to life on the page as she laughs, cries, and becomes enveloped in the storyline right along with you. She's entirely at home when writing sassy heroines and alpha males that rise from the ashes of their pasts.

K E Osborn comforts herself with tea and Netflix, after all, who doesn't love a good binge?

Explosive. Addictive. Romance.
http://www.keosbornauthor.com/

Made in the USA
Coppell, TX
06 October 2024